PRAISE FOR MARIE-CLAIRE BLAIS AND THE SOIFS CYCLE

SONGS FOR ANGEL

"A richly layered, emotionally resonant text, one that rewards readers who come to Blais's work for the first time as well as those who have journeyed with her from the beginning." —*Literary Review of Canada*

"*Songs for Angel* is a daring aesthetic experiment and a powerful appeal to solidarity." —*The Walrus*

A TWILIGHT CELEBRATION

"One of the most distinctive and original living writers of fiction."
—*The New Yorker*

"A sublime and visionary novelist." —*Le Journal de Québec*

"The most ambitious thing attempted by a literary writer." —*The Globe and Mail*

THE ACACIA GARDENS

"*The Acacia Gardens* is a sublime evocation of human existence in all its darkness and light, and even achieves a kind of dualism that escaped its modernist antecedents." —*The Globe and Mail*

"… moral complexities and the grandiosity of Blaise's language give this book its appeal." —*Toronto Star*

"A magnificent song of pain, full and hypnotic." —*Nightlife.ca*

"Without a doubt Blais is the greatest living Quebec writer at present, she will certainly leave an incredible and inexhaustible legacy for scholars of her work." —*La Presse*

NOTHING FOR YOU HERE, YOUNG MAN

WINNER, GRAND PRIX DU LIVRE DE MONTRÉAL

“Resilience and memory are at the heart of this ‘saga’ where voices intermingle … driven by powerful prose.” —*Huffington Post*

“The powerful, lyrical, and unclassifiable prose of this great writer will not leave you untouched.” —*La Librarie*

“One of the strongest books [in the series]. Every time, every book is an experience in itself.”—*The Montreal Gazette*

“A powerful novel. Dense and charged.” —*Voir*

“Long spiralling sentences are carried by a grandiose prose.” —*Chatelaine*

MAI AT THE PREDATORS’ BALL

WINNER, GOVERNOR GENERAL’S LITERARY AWARD FOR TRANSLATION

SHORTLISTED, THE COLE FOUNDATION PRIZE FOR TRANSLATION

“[A] hallucinatory and poetic story, ripe for underlining and rereading … *Mai at the Predator’s Ball* will reward you.” —*The Globe and Mail*

“Spencer admirably captures what one might call the ‘breath’ of Blais’ prose, although this is a somewhat misleading term, since, unlike the oral style of Joyce’s paradigmatic *Finnegans Wake*, Blais’ narration, exploiting the French tradition of the segmented sentence, is very much a written form. This difference in language and literary tradition presents the translator with a serious challenge, which Spencer has met with wonderful skill.” —The Cole Foundation Prize for Translation

REBECCA, BORN IN THE MAELSTROM

WINNER, GOVERNOR GENERAL’S AWARD FOR FRENCH-LANGUAGE FICTION

“There is only one way to read the latter novels of Marie-Claire Blais. Slowly. One word, one phrase at a time, and then the next … Once it all starts to make sense, you feel utterly grateful and deeply connected, in tune with humanity, mesmerized, ready to go on and on.” —*The Walrus*

"There is pleasure in the rhythm and poetry of the language … this novel keeps company with James Joyce's *Ulysses* and Virginia Woolf's *The Waves* or *Mrs. Dalloway*." —*Winnipeg Free Press*

"… brimming with tenderness for humanity and an almost religious elevation." —*The Globe and Mail*

"The experience is the only goal; the journey, the reward … a coherent vision of the world." —*The Montreal Gazette*

AUGUSTINO AND THE CHOIR OF DESTRUCTION

WINNER, GOVERNOR GENERAL'S AWARD FOR TRANSLATION

"… an enriching and stimulating read, a tour de force that will fit in comfortably with the rest of Blais' finest." —*Quill & Quire*

"The acceleration of our lives … deftly translated by Nigel Spencer. These people do exist. On the page, however, they take on surreal dimensions, the fragments of their lives woven together through Blais' dark, magical prose." —*The Montreal Gazette*

"Nigel Spencer has performed a tour de force in *Augustino and the Choir of Destruction* … Spencer has risen to the extraordinary challenge of rendering Blais' uninterrupted stream of hallucinatory prose into an accomplished and lyrical translation." —Governor General's Jury Citation

THUNDER AND LIGHT

"Blais is a writer attuned—there should be a stronger word—to our times … Readers will be stunned and startled by Blais' prose. Her characters, each an international mix of intellect, passion, and problems, are constructed with wisdom and compassion." —*Quill & Quire*, STARRED REVIEW

"The inconsolable vision of the human condition expresses itself in powerful poetic prose, with a sort of multi-voice delirium that becomes an incantation, a prayer almost, and that attains hallucinatory dramatic density … We are with a writer at the far reaches of language, in the dazzling fracas of beauty." —*La Presse*, FIVE-STAR REVIEW

THESE FESTIVE NIGHTS

WINNER, GOVERNOR GENERAL'S AWARD FOR FRENCH-LANGUAGE FICTION

"Marie-Claire Blais's best, and without a doubt, the richest and most impressive tableau d'époque I have read in a long time ... Blais has modestly, generously, written The Divine Comedy of our time." —*Le Devoir*

"[*These Festive Nights*] resounds with what has become a Blais leitmotif: the spiritual thirst born of hardship, and the hunger for redemption in a brutal world." —*The Gazette*

"[In *These Festive Nights*] Marie-Claire Blais appeals to the best part of who we are. It's a book that we finish reluctantly and with a deep sense of gratitude for the characters who, like the heroes of Sophocles and Shakespeare, are the messengers of a hidden truth of fundamental concern to the human heart."
—*Magazine Littéraire*

Together by the Sea

ALSO BY MARIE-CLAIRE BLAIS

FICTION

The Angel of Solitude

Anna's World

David Sterne

Deaf to the City

The Fugitive

A Literary Affair

Mad Shadows

The Manuscripts of Pauline Archange

Nights in the Underground

A Season in the Life of Emmanuel

Tête Blanche

These Festive Nights

The Wolf

Thunder and Light

Augustino and the Choir of Destruction

Rebecca, Born in the Maelstrom

Mai at the Predators' Ball

Nothing for You Here, Young Man

The Acacia Gardens

A Twilight Celebration

Songs for Angel

NONFICTION

American Notebooks: A Writer's Journey

Together by the Sea

MARIE-CLAIRE BLAIS

Translated by Katia Grubisic

First published as *Une réunion près de la mer* in 2018 by Les Éditions du Boréal
First published in English in 2026 by House of Anansi Press Inc.
houseofanansi.com

House of Anansi Press is committed to protecting our natural environment. This book is made of material from well-managed FSC®-certified forests, recycled materials, and other controlled sources.

House of Anansi Press is an eBound Digital Certified Accessible publisher. The ebook version of this book meets stringent accessibility standards and is available to readers with print disabilities.

30 29 28 27 26 1 2 3 4 5

Library and Archives Canada Cataloguing in Publication

Title: Together by the sea / Marie-Claire Blais ; translated by Katia Grubisic.
Other titles: Réunion près de la mer. English
Names: Blais, Marie-Claire, 1939-2021, author | Grubisic, Katia, translator
Description: Translation of: Une réunion près de la mer.
Identifiers: Canadiana (print) 20250235587 | Canadiana (ebook) 20250235595 | ISBN 9781487006358 (softcover) | ISBN 9781487006365 (EPUB)
Subjects: LCGFT: Novels.
Classification: LCC PS8503.L33 R8313 2026 | DDC C843/.54—dc23

Cover and text design: Lucia Kim
Cover image: iStock.com/THEPALMER

House of Anansi Press is grateful for the privilege to work on and create from the Traditional Territory of many Nations, including the Anishinabeg, the Wendat, and the Haudenosaunee, as well as the Treaty Lands of the Mississaugas of the Credit.

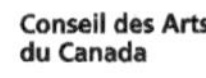

CERTIFIED
CANADIAN
PUBLISHER

With the participation of the Government of Canada
Avec la participation du gouvernement du Canada

We acknowledge for their financial support of our publishing program the Canada Council for the Arts, the Ontario Arts Council, and the Government of Canada.

Printed and bound in Canada

To René de Ceccatty, with gratitude.
With thanks to Sylvie Sainte-Marie.

And for Sushi, a remarkable artist.

Together by the Sea

Mai has no idea, Daniel thought, what a great present, what a surprise, Mai's eighteenth birthday, it'll be wonderful, all of us there by the sea together in just a few days at old Uncle Isaac's Grand Hotel, why don't you come, Uncle Isaac said, you can have the gardens, the beach, the breathtaking beauty of the whole place, I'll be a hundred soon, only fools cling to their empire and what a balm on my dusty old heart it'll be to celebrate a young girl like that, my grandniece, all of your children have been treasures in my life, Daniel, all money does is pile up, it's an inert, heavy thing for a man, you have to know how to spread it around otherwise you get lost, all we have in the end is love, as you can see, Daniel, my days have been full of love, that explains why I've lived so long, don't you think, imagine, you and Mélanie were barely thirty when you first came here, after that near-fatal accident in New York, you loved those hallucinogenic drugs when you were young, dangerous stuff, but they let me in on so many secrets, Daniel told old Isaac, misfortune and mortification, I saw Great-Uncle Samuel, the saddest thing, it was unforgettable, I saw him, though all that happened long before I was born, I saw him get shot and stumble backwards in the snow, I thought I heard voices full of disdain as he groaned in the snow, I thought I heard, I thought I saw my parents' past, my grandparents, I knew they tried to hide everything from me, that pain, the indignity of my great-uncle gunned down in the snow, and the rabbis, those hallucinations were a gateway to such terror, and as Daniel walked along the water with Isaac, the old man beside him shuffling the sand with the tip of his cane, his eyes still bright as ever beneath his straw hat, or was that the valiant expression of tenacity, his determination to live a life that would be so long and so full, he said so himself, I wake up with a new project every morning, I think we should rebuild the tower on my island, the Island No One Owns, I'm organizing a meeting with students from the faculty of veterinary medicine, it seems fair for them to have a share of my estate for their research, that would be good, yes, though it's so tempting to tip into idleness, so inviting, from the moment I wake up in the morning all I want to do is to watch the eagles and the sea, ask my gardener how many panthers we still have, Uncle Isaac went on, and I remember, you only had two children then, they were young, Samuel and Augustino, this was before Vincent was born, and Mai was much later, Samuel wanted to be an actor, I remember, old Isaac said, and the *Lumière du Sud*, I remember the boat too, you almost lost it in a storm, you see, Daniel, I remember everything, what was I talking about, the Florida panther, I was able to save a few, no, it was Vincent we almost lost during a storm, Daniel said, the power went out suddenly on the island and we couldn't get help, Vincent was only a few months old, he had a seizure, one of his first seizures, he was barely breathing in my arms, ah, I only remember the boat, old Isaac said, they're ingrates, aren't they, that's why I never had any children, I didn't want to be disappointed, and anyway I always liked animals better, you always liked architecture most of all, Uncle Isaac, to each his own Uncle Isaac always said, but you must have something, a passion, something absolute, yes, yes, I remember you and Mélanie there on the pier and then one of you went in for a swim, the ocean seemed so cold to me even in the summer, after a hurricane I had to rebuild the pier and all these footpaths that go down to the sea, the summer cyclones destroyed everything, the long wooden paths, beneath the cloudy black sky of the windy season, Uncle Isaac said, what season is it now, I think it's fall, no, dear Uncle Isaac, it's summer, dear Uncle Isaac, so that's why my forehead is all sweaty under my hat, it's still summer, this sweltering heat, I should have guessed, Isaac said agreeably, you know I never liked summer, there were too many visitors on my island, the guests were after some of this cool ocean air, and I didn't like remembering Jean-Mathieu's ashes, the little boat that docked here, and the sailor, no, I don't like that memory, Isaac said, what astounding artists they were, such great poets like Jean-Mathieu, my friend, he could have been my son, I knew him for so long, I didn't like that they were laid to rest at my place in the summertime, no, I don't like that memory, the sailor scattered their ashes in the water and it made me sad, I was up in the tower, meditating, wondering what it is we're doing on this earth only to find ourselves poured out over the waves like that, in the unfathomable water that will erase all our names, eat away at our bodies little by little, I never dared knock on his door but I believe Jean-Mathieu was hiding there, in his room, sometimes I could even hear him sigh, I remember everything, old Isaac said, I've kept them all close to me in my tower, all my dead still squirming with life, it's my secret, they share my life, what is there to do at the bottom of the ocean, can you tell me, dear Daniel, when you make up the guest list for Mai's party, don't forget anyone, they're all there wriggling, full of life, just like me, make no mistake, they may be disaffected souls, confused by having met a sudden end, and why should that be the end we might ask, don't be fooled by appearances, they're forever trying to hide from us, they're just like us, with their faults, sometimes they're unkind, don't forget them on your list, Daniel, they're men and women, living souls, I'm telling you, living souls. Carlos saw Mama, she didn't come toward him, he was getting out of juvie that day and she stood in a halo of yellow dust, maybe she couldn't walk to him because she had gotten so fat, she often said during the Sunday visits, you see why I'm so heavy, it's the grief, the tears I can't shed when I think of you, and now my legs are swollen, and Mama waited for Carlos, unmoving, one hand on the door of the old-model convertible, ragged sounds rose from the car stereo, like howling, thought Carlos, it was El Toque's music, it was his car, he always had to have the stereo blaring when he drove into town, El Toque had probably stolen the car, thought Carlos, his brother was a thief too although he never did time, no, that only happened to Carlos and now he'd been released, I'll be there, Lazaro had said, you'll pay, and Carlos looked around in fear, his mother just stood there against the low grey sky in her purple dress wearing the shoes she'd always worn for the Sunday visits, no, Mama wouldn't help him, she was massive, my legs are swollen, she said, try to understand the pain of a Christian mother with her son in that hole, and you were lucky, you had a good defence, some of them are in for life, did you think about that, son, in your flimsy little brain, Mama you know there was no bullet in my gun, the Cuban's gun, it was Lazaro, I was just trying to rile him up, you know that, Mama, he could already hear himself saying the words, Lazaro was my friend, he wanted his watch back, that Lazaro, a Muslim immigrant from Bahama Street, the Adidas watch, every night he watched me, Lazaro the Egyptian, that was no reason to use that Cuban's gun, Mama would say, and don't lie, there must have been a bullet *because* he was wounded, you shot him in the knee in broad daylight, there must have been a bullet, no, Mama, I didn't know, I didn't think it was loaded, but Mama couldn't hear anything because of that music, his brother's music on the car stereo, Lazaro had sworn to get back at Carlos as soon as he got out of prison, within an hour of him getting out, where was he, Carlos looked around, there was a whole landscape of grey fields, a few grey houses maybe further on, but it was mainly his mother he saw, she was enormous there by the car, an old model, a classic, El Toque liked those fancy cars, convertibles mostly, in that hostile grey landscape there was no Lazaro, the Muslim who'd immigrated to Bahama Street, no, or anyone who looked like him, he always dressed in black, none of them were there, thought Carlos, bag in hand, he had almost nothing to his name, he was wearing the same clothes he'd had on when he was locked up, they still smelled like that day a few years before, his first day in jail, he'd been still a child almost, he was grown up now and his clothes were tight over his muscular body, it occurred to Carlos that his mother wasn't rushing to welcome him with open arms not because she was heavy, she was so heavy, no, it was because she was ashamed, she didn't want anyone to notice them, her and her son, it was shame that made her unmoving body so heavy, next to the vintage car, she would probably close the roof on the old-model convertible, she would close the sunshade so no one would see her and her son driving down Bahama Street like some dismal procession, down Esmeralda, yes, thought Carlos, so that the Black people in the neighbourhood wouldn't see them, safe from judgment, safe from shame, he thought, a day of mourning like when the processions go by, gloomy but singing, thought Carlos, no one would celebrate his return except maybe Deandra and Tiffany, his sisters, the twins, if they were at Pastor Jeremy's house, they'd be cuddling Polly, obviously Polly wouldn't remember him and neither would Deandra and Tiffany, they'd never come visit on Sundays, they've got too many boys in their harebrained heads, said Mama, they're starting to look like Venus when she was their age, our children aren't ours anymore, they're heedless heathens, you have to drag them out by the hem of their coats to get them to come to the Coral City Temple, and as for Polly, Deandra had written to Carlos that he'd been away so long that the first Polly was no more, she had been replaced by a second and then a third Polly, but Carlos thought it would always be the same Polly, his Polly, dogs' lives were shorter than humans' but it would surely be the same Polly, thought Carlos, she couldn't forget me, her master, she used to run with me in the waves, even from a distance Mama seemed unhappy to see him, silent and massive as she listened to the music on the stereo, one hand resting on the door of the old convertible, her face heavy and closed, there was a new crease to her mouth, her lips barely moving, as if she couldn't wait to get home, or maybe it was because Carlos was finally free, Lazaro's mother, Caridad, had said, let's leave this calamitous country, come with me, my son, otherwise you'll end up like your father and your uncles, they're going to die as martyrs, tomorrow you'll be attacking pious innocents in their temples, but Lazaro, the immigrant from Bahama Street, said that his mother was wrong to disobey the laws of men, his religion was his cousins' and his father's, Lazaro was the son of a vengeful tribe, said Caridad, saddened by how things were turning out, Carlos continued to look around, thinking that Lazaro might be hiding nearby, it had all happened at noon, the town bells ringing, it was noon when Carlos thought he was firing an empty gun at Lazaro all dressed in black, the watch, the Adidas watch, Carlos repeated, was it true, that bang, the Cuban's gun had been loaded, they'd lied to him, he was going to tell his mother once they were in the car, Mama, I just wanted to scare him, we weren't in the same gang anymore, we were afraid, we were spying on each other, I just wanted to scare him, Mama, and Mama would say, you didn't shoot at nothing, you saw him fall to the ground holding his bloody knee, what are you telling me, son, when you threaten to kill someone who used to be your friend, when you shoot your gun, that's homicide, my empty-headed son, Mama would say, did I bring you up with your brothers and sisters so you would start a life of crime so young, no, that's not how I raised you, Pastor Jeremy either, he's a holy man, they said so at the sermon at the Baptist church, a holy man, your father, and your friend Lazaro is no better than you, Caridad his mother talks to me sometimes, she says her son has gone back with his father and his uncles and they're all killing for Islam, she doesn't know where he is, and when he was in the car, the old-model convertible, Carlos would ask his mother, you must know where he is, Lazaro, Mama, you must know, and his mother would repeat that Caridad's son was no better than Carlos, an unspeakable grief for his mother, she still had her craft shop on the island but when she spoke of her son she wept, what did we do to heaven to have such children, why did we have them, we want nothing more than for them to be brothers, not enemies, you, Carlos, you shot him first, the noon bells were ringing and planes flew so low across the sky they couldn't hear a thing, you shot Lazaro, I thought it wasn't loaded, Mama, Carlos would repeat, and Mama would turn up the volume on the radio in the classic car, she couldn't hear him, she couldn't hear him anymore, and Carlos's heart tightened even more until it was nothing but a dry pit, hardly beating, what if Lazaro comes back, Mama, they say he comes back sometimes, that he's planning to, maybe I wouldn't even recognize him, why would he come back if he's got it so good over there, a fighter, a terrorist, you think it's good, Mama would say, he has so much violence to repent for, so many crimes, he can come back but he'll kill his mother, she went against the law of his forefathers, she refuses to wear the veil, or he'll kill you, yes, you, Carlos, if he comes back, we don't know, how can we know, he's so far away, no one can reach him, and Carlos would repeat, you must know where Lazaro is since you see Caridad, his mother, we're just two grieving mothers, Mama would say, turning up the music in the old car, we don't know where he is, we don't know anything about him except that last year he went over to see his uncles and his father, but we've seen him hanging around, all dressed in black and his face half hidden under a black bandana, we don't really know anything about what becomes of our children, no, it seems that life and experience are there to take them away from us one by one, to lead them off course, but Venus would come visit me on Sundays, she came with Rebecca, she always had bangles around her tattooed ankles, yes, either Venus or Rebecca, and her brother, Venus's son, he was still a baby, she brought him too, hang in there Carlos, she told me, I know a lawyer who'll represent you, her name is Perdue Baltimore, yes, thought Carlos, my sister Venus always came to see me on Sundays, we talked through the phone on either side of the glass and when she headed back out to the hallway with Rebecca and the baby, to the outside world, it was burning hot out there while inside we were always freezing, to her shiny car out in the sun, I could hear the bangles on her tattooed ankles, and I would cling to the bars thinking, Venus, Venus, come back, don't leave me, it's fierce in here, it's like an arena, the lions, I can't sleep, I'm scared, it feels safe to be near you, your daughter Rebecca, the baby on your shoulders, and Mama would say, your father forbade Venus to come see you, you weren't a good example for his children, but Venus never listened to him, your father is a holy man, she defied him again like in the old days, yes, like the old days when she used to sing in Uncle Cornelius's mixed club, Venus, Mama would say, that was a rough spot, your father was right, a girl could turn bad there, become an escort and who knows what else, the very picture of sin, Pastor Jeremy always said, she didn't listen to him, went and married Captain Williams, she wasn't even twenty and he was already ravaged by time but a handsome old man all the same, he had a fine bearing, though I don't know what she saw in him, other than the breath of decrepitude, he had a lot of money, he was a businessman, though you should have seen what kind of business, said Mama, it was always going to end badly, he was killed at sea by a rival gang close to his estate in the mangroves where Venus waited for him at night with his whole menagerie of pets, the dachshund always at her feet, the hummingbirds, the iguana she wore on her head, he had a mansion, an estate, he worshipped Venus and they lived like that in their counterfeit kingdom of happiness, he was a painter too, in one portrait he'd painted of the two of them he'd swapped their skin colours, she was white and he was Black, that was what love was, he said, an exchange, but could a white man know what we feel, could he, tell me, Carlos, well, he loved Venus and that was enough to please me, though not your father, he said that Captain Williams was a reprobate, he wasn't a husband worthy of Venus, Captain Williams's sailboat floated back alone to the estate in the mangroves flying a black flag, it was quite the drama, mothers know everything about their children, not that I witnessed it but I was told, all that drama, the captain would head out to sea all the time for his sketchy ventures, worse than sketchy, Mama would say to Carlos in the car to the droning of his brother El Toque's music, what I do know is that Rebecca isn't his daughter, she knows nothing about it and just keeps getting prettier and prettier like her mama Venus was and she sings so well in Coral City Temple just like Venus used to, just like Venus, yes, Rebecca isn't Captain Williams's daughter but his caretaker's, that boor, one day when the captain was gone he had his way with her, and so Rebecca was born, Venus always kept a gun under her pillow, but the captain was away at sea for a long time on business and the caretaker had his way with her, your father can never find out, Carlos, no, and my Rebecca must not know, she believes her father is the Jamaican fellow with whom she shares her life now, a more virtuous life than before, I must say, that's how it would be, thought Carlos, Mama still wasn't coming any closer, come on, she said, as if she were just suddenly seeing him in front of her, get in, get into your brother's car, here's an apple, you must be hungry, as soon as she sat down in the car she'd turn up the music and Carlos would see a less leaden light gleam over the fields, the road lined with grey shacks, and before long they'd be on the freeway and Mama would say, even with my swollen legs I came all the way to Atlanta to fetch you, it took some patience, you know I've never seen the city, I didn't stop, went straight to your jail out in the country-side, straight there, straight to your fenced-in suburb, I couldn't stop, my legs were too heavy, here, eat the apple, don't look at me like that, it took some patience to get here, Mama would say to Carlos in the vintage convertible, yes, he thought. Tonight is the opening of the new bar, Robbie's bar, Le Fantasque, said Yinn to Geisha, who was wearing a black wig with short hair spiked above her forehead, because of the heat, she said, and a short-sleeved dress from which her round arms bulged out, she felt puffier without the opulence of hair from the blond wig against her cheeks, she told Yinn, and Yinn kept telling her that she was still the same slim girl as ever, the same Geisha audiences loved for her uncommon, snappy, cheeky beauty, said Yinn, Geisha had a spicy way with words, oh yes, her voice that caught gently, she roused senses that refused to lie dormant in old and young alike, Geisha turned to Yinn, listen, Yinn, there's a message for you on my phone, a disturbing message, maybe we could put off Robbie's opening and our party for Robbie until tomorrow or even a bit later, but Yinn was busy getting ready for the opening and there wasn't time to read the message, and who would send them disturbing, worrisome messages anyway, we're not even going to answer, let's put some balloons outside too, said Yinn, decorations everywhere, Robbie wasn't expecting the bar to open tonight, he was going to be so surprised, if Robbie could still be surprised, said Yinn, he's been out at every march, he went out for the big San Francisco march for trans rights, though we have to keep doing it over and over again, said Yinn, Robbie's sense of humour wasn't the same anymore, he didn't have the same sense of awe he once had, he smiled less, he was tired, he's working nights too, said Geisha, he still dreamed of finding a husband, a navy officer, some lieutenant who would take him to live in Alaska, it's not as hot there in the summer as it is here, said Yinn, stop thinking about the message, Geisha, come help me, we have to go buy balloons, come on, focus, how do you go about decorating a bar called Le Fantasque, it's all about mischief and play, that's always been Robbie through and through, Robbie has an eroticism about him, who could have sent you that message on your phone, asked Yinn, who's it from, but Geisha didn't know, there was no name, she said, just a strange drawing, like an ink scratch, nothing, you couldn't really tell, but the tone of the message, it was the tone that got to her, said Geisha, it made her mad, or afraid maybe, or annoyed, and Yinn said, tonight is the opening of Robbie's bar, this is my gift to Robbie, my way to thank him for his activism, I don't have time to read it, said Yinn, I'm not done sewing my dress for tonight, you'll see, it looks downright imperial, Geisha, my mother is going to help me with the gold stars and the sequins, it's her style, more decadent than mine, and I'm going to do my makeup to look more exotic, the eyes, the dark arch under the eyebrows, you've got to have some mystery, you always have to hold something back, especially when we leave so little to the imagination otherwise, my lace underwear, we reveal everything about our bodies, listen to me, said Geisha, we got a message, this isn't the kind of thing you get every day, can I read it to you, Yinn, I feel like I should read it to you, there will be a few young ones up on stage tonight, baby queens, and the audience will be young too, out of caution and consideration for everyone who comes to our shows, should I read you the message, it's kind of scary or disturbing, we get all kinds of messages every day, said Yinn, why is this any different, it's just so much garbage, don't think about it, Yinn spun around and Geisha could only see the long, slender legs as Yinn strode toward the bar, a dancer's legs, not a man's, thought Geisha, and in the light-drenched garden Mélanie heard from Vincent, he wouldn't be able to leave his patients at the hospital, he wrote, though he would have liked to, he had a volunteer friend working in the refugee camps in Jordan, he would have wanted to be there to look after the children, many of them with respiratory diseases, his friend was a dermatologist, she had created a gel to heal their hands and their feet, all you could see during their endless exodus were bodies draped in dark clothes but often their feet and their hands were uncovered and they were infected or they had eczema and the gel soothed their skin chapped raw by the dry heat, winds, the stinging cold, Mélanie read her son's message and it was like Vincent was close to her again like he used to be when he was small and she had to call him back, be careful, don't get out of breath, warn him to stop if he felt faint, and all he wanted to do was run away from his parents to go play or tussle with his friends, go outside, swim with his friends in the pool or in the ocean even though she told him not to, it was like she was back in those early days again after Vincent was born and she lay with him in the bedroom with the blinds closed, for the longest time she just lay there and listened to him breathe, the whole house was celebrating the birth of her son as the millennium turned, the disturbing new era into which he was born, that evening she had her women's meeting, that much hadn't changed, her activism, all the meetings and lectures, those early days, so close to Vincent, so close to his breath, she hadn't had time to write her notes for the evening, she'd taken Samuel to school that morning in the van, she'd put the tennis balls away and packed a sandwich in his backpack for lunch, she'd been so young then, dressed as she was now in beige shorts and a white shirt, she and Daniel were so much in love, they had to tell Augustino not to come to their bed at night, he was too old, around her people were saying that Vincent was dark like his Italian grandparents, the family thought he looked like them, no one mentioned his halting breath, no one talked about his difficult birth, born of their love, of sensuality, born of the carelessness of youth and the blaze of their passion, at first he seemed as strong as her other sons, but then suddenly there was that little spasm, his face, was he breathing, he wasn't breathing, maybe it was modesty, women didn't talk as much about childbirth, how hard it was, Mélanie thought, it was supposed to be triumphant, the only thing to do really was to forget everything, there was such a weariness sometimes, a disgust that you could never overcome or define or even name, she felt it there in the half light of the bedroom next to Vincent, touching his damp forehead with her finger, Mélanie felt guilty, it was hard and she'd felt somehow removed from motherhood in the warm half light of the bedroom with the blinds closed, the pressure of Vincent's little body against her brought her back to herself, this new being, he belonged to her, she had given birth to him, brought him into the world, and now there he was, wailing for her to take care of him, should he even have been there at all, and so demanding, with that defect, would he even survive, wouldn't it be better for her to remain cold, detached, to keep him at a distance, his breathlessness might steal him away, that night or the next day, Mélanie touched a finger to Vincent's damp forehead and felt the chill of death although her child was alive, he was fierce and struggling, wasn't it better to push him away so that she would suffer less if she lost him tomorrow, and then all at once it came back and they were as one, mother and child, surrendering themselves together to the impossible future with the same gloomy certainty that they would both be kept alive, Mélanie thought, in spite of everything, and they were alive still, although the fear rushed back so easily, just an email or his voice on the phone, no, her son couldn't leave tomorrow for the refugee camps in Jordan, let another doctor go in his place, she kept reliving his difficult birth, inside her, in her body, Mélanie thought, she couldn't forget the torment of his laboured breathing, it felt like yesterday, it was now, and as Daniel walked along the water with old Uncle Isaac he remembered his dreams the night before, relentless dreams in which Augustino was near him, where were they going, what streets, what houses, everything seemed askew on the roads, rows of houses like shoddily built attics emerging, where were they, Augustino's words to his father seemed crucial, metaphysical almost, they were walking through the greyness of a destroyed city, Daniel didn't know which city, were they on another continent, there was nothing friendly or familiar, Augustino asked his father what he thought of his beliefs, or were they his own, the faithlessness of an atheist son, there was no cure for our longing for God, an insolent, impertinent longing, Augustino said, it had become a leaden longing we no longer had time to think about though it was there, hovering beneath our crude material pleasures, yes, just as insolent, just as impertinent, an inconsolable longing, Augustino said, Daniel could hear his son's voice clearly, he was speaking like a teacher, there was something revelatory in his voice, only to his father could he could speak like that, in some previous life, Augustino said, a divine love enfolded us, swaddled us, a love so deep that it was at once a mother's love and a father's, the love of a son or a daughter, is there not in that pervasive whole that was lodged for so long within us and which is so complete in its soothing unity the faint memory of mourning that love, of its loss, then Augustino fell silent, Augustino, tell me more about this doctrine, Daniel asked, or is it just another one of your inventions, something in your books, right, in your books, but there were no more words, Augustino was gone again and the pain he had described so clearly, inconsolable, he had said, that was the same pain his father now felt, hearing Augustino's voice again and his reprimands when he woke up, he told himself he had woken too late to start writing, it felt vindictive that his son would come to him in a dream only to tire of him and leave so quickly, where had he gone, in some desolate, abandoned city, his last words had been, oh Papa, you can't understand, you don't understand anything I'm telling you, then he was gone, what had he been wearing in the dream, he was cold, he had no shoes on it seemed, old Uncle Isaac asked Daniel if he was finally making any headway on his book *Strange Years*, did he come and write by the ocean sometimes like Adrien had been doing for so many years there in his deck chair even though his *Faust* wasn't finished yet, he kept editing it over and over, Isaac said, Daniel wanted to tell his uncle that sometimes writing books was a slow process but the old man was already talking about his travel plans, he was headed on a photo safari in Africa, he said, not a hunting expedition like those nasty hunters, no, just to see them, my lions, my zebras, the old uncle said, as if he had created a fleeting animal paradise with himself as lord and master, because there are so few of my zebras now, so few, even though I'm old, I'm almost a hundred, as I was saying, Daniel, I'm going to see them with new eyes, lions in the wild, in the bush, their wide eyes, wide open, yes, like my Florida panthers when they come visit me here on my island, the Island No One Owns, will those veterinary students know how to protect them as well as I do, how heartbreaking it is that we have to leave this life one day without knowing what happens after us, Daniel, you know how dear all of this is to me, my heart, whatever you think of the heart, it's an organ that never wears out, believe me, dear Daniel, you will hear mine beating beyond life, you will think, there it is, I can hear tough old Uncle Isaac's heart, what does he want now, does he want me to save one of his panthers, one of his foxes, and I hope you'll go save them, I am entrusting this mission to you, just like the veterinary students, the young researchers, listen to me carefully, you better forget about Augustino, it's eating your soul, it's better to forget about him, otherwise it'll be your own heart that breaks and stops beating, as smart as he may be, your son is a rebel, a renegade who divides people, but Daniel wasn't listening to old Uncle Isaac anymore, he was watching the egrets wing above the waves, they looked like white herons, Mère had seen them once, admired them, it felt like only yesterday she had come out to this pier nearby with the children, nothing ever changed, no, nothing, Samuel's boat was still at the marina, *Lumière du Sud*, Daniel thought, light of the south, all his children were grown, even the one whose uncertain return he still awaited, they were all alive and their parents too, the two of them, Daniel and Mélanie, sometimes it seemed like nothing ever really changed, even though Augustino had left, Daniel thought. Petites Cendres was helping Geisha with the decorations at Le Fantasque, at Robbie's bar, he thought Robbie was funny and eccentric but that much swagger could be a dangerous thing, his reputation as an activist was intense and he had started getting threats, enough was enough, thought Petites Cendres, the bar was going to be amazing, it would draw crowds, said Yinn, Robbie's bar, with a screen, electronica all night and outrageous videos, a dance floor swirling with colours and sounds loud enough to crack your skull open, Robbie loved the noise, the screaming, the party, the all-encompassing frenzy of the night, whether we're singing or dancing, it swallows us whole, said Yinn, as if we were dancing in fire, yes, Robbie is cocky, thought Petites Cendres, I need to talk to him, I have to calm him down, sometimes it's better not to be so loud, to make less noise, fewer words, a quieter life without too much emotion, to keep the anger as quiet as you can, yes, thought Petites Cendres, he was thinking too that there had been far too much Black blood spilled, his own and that of his brothers and sisters, if you were attacked in a church or in a Black or Puerto Rican drag club, whether you were praying in a church or dancing in a club, it was the same Black blood that was shed, always the same, there was no place to hide anymore, there was nothing sacred, even pastors fell in a hail of bullets, dancers moving under the lights beating down, it was always the same Black blood, defenceless, Petites Cendres's blood dripping while the white supremacists laughed, though that trans woman in Harlem had been killed by Black fire, the woman, Islan, her Black blood mingled with mine, thought Petites Cendres, and Black parents abandoned their children, they kicked them out in the street because of their sexual orientation, it was in a Black church that the pastor refused to hold Julion's funeral, no forgiveness for difference, let him go unburied, Julion is a degenerate, and then there's Robbie strutting around, the freedom fighter, can we not get some rest, thought Petites Cendres, we can't get a break from Robbie, from all the noise, yes, thought Petites Cendres, it was drizzling, a short, sweet summer shower, refreshing, he felt raindrops on his skin, his bare shoulders peeking out from his denim blouse, his head was getting wet, his hair, Yinn and Geisha were already inside, their gowns tangled in the great loops of balloons they would hang up on the walls before nightfall, there was another club opening up across the street, Decadent Friday's, Petites Cendres remembered dancing on the tables with Robbie at the Garden of Eden, they'd set it up like a tropical garden, the club had a lush green garden and even a swimming pool with gushing blue water, he remembered laughing with Robbie as they danced on the tables, their bodies swaying, more naked than naked in tiny Diesel G-strings, their cocks looked swollen under the silky fabric, Robbie strutting around, delighted, for his clients, clattering up and down the counter in his black boots, Petites Cendres was barefoot and the men relished the sight of the pink soles of his feet, their animal scent, bending over, languorous, the dancers syncopating their movements with sighs, high on the rutting desire of their clients stroking them, they welcomed the caresses with flirty, childish pouts as fingers and hands burrowed under their waistbands, the thin elastic that kept their thongs from tumbling around their ankles, and wads of bills brushed over the proffered skin, the dance went on and the next client tugged at his G-string, Petites Cendres hoping for a bag of powder, blow or money, already he could see himself and Robbie getting rich, that was back when he could still get full price, even though Black and mixed boys got less than others, but that was before he got the news from Dr. Dieudonné, he'd come to hate the doctor, we hate messengers no matter how politely they inform us that despite our youth we are on the brink of death, though Dieudonné only said to be careful, take it easy, Petites Cendres saw scantily clad young men with beautiful muscles heading into Decadent Friday's, their feline beauty, thought Petites Cendres, just like us when we danced on those tables, sensuous and greedy, Robbie and me, before Robbie became an activist, so intense and so distant, we moved across the tables through the smoke, women came too and one of them pointed a finger, a fingernail, at our indecency, like the men, bold as brass, what was there was so captivating, they wanted to touch, to take, but at the same time it was out of reach, they weren't allowed to take or touch, we were just making a living, he thought, when that finger curled toward me I thought, ah, there's my dust for tonight, now I won't have to work the hotels, begging, humiliated, I won't have to let them whip me, beat me, I won't, let's get up on the tables, Robbie, let's have a little fun, we're like sheep sold to market for next to nothing, you and me, Robbie, you know, leaping ewes, sheared and sold, with a little blood sweat and tears thrown in, don't you think, Robbie, and Robbie, complacent as hell, without an ounce of rancour in him, looked at me and smiled, thought Petites Cendres, do what you have to do and shut it, brother, he said and walked toward the men, sometimes lying back so that their hands propped him up, so many hands, as if he were saying, it will be fleeting but here is my body, an offering on your bed of hands, do what you will, but his subservience was a ploy and Robbie leaped up in his black boots, his G-string stuffed with gifts he seemed to want to share around, streaming with sweat, his body dripping in the yellow beams of smoke, he stood up, proud and weary, yes, that was how we lived, night after night, thought Petites Cendres, and Dieudonné had said, curtly but not without respect, if I were you, Petites Cendres, I'd stop all this right now, you see, there are a few symptoms, though I'm not sure yet, we have to run some tests, you see, Petites Cendres, words, they're just words, thought Petites Cendres, who'd begun to hate the doctor though that was unfair and he knew it, he hated Dieudonné's words, the courtesy with which the Haitian man spoke, they were only words, after all, thought Petites Cendres, but it was him, Dieudonné was the one who had said the words, what was he supposed to do, how could he not hate him, how, thought Petites Cendres, there's someone we've seen hanging around at the shows, at the cabaret at night, Geisha told Yinn, he's not a regular, he shows up around midnight, I see him and I wonder what he's doing in our neck of the woods in his black leather suit, he's maybe twenty years old and he seems to be checking things out, he was asking each of us if we bring people back for orgies after the show, what kinds of things we do, sometimes one of us allows ourselves to be misled by his appearance, we let him kiss us, I've been telling everyone to watch out, it's a traitor's kiss, listening to Geisha, Petites Cendres thought that death was like that, a traitor, although the boy Geisha mentioned might have been just a fly-by-night drawn to a bit of pleasure, nothing more, was Geisha worried about unknown pleasures being discovered by a stranger who might work his way into the group, was Geisha thinking of the lovely Samantha heading off at dawn in her airy green dress with a stranger on her arm only to be found a few days later in a ditch in Georgia, Yinn had drawn wings on the photo of her that hung on the wall at the Porte du Baiser Saloon, like on the bathhouse wall and around the plastic-coated faces of Herman and Fatalité, with the words, Petites Cendres could read them still, *rest in peace Samantha, rest in peace Herman, rest in peace Fatalité*, Samantha's blond hair all undone, lying there like that, in the ditch, her feet in the mud, oh, little flower of the streets, Samantha, thought Petites Cendres, why had things turned out that way, what sweet words caught your ear and took you away forever, Samantha, thought Petites Cendres, what love potion poisoned you, Samantha's parents said we have no son, we haven't seen him since he chose this, we blame you, you are all guilty, damn you, damn you all, and the bar was damned, the devil dressed to the nines and whispering, I'm one of you, but he wasn't, the venom of hatred was his bait, people like you, it would be better if you didn't exist, he said as he kissed Yinn or Geisha, if you only knew how much I hate you, I will rid the earth of your kind, no, no one had said that, thought Petites Cendres, we felt cold around him, a cutting, hurtful word barely uttered, yes, thought Petites Cendres, but we knew, the murderer was one of many, he had gone to pray in the mosque that would be set ablaze a few days later in Port St. Lucie, in the Muslim neighbourhood in Fort Pierce, he knelt on the stone ground and prayed, praying, he was insane with hatred, when had he felt that, when had he been attracted to men, boys, it was a serious sin for a Muslim and he couldn't admit it, praying, he prayed on the ground, prostrated himself, and in the house of prayer he gave in and sought revenge against all unholy temptations, he would not be one of those perverts, those freaks, he would recover from his temptations by putting an end to their existence, the mosque was set on fire, it burned down overnight, swallowed up by the flames, the murderer was still wandering around, or maybe none of it was true, thought Petites Cendres, Yinn and Geisha had been dazzled by how well their show did in Vegas, it was delirious, they kept repeating, we'd come back in a heartbeat, anytime, the queens got their flowers, ovations, Yinn and Cheng, prince charming, an Asian prince, the show was pure theatre, they would go back, for sure, after Robbie's bar opened, Yinn was bursting with artistic pride for Cheng, the bond they shared irked Petites Cendres, master and disciple, he couldn't dance like Cheng, all syrup and slowness, he didn't have his poise, who was Petites Cendres to Yinn anyway, a forgotten love, a meaningless fling, an affair, a bit of hazy tenderness, but although Yinn wasn't interested anymore, or worse, all that was left was a kind of tepid detachment, still Yinn stubbornly protected and defended

Petites Cendres against everyone, under Yinn's wing or armour, as if Petites Cendres were curled up under a butterfly's veil, in a velvet lair, Petites Cendres knew it, he was loved and protected, if it hadn't been for Yinn he would still have been lying around in Dieudonné's clinic, you could look out at the sea and at the sky without seeing them, healing in a crystal cage, or else he would still have been out on the street if not for Yinn, holding up the lamppost across the street from the saloon with Louisa, offering customers a beggar's dope, Louisa was only a homeless child, Petites Cendres should have kept her close, looked after her, led her home when the day dawned purpled and grey above the saloon rooftop, why hadn't he, hadn't he said, Herman, Fatalité, aren't you ashamed to surrender to these charms, where are they now, six feet under or scattered out over the waves, flecks still warm, Louisa, don't you regret it just a little, so do we all march from one hardship to the next until the ocean dries up, the seas, the rain that falls at night on the houses and streets of our town, Yinn had left a few days before with Jason and Jason's two daughters, Lily and Line, for their triumph in Las Vegas, with Geisha, Cheng, and Cobra, without giving Petites Cendres a second thought, they all knew he was immobile in his hammock at the Acacia Gardens, Jason's two daughters were too attached to the mother and father figures that Jason and Yinn provided, the stability of the couple, they were still so young, Yinn's fondness for children, or at least the way Yinn played at being fond of children, Yinn made puppets but was a kind of dream puppet, listless under the long hair, a body held aloft by masterful strings, and the children were obviously delighted by parents like that, they travelled together like a stunned, submissive retinue, on stage Yinn was all lush femininity, the most exquisite mother, glistening, that was how Yinn and Jason lived, Jason had lost his baby fat and his once-round arms and now was just as slender as Yinn although his arms were still covered in tattoos, they were so close now in their domestic life, family, sisters, children, Yinn's mother loved them all, all those misfits together at last, she sewed their costumes for them for the comedies and for the tragic nights, Somo meanwhile was both teacher and school for those lawless, bohemian children, Somo, her name was Somiko though everyone called her Mama the First, she was as dominant as her child though her authority was more nuanced than Yinn's, that's how it was, thought Petites Cendres, he was nothing more than Yinn's forgotten love, an object forgotten in a cupboard, or had he been a plaything, an indulgence in the secret spot on the heavenly cloud on which he rested his wide forehead when he slept, could that be it instead, thought Petites Cendres, Petites Cendres was Yinn's refuge, a haven, and in the sunny garden among the orchids, the ornamental plants Mère used to love giving to her friends, to Olivier or Tchouan when she went to visit or when they came to the house, but those days seemed so far away now, Olivier couldn't go out anymore, Mélanie thought she heard her mother say to them once over a cocktail, you'll see, my daughter will be at the head of a political party one day, you'll see, my daughter is a leader, or was that in the tearooms Mère used to go to, in Africa, my daughter knows how to organize community work, programs to reduce poverty, you'll see, my daughter, but then there was only silence, Mère, Esther, Mélanie's mother was no longer there to encourage her daughter, to feed her fervour, their lives had been intertwined for so long, bound by the same drive and

Mélanie now felt the absence of that force so sharply, a sudden rift in her life, Mélanie had only one regret, almost toward the end, the two of them were alone in the room that Marie-Sylvie de la Toussaint had finally vacated shortly after the theft, Marie-Sylvie, Mère's caregiver, had stolen her jewellery, after all the lies, Marie-Sylvie had finally left Mère's room with a devious look on her face and her head held high as if she were saying, you're rich, you owe me this, you've forgotten what misery I come from, with my brother, he's sick in the head, he never sleeps, you've forgotten that we crossed such stormy seas, what we sacrificed when we had to leave Haiti, our country, what would become of us in the promised land, lowly servants, your servants, you owe us a bit of stolen jewellery, you owe us, no, Marie-Sylvie hadn't said that, she had said to Mélanie, maliciously, I leave her in your care, your mother won't live much longer, Mélanie, the words had felt like an insult, a blow, not much longer, Esther, what haunted Mélanie was that she wished she had kicked Marie-Sylvie out of the house sooner, she didn't want to offend Esther, she wouldn't have approved of Marie-Sylvie being put out of the house like that, no, Esther would have said, you mustn't, but she treats you so poorly, Mélanie would have told her mother, yes, that was a regret, though there was nothing for it now, Mélanie thought, painful as it was, and she thought she would give Tchouan orchids and ask after Olivier's health, she wouldn't forget them, or would Olivier see the gesture as an affront, giving Tchouan flowers when her husband couldn't walk anymore, though he was lucid as ever, he could be ruthless, with himself just as with everybody else, the hibiscus with their open corollas shone in the sun, it was time to move them into the shade, Mélanie thought, before Mai got there, that would be a bouquet for Mai's birthday, she used to stick wild roses in her hair and behind her ears, they withered so fast in the heat and the stems were thorny, and Mélanie was reluctant to grab the soft bunches that dropped from the trees that were heavy with them in the summer, it felt like yesterday, Mélanie thought, Jermaine would come over to play with Samuel, back and forth from one house to the other by the ocean with the dogs, the birds on their shoulders, and then in a leap of time that relinquished nothing all of a sudden they were grown, both of them were artists, Jermaine was a filmmaker and director, he had his own production company and Samuel was a choreographer in New York, they didn't see each other as often, it seemed unthinkable, they'd been so close, inseparable, time destroys everything we love, even childhood friendship, yes, all of them, all the women had to join their voices together, Mélanie thought, Jermaine did live far away, in California, where he had his company, but why let go of those beautiful friendships, although time devours what we are and what we become, it devours it all, one instant and the next, we need to be more resilient, more resistant, yes, and we need to finally elect a Black woman president, it's her, Donna Africa, we'll fight for her, Donna Africa, she is a gift to an unsympathetic, hostile, racist society, she lived in the South when she was young, and in spite of how forgiving she is it'll be a rough go, we have all the technology at our fingertips, yes, and above all we have Donna Africa's passion for citizen involvement, she says it was the assassination of Martin Luther King that inspired her to ask for that engagement, to demand it, I'll talk to Olivier about it, he was one of the first African American senators, I wish he weren't so withdrawn, so impatient, it's this wheelchair I'm stuck in, he would say, that's the cause of my impatience, dear Mélanie, please don't be angry with me, my dear wife complains about me too, I can't even write like this, it's such a burden, don't hold it against me, like Jermaine, my son thinks I don't love him anymore, God, how can he believe that, Mélanie was still thinking of her, Donna Africa, the thrill of the crowds at her speeches, history was mostly an account of white people's exploits, the names of the country's first Black politicians got left out, what about Hiram Rhodes Revels, the first Black senator, born in North Carolina, he came to Washington in 1870, for a long time he'd been an Episcopal minister, preaching about racial integration, but no one listened and when he became senator they wouldn't listen to him either, nor when he was working for integration in the schools, but no dedicated life is wasted, Donna Africa said, none, and today her name was revered, Mai's future couldn't belong to greedy despots, no, but to the claims of this woman making noise in the Senate, Mai's heart would rejoice tomorrow for her, for Donna Africa, Mélanie thought, the warm afternoon air was fragrant with orchids, with roses, their perfume surging from thorny stems, the wild roses Mai had once worn in her hair, soon Mélanie would be able to hold her daughter, she would be there, they would meet her at the airport, Mai was quiet but she was more open than Augustino, and she was more than her child, she was her sister because she was a woman, or would be soon, a complicity already threading between them, like on that day when Mai had confided to her mother how bad she felt that she hadn't been a better friend to Tammy, they were sailing the *Lumière du Sud* while her friend was starving to death in a private clinic on an island where her parents had sent her, they didn't want to see her, a cadaverous child who refused to eat, Mai would always feel guilty for not having loved her enough, could her love have saved Tammy, that's how we live, on the cusp of such chaos, with our failure to reach out to those we should be supporting, Mélanie thought, she herself couldn't bear the hollow absence between herself and Augustino, she was heartsick, really, perhaps all you needed to do was hold out your hand, but that hand clasps only empty air, she could call out, shout, but Augustino wouldn't hear, he wasn't deaf to the cries of others, he was charitable, generous, but as time passed, Mélanie became less and less aware of him, just as in our memories the faces of those we've loved and lost slip away, only the living are real to us, Mère's features, the kindness in her expression, had never really faded, the music she listened to brought back her face, the light in her eyes, Mélanie used to listen to Schubert near her mother, often in the evening, before nightfall, the cicadas still humming, and Mère asked if Mai was back, no, not before midnight, Esther, Mélanie said, she does go out a lot and she comes home late, Mère said, isn't she a bit young to be going out like that, or else Esther would ask for a fresh pitcher of ice water on her bedside table, I won't sleep until the little one comes home, she would say, rising from her pillows with a smile, as if Mai were the cause of a great unfulfilled happiness, you see, Mère told Mélanie, I can't bear to see them grow up like that, they leave one by one, like Samuel and Augustino, to know they're leaving home, when I see them again, the music, the softness of Mélanie's voice soothed Mère, and Petites Cendres saw the workers bringing the special pool table in to Robbie's bar, they used to play pool with Fatalité, thought Petites Cendres, he could still hear the trundle of the balls on the green felt, we would be watching movies at the same time, we danced for hours out there on the dance floor, every Sunday, yes, it was always cocktail hour, euphoria o'clock, we would dance and smoke weed, and there was a little bit of illicit love too, knowing Fatalité, a stolen embrace here and there, those sneaky dancers who came in on Sunday after swimming in the sea, they smelled like sweat and salt, the flavour of that skin, the raw tang Fatalité held onto for a long time, Petites Cendres remembered a recurring dream he used to have about Fatalité, almost every night, as if Fatalité were telling him, don't forget me, the lamp hasn't gone out yet in the apartment upstairs, or has it, has another tenant moved in where my ghost reigns, in the dream Fatalité was on the bicycle she used to ride at night, its wheels festooned with colourful baubles, it looked neon-lit, buoyant, but, glitzy as it was, the bicycle was headed for the tracks, the trains speeding by, and Petites Cendres was shouting, don't go that way, Fatalité, don't go toward the train tracks, and as if Fatalité were suddenly concerned with elegance she bent at the waist to greet Petites Cendres, he could hear a laughing goodbye from her wide red mouth, or maybe she was saying see you later Petites Cendres, maybe tonight at the cabaret where Yinn waits for me every night, the bicycle, the tracks, the trains, everything vanished into a grey glow, but Petites Cendres knew Fatalité wasn't there in front of him anymore, when he woke up, he told himself that he would have forgotten the dream in a few days, Fatalité's wide mouth and her kisses and conquests, only a few days and the memory like so many others just as painful would be gone, erased, but it wasn't like that, Fatalité boldly ran him down on her bicycle, rolling over him with her multicoloured wheels, always asking if the lamp was still lit upstairs, asking, insisting, thought Petites Cendres, as if she were begging for the very breath of life to be given back to her, my life, my wicked life, she seemed to be saying, and Carlos saw that they were getting closer to her house where Mama and Pastor Jeremy and all their children lived, the old-fashioned car, the car his mother drove was going to turn the corner onto Bahama Street, and from their porches they would all see, they would be watching in silent disapproval, look, he's back, that delinquent Carlos, don't frown like that, Mama said, don't slump, they all know who you are, Mama would say, they're your brothers like you're their brother, even that Lazaro, he's forgotten what you did, we still don't know where he is, but Mama, it wasn't a crime, there was no bullet in the Cuban's gun, those white men didn't see it that way, said Mama, they're always more than ready to accuse us, Carlos didn't dare mention Polly, his dog Polly, even though Mama had told him several times that the twins had found other dogs named Polly, my son, don't you remember you stole her, not just the puppy but the bike too, you really are rascals, you and your brother El Toque, he's making a career out of stealing, I think this old car is one of his felonies, yes, I think so, El Toque doesn't have a job, so how could he have bought a convertible, tell me that, it's a classic, it's really old, replied Carlos, if I were him I'd sell it, it's worth a lot of money, said Carlos, he knew his mother wasn't happy, you've just arrived at your parents' house and already you're doing business, she replied gruffly, two more delinquents in your father's house, Pastor Jeremy, his reputation in the church is so honourable, you should be ashamed of yourself, son, causing your parents so much grief and disappointment, your parents are good people who've lived by the Lord's doctrine, a faultless, upright life, especially Pastor Jeremy, he's a holy man, I do have faults, they say in church that impatience is a sin and God has stricken me with the fault of impatience, Carlos listened to Mama, she did sound impatient, or annoyed, resentful, he could hear the exhaustion in his mother's voice, Mama never asks me what it was like in juvie, he thought, no, she doesn't want to know if I got beat up, she doesn't want to know about the Aryan Brotherhood giving the Black boys cigarette burns, she doesn't want to hear about any of it, in Chicago, said Mama, every day mothers lose their sons and daughters and the police get off scot-free, that's the truth, she said, but the Aryan Brotherhood guys aren't even men yet, thought Carlos, what are they going to turn into with their juvie-hatched gangs, Mama doesn't want to hear about it, my son, she said, I hope that you've been rehabilitated and that from now on you'll stay on the straight and narrow, there's a job opening in an auto shop, starting tomorrow, there'll be no lazing about in my house like in the old days, hunched over the table yawning and doing nothing with your dog, I don't want any more of that in my house, no, Mama won't ask me any questions, thought Carlos, she doesn't want to hear about the Aryan Brotherhood and their vicious attacks, I still have scars, no, she doesn't want to know anything, and in the convertible, in his brother El Toque's stolen car Carlos looked up at the sky, it felt good to see the egrets flying out to sea, the pigeons and the doves, he hadn't seen the sky for a long time and just breathing the air was a comfort, the smell of the sea, so close, there was the cloying smell of knapweed too, that and the hum of the engine nearly lulled him to sleep as Mama drove along Bahama Street, Esmeralda Street, and the neighbours on their porches watched them go by, dumb and dazed, he thought, let's put the roof down, said Mama suddenly, let's open the sunshade in the back, the neighbours have seen enough of us, it's just spite, rubberneckers who've got nothing to do all day but smoke hash on the balcony, when are they going to get a job, meanwhile their wives are working themselves to the bone, when are they going to man up, louts, the lot of them, they do nothing but stare into space all day long, they're soft, they're stunned, it's a disgrace, said Mama, their wives are out killing themselves for them, let's take down the roof, said Mama. What was it like, the sound of Fleur's flute, what were the notes he was playing in the street with Kim sitting next to him lazily riffing along on her tambourine with her big dog at her feet, since Fleur made it big in Europe now he was even renouncing his name, Fleur, he went by Andrew, he had disowned everything, thought Kim, it was insulting, it was an affront to Kim that they no longer existed for him, Jérôme the African, the craftsman Rafael, Kim, Brilliant, they had all been swept away along with his past, unhoused, a vagrant, a wandering minstrel, day and night, only yesterday he'd been dressed in rags with hibiscus in his hair, Kim was filming Pearl Saved from the Waters, her daughter's first steps on the beach, it was outrageous to think of Fleur flicking off his phone, the screen going dark, as if the images were too much for him, unbearable, by the ocean with the herons Kim looked healthy with her child in the sun, Pearl Saved from the Waters, her first steps, he had roamed the beach forever with all of them, Kim, Max the dog, Jérôme the African, no, the past had to be summoned, it had to be exorcised, thought Kim, what a mistake, a missed opportunity, Kim would never see him again, he had betrayed her for his concerts in Europe, his music, maybe he was rich now, he knew what money was, that was for sure, thought

Kim with a touch of disgust, he had probably learned how to be an educated man, polite, yet he was humble, the humility of those who have been deferential for so long, who are used to lying, like when the two of them were still panhandling together, it wasn't always deference, some submissiveness maybe, but always dignified, when they were offered heroin they refused, while on the other hand Jérôme the African would shoot up with dirty syringes, Jérôme might have been the only one in their group who did, Rafael only sold to get high, for weed, she would have preferred to live somewhere other than a loft crammed full of women and children, every one of them Rafael's own, she wished she'd never left Old Salt's boat, the smell of fish and ocean, and the murderers who'd done him in, Old Salt loved them so much, Kim and Fleur, and the yellow bicycle, a gift for Kim, he'd said to her, I love you like a daughter, Kim, take whatever you want on this boat or live here with me, don't stay out in the street anymore, you and Fleur, they still hadn't found the suspects, killing a poor man like that, an old man, and Pearl Saved from the Waters walked, her first steps ungainly and perfect, thought Kim, her daughter, Rafael's daughter, walking, how bleak to think she would never see Fleur again, he acted so cold, Andrew, he was unreachable, a concert musician now, transplanted into a world that wasn't hers, a world of music and banquets, and she was so alone on her island with a man who distracted her, he entertained her but she didn't love him, Kim would never have children with him, with Fleur, they would never see each other again, everything was falling apart, the sky, the earth, thought Kim, she sprang to her feet, Pearl Saved from the Waters was toddling toward the waves and Kim scooped her up, no, you can't go that far, my love, no, Kim moved awkwardly on the sand, tangled up like she'd always been, when she was with Fleur, that khaki shirt she wore and her studded boots, maybe she had that sour smell he didn't like, she was awkward and heavy, anonymous, like all of Rafael's wives, she thought, she would have been Fleur's one and only, she wasn't like other women, but often, even when he was busking, Fleur hardly looked at her although she was right there with him, so close, his flute and the scatter of the tambourine in the scalding, still air, especially in the summer, and he would stop playing and turn to her, and cry, what are you thinking, this is music, we have to take it seriously, why hadn't she answered him firmly, I'm wide awake, I think I love you, but he would have laughed, maybe, and moved away from her, tipping his head back in his hoodie, it has to be beautiful even for people just walking by on the street, you don't understand, Kim, my parents were junkies, said Kim, there was nothing but shouting in our house, yelling, and I hear it when I play the tambourine, but maybe she'd forgotten to tell him about her parents, she was embarrassed, they were hopeless junkies, she'd never see them again either, they would forget to feed their kids, they forgot when it was time for school, they were so out of it that one day the kids had to call for help because their parents were lying there on the kitchen floor, they wouldn't wake up, children of junkies, such trash, thought Kim, her honour, Kim's honour even with Fleur would never be redeemed, even if Old Salt had said, go on, Kim, dear child, don't give it another thought, your parents lost custody of your siblings anyway, why don't you come stay on my sailboat with Fleur, come in from out of the storm, that way you wouldn't get so cold at night, I can't see my children, they're on the other side of the Pacific, how could I sail that far at my age, Kim kissed Pearl Saved from the Waters on the cheek, the salty taste of her daughter's tears, she was looking more like her father, she was getting darker, the Mexican's daughter with that golden complexion, you'll play in the waves later, said Kim, Pearl Saved from the Waters wobbled back in her bare feet and came to sit against Kim's dog, playing with the rope Kim used as a leash, and Kim continued to film her on her phone, the baby was annoyed by her mother taking pictures, her eyes trained on the rope around the big dog's neck just as they had focused yesterday on the budgie's beak and wings, Orange was the budgie Lucia had given her, she stared at the dog, looking at the animal and the rope so seriously, with such attention, too bad for Fleur, thought Kim, he'll never get to see Pearl Saved from the Waters, she's so good at understanding the language of animals, she's like a little animal herself, primitive and untamed, she's at one with the bird, squawking, Orange the budgie, the bird loved a good show, just like them, the public performances, Rafael would hold out his arm to let Orange claw on, he sometimes did the same thing with the autistic kids when he took them out to the pier, it was therapeutic for them, he said, for those children whose speech seemed to be caught in some private drama in which words, the very desire for speech, had been broken, Rafael could hear them cooing with the bird, the budgie, that instinct was what he had tried to instill in Pearl Saved from the Waters from the moment she was born, Kim thought, he was entertaining and generous, he distracted her, but he was also a liar, he rejected any authority, it's time to head out to sea, he said, we'll buy a boat, the coast guard has forgotten me, nothing is going to happen to us, you'll all be safe, I'll travel around and work, our sailboat bobbing high on the waves, how quickly he forgot, thought Kim, Rafael was as defiant and stubborn as ever in his plans, he was just a lawless sailor, a man without papers, though he could forge them, if he were caught he would be punished to the fullest extent of the law, a fake refugee from Mexico, he was no less a fraud than Jérôme the African who had washed up on the shore in a cargo ship full of Haitians, but Jérôme had been a child soldier, he said so himself, a killer, he sang about it all day long, high as a kite, biking around with his clinking bottles, water, who wants water, he had been deprived of water, that was a favourite torture inflicted on child soldiers, they had neither water nor rice nor bread, only the sharp rattle of guns, and even here, even in the country that had taken him in, he was a man without a homeland, even here he kept being pushed back toward the ocean, toward emptiness and death, and Rafael repeated to Kim, those immigration officers won't get us, we'll be invisible at sea under the clouds, under the sky, invisible, Kim, don't be afraid, there are borders they can't cross, we have a big, strange family, if we formed a human chain, they wouldn't be able to cross the wall of bodies, that's what we'll do, we'll leave with our animals, it'll be a real Noah's Ark, I'm telling you, Pearl Saved from the Waters will have a rabbit, budgies, whatever she wants, as Pearl Saved from the Waters took her first hesitant steps, falling back and rolling on the sand, Kim thought of Fleur, Fleur who would never see her daughter, Fleur, a composer and concert musician who only yesterday was a beggar, dressed in rags, hibiscus in his hair, Martha, his mother, hated it so much, she had lost Fleur too, he went by Andrew now, his picture was splashed all over the arts section of newspapers Martha read and promptly destroyed, she had enough to worry about without Fleur, or Andrew, she said to Kim, and above all, don't cry for him, Kim, dry your eyes and harden your heart, he'll never give you anything, he'll never give me anything either, and I have other things to do than wait for a son who treats me that badly, Martha told Kim, Martha asked Kim for help, Father Alfonso was finally back in his parish on the island after being sent to New England, an undeserved banishment after he spoke out against pedophile priests all over the world, for a long time he was exiled, punished so that he would keep quiet about those crimes, Alfonso was with Martha again, with Fleur's mother, together they hid the refugees in his church or in Martha's house, those poor people constantly persecuted, her son knew nothing about the work she did, thought Martha, she was risking her freedom and Father Alfonso's, Fleur was an egotist, though not a criminal like he had been when he lived on the street, that was something at least, he wasn't stealing from anyone, really he was a good boy but music had taken him away, it was no consolation to hear people who were more educated say that her child had talent, even very young, Fleur was phenomenal, it bothered her, though she'd been so proud of him once, the admiration her son got when he played flute or piano, he had been born into music, he couldn't escape it, it was a straitjacket, he was eating well now, thought Martha, he wasn't scrounging through dumpsters anymore, he was dining at Europe's finest tables, she should have been thrilled, but the shadow of shame never left her alone, even when she imagined her son suddenly elegant, the same baleful shame crept into her mind, she still thought of him when she took in refugees at her house or in Alfonso's church, always him, those refugees who were endlessly abused, her own lost son could have been one of them, there were so many young men who looked like him, they might not have been as talented, but they were young and healthy, they had no other choice than to be invisible so that they wouldn't be deported, whereas Fleur belonged, he had a mother, he had a country, but he didn't care, Martha wrote him messages all the time on her phone, I know you refuse to remember us but your friends are asking after you, your friends in Lizzie and Seamus's Cajun band, there'll always be a place for you, on violin or piano, they're asking after you, wondering why you're taking so long to come back, and we see poor Kim everywhere with the dogs, Max and Damien, even Damien, your dog, your German shepherd, he's so intelligent, how could you forget him, you loved him so much, we see her on the beach in the evening with the baby and the dogs, as if she were waiting for you there in front of those cruise ships gleaming in the night, some of your friends, musicians, Black guys, they work on the cruise ships, playing for tourists with their jazz bands, you've forgotten all about them, it's time to close up, I never close the pub until late at night because the sailors stay so late, I can hear the music and the laughter gliding out over the water from the cruise ships where Black musicians toil, those old, toothless men shucking their voices, you used to like coming with me, once a month I'd wash you from head to toe to the sound of that music melting into the night, your own mother, I washed you, I'd scrub you clean, and you'd run off again, back to the street, your haunts, your friends, that's how I wash the refugee children, I look after them as best I can even though I know what fate has in store, I may not have a son anymore but I have all those children who want me to be their mother, and Alfonso, the priest who rebelled against his church, he tells me you'll be back but I don't believe it, I don't believe him, he's an idealist, his heart is too pure, Alfonso, he's still my best ally against the scourge of injustice and deportation, and here we are, standing up to evil, there are two of us but we are legion, I want you to know what's going on here where I am while you're halfway across the world, you say you're writing an opera about a tragedy in a high school in Germany, what good is that, don't waste your time, or maybe I read that somewhere, that you were composing that opera with a young composers' grant, no less, you're drunk on success, one triumph after another, while here you would be appreciated and surely well paid in Lizzie and Seamus's Cajun band, they don't just play here, you know, they get around, but you're probably too good for them now, that's not how your grandparents raised you, that's not how my husband and I raised you, we're divorced now, even with all your talents we wanted you not to become vain or proud, you were such a sweet, simple child, do you remember, I used to embroider your clothes when you had a concert, a piano recital, you played barefoot, yes, it was so simple then, so spontaneous, and I would run my hand through your long hair, that's how you liked it, I didn't mind, if you hadn't met your friend Clara, that virtuoso violinist, you really looked up to her, you turned your back on us, your parents, you respected your father, your grandparents loaned us money, they were just poor farmers, you loved them, you loved us all, even though in some ways we were unworthy of you, we didn't know how to guide you, where or how, we were dazzled and defeated, powerless, we didn't understand you, yes, that's how it was, I'm afraid, I admit it, from the moment you were born, was that our fault, you were misunderstood but was that really our fault, tell me, and as they drove down Bahama Street, Esmeralda Street in the old-fashioned car Mama said to Carlos, don't look at anyone, don't look back under the blinds, don't let anyone see us, men on their porches while their wives slog away for them, good-for-nothings, sloth is a vice, my son, you've got to get a job, tomorrow, and don't be seeing those trouble-makers, no, you'll go and beg your keep from that garage owner, though he's a white man, you'll go tomorrow, I tell you, the director of the juvenile detention centre told me you liked fighting but the gang boys scared you, they burned your skin with hot coffee, back in Lazaro's time I told you not to join the Aryan gangs, I told you that, how many times did I tell you, you're going to show me where the burn is, the director told me you had a huge scar on your shoulder, the skin wouldn't heal, in the infirmary they told you you'd need morphine for the pain, you never told me any of that when I came to see you on Sundays, you were always quiet and vague, I wondered why I bothered coming to see you at all so far away in Atlanta, I never even stopped in the stores in the city, even though I love them, your father doesn't approve, but I'm a woman and always will be, the thing about the hot coffee, I didn't know, that Aryan Brotherhood, they're hooligans, who knows how they came up with the idea of the hot coffee, and what you did, you've always got to be fighting, just like with Lazaro, you used to love boxing, it wasn't always about conflict, you learned to box with your brothers, really, I hardly recognized you back then, though I won't stand for you being insulted, hot coffee thrown on your shoulder, if I had been there, tell me again what you did, or it's fine, don't tell me anything, sometimes silence is better, I know one day you'll talk, you're my son after all. Donna Africa, Mélanie thought as she walked among the flowers, gathering a bouquet for Mai's birthday, perhaps she would go surprise Mai at the airport with the flowers, they smelled so lovely, Donna Africa said in her speeches that everything had to be shaken up, shaken loose, African Americans had been misled, poor people deprived of their rights, their right to vote, their rights had always been undermined, even their right to live, to exist, were things really that different now from the days of enslavement, yes, she shouted, everything had to be shaken up, the fortresses of lies behind which the leaders hid, the women and the men in the opposition, the party she called the party of indifference, but from indifference, you will see, will come the party of terror, many of us have begun to feel it, the assassinations have already begun again, many times, yes, they will try to reject our Blackness, our entire heritage, and those who defend us will perish along with us, her detractors said Donna Africa's reaction to injustice was too emotional, it was that sentimental side of women, that's how she was described in political circles, Mélanie thought, Senator Donna Africa was a passionate, overly emotional woman and emotion was a regrettable female flaw, wasn't it, in Kenner, Louisiana, in the New Orleans suburb where she was born, that day Donna Africa had seen thousands of people weep in their homes and in the streets, how we wept for that man in 1968, he was our family, he was our country, you who have come here in droves to hear me know that I have been fighting for you for a long time, since that day in 1983 when I was coming out of university, who in their youth doesn't dream of changing the world, I've been with you since that day, rise above your oppression and stand with me, Donna Africa was saying to those who had gathered to listen, and Mélanie thought she was right, our most serious fault was our indifference to the past, the nation was recruiting the indifferent for the party of indifference, we ended up feeling nothing at all about the mistakes of the past, they were more than mistakes, the heinous acts we allowed, what we tolerated, as if it had become a part of us, an impersonal racism, the racial inequality or any form of prejudice that was accepted and acceptable, it spread through indifference, we no longer felt anything in the party of indifference, Donna Africa said, we had to shake ourselves awake out of that inertia, the oblivion of our indifference, she said, Mélanie thought back to another time, Mère listening to Puccini, her unfathomable joy when she listened to those operas sitting in the swing by the pool while the children played, the memory of Mère listening to the music revived a whole era for her, she remembered her mother young and flourishing, lit from within, blossoming, the music she loved opened her up, on those afternoons, when Mélanie was writing anti-war pamphlets, at the time of what they called the interminable January war hanging over them like a black cloud, Augustino, Samuel, and Vincent played in the pool under their grandmother's watchful gaze, she only seemed to be paying attention to the music that filled the air but her eyes never left her grandsons for an instant, the summer afternoons blurred into the gripping anxiety Mélanie had felt that day, hours glued to the television set, the same event unfolding again and again, an infinitesimal drop of plutonium had seeped off course, spreading over the fields of the Ukrainian Republic, wiping out thousands, humans and animals, and children, the children went bald, they had leukemia, and the unborn animals, the occupier was near but still unseen, no one knew it was coming because we had forgotten, the events dated back to the twentieth century, in those days Mère was more frivolous, more worldly, Mélanie couldn't bring herself to tell her that she was imagining Augustino or Samuel without their blond curls, without eyelashes curled around their eyes, the occupier was near, the drop of plutonium was silent, the occupier was close but there was not a sound, the thunder of the cavalry, the interminable January war had been raging for months already, a drop of plutonium across the fields and forests of Ukraine, though what mark did that leave in the infinite game of massacre, almost nothing, Mélanie thought, her sons had grown up and the drop of plutonium had crossed the Atlantic, landing on other fields, other forests, on the heads of other little children who went bald, they were diagnosed with leukemia, just one drop, what did it mean in the grand scheme of things, no one expected the occupier to return, that was the thing, Mélanie thought, indifference, the forgetting erased everything, we were living in a coffin of indifference, as Donna Africa described it, and there was the weather, too, it was so nice that day it was easy to forget, the children played in the green water of the swimming pool, Mère listened to her music, the swing swayed under the blue sky, we could forget about a drop of plutonium drifting and spreading slowly over the planet without a sound, and we also forgot about the occupier, a nuclear superpower with a giant arsenal, they were still there, more present than ever, closer than ever to the population, the poor men and women and children, the plants and animals, the poor fields frozen under the snows of Ukraine, without making a sound, who knows, Mélanie thought, perhaps the droplet of plutonium had pushed against headwinds across the Atlantic to mingle with Vincent's breath when he was born, as the leaves fell from the trees, as the fruit rotted on those trees, in Ukraine, in the ghostly villages and towns people were leaving behind, people said those who stayed could barely digest anything from the radiation poisoning, yet they still drank vodka, where there was still life there must not be despair, but how could they live if they couldn't sell or consume what the land produced, how could they survive, even for a time, already bald and riddled with cancer, they knew it but they couldn't change a thing, yes, that was how Vincent's breath had been broken, without a sound, he couldn't breathe but Mélanie never said a word to Mère about how anxious she was, and Esther on the swing listened rapturously to a love duet that made her forget the painful end of her marriage, the divorce that tore her two sons away from her, Puccini's duet offered the ecstasy of a brief escape from an existence where divorce was a failure, the failure of love, not its redemption through music that sang the beauty of a passionate encounter between a man and a woman, but Mère took no solace, Mélanie thought, she had loved her husband and not seeing her sons was harrowing, the music did help her to overcome the sinking feeling of having been betrayed by her husband, he left her for a younger woman, a mistress, that was all, Mère thought, she had been betrayed by a philandering husband who chose a young lover, she could hardly bring herself to admit it and she would never have confided in Mélanie how angry she was at the thought of her husband, she knew Mélanie looked up to her father and her faith in him had to be upheld, Mère was a patron of the arts, she ran a museum, one day she would be able to live without him, he didn't understand the extent of her ambition and her selflessness in wanting to fulfill it, the Puccini duet, the love song in the opera Mère was listening to on the swing, that was the reward, the blessing of thinking only of love that radiates without destroying everything around it, a mother and her family, destroying everything, or was it before that, Mélanie thought, when Augustino fell asleep on the veranda and Mélanie comforted him, don't cry, Augustino, it's only a storm, it'll pass and soon the sun will come out, this evening, we might be able to go to out on the boat with Papa, already when he was just a baby she had brought him to all their friends' houses, in winter too, during the Christmas holidays, she would be wearing fine wool clothes, he was so small, how was this her son, Augustino, she took him out so he would be less shy, more sociable, he was always huddled against his mother's legs, he didn't want to see anyone, was she too lenient, had she been too soft with Augustino, she never scolded him when he sulked or when he threw a tantrum, as she watched Esther on the swing Mélanie thought of those years when Mère had travelled so much, visiting cities and ancient museums, what would she think, what would she have thought of the ancient city of Palmyra, if she saw it now, the fortresses she had once contemplated, fourteenth-century souks, concerts in Homs and Damascus, so much of the splendour she had become accustomed to as she travelled around discovering new museums was gone now, Mélanie thought, the fourteenth-century mosques and their pious visitors or the hotel she had visited that had been a palace in the sixteenth century, everything had been demolished, vandalized, either by conquerors bowing to mad dictators intent on driving out rebel forces or by tribal bands destroying famous works of art with axes, and in the depth of the silence that follows looting you could still hear the cry of an animal or a child, a last sigh perhaps, and that was the sigh, barely audible, that Mère would not hear when she shut herself up in her room and never came out again, much later, when she no longer had the curiosity to travel, she was so tired, Mélanie thought, although she had taken such pains to make the room as pleasant and lovely as a Matisse painting, you could see the sea behind the blue curtain, the palm trees that looked blue too from the gleam off the water, the sea looked like it had been freshly painted, or was it just Mère who saw the room that way, the window with its blue shutters, the sea that seemed to be set apart by a red line, as Matisse would have done, that red line reining in her desire, keeping her back from heading out to sea, she would never leave again, not to the ancient museums of Palmyra, not to a concert in Damascus, beyond Matisse's red line, that was how she imagined it, although she could hear the sea, the ocean, perhaps there was nothing left. Evening will come, and night, and the pool players will face off in the lanterns' red glow, thought Petites Cendres, Robbie's bar, Le Fantasque, will be open until dawn, for all-night raves, the sun setting at dawn as it sears our eyes, I can feel it, I can see it, it'll be great, we'll only be thinking of love, as Yinn says, we'll forget about that hateful message, thinking only of love, we all love each other, as Yinn says, does he still believe that, here we are tangled up in balloons to hang on the doors, Geisha and I, the windows and doors are only for closing time, there will be no doors or windows otherwise, people will be able to come in off the street to dance with us on the dance floor, even with the fans the air will be so hot that we'll have to take off our clothes as we dance, like the girls who come in here, they end up wearing only their baseball caps, half naked, they'll dance around for a while to the blaring rock music then head off to other clubs, other bars, unleashing their dancing bodies, one of them will stand waiting for a long time for a man in front of the pool table but the man won't see her and he'll leave with another man and the waiting girl will be sad with a beer in her hand, that's how it always is, thought Petites Cendres, so many nights flashed through his mind until he was saturated with them, but like the girl staring at the pool player he had waited at the end of the late night that stretched until the paleness of dawn because sometimes the sky after a violent storm goes white and ugly, yes, hoping for Yinn's hand in his, almost nothing, a disillusioned smile and the sip of a cocktail, the last of the night, the cherry cocktail, hoping Yinn would say to him through the rising steam of the white dawn, my dear Petites Cendres, will you have a nightcap with me, in the bar the big-screen TVs will bring us back to the songs, the wailing trumpets, all those Mardi Gras in New Orleans, armfuls of necklaces in the streets, a necklace of roses too, I'll be dreaming of that, as if the necklace were a gift from Yinn's own hand, petals between fingers against my cheek, as Petites Cendres day-dreamed, under the decorations at Robbie's bar, at Le Fantasque, he saw a man and his son coming down the street, a father walking his son home from school, father and son chatting quietly, the boy hopping from one leg to the other, are you still working hard in school, asked the father, he spoke with a foreign accent, yes, Papi, replied the son, but I'm also having fun with friends, we're going to a cabin by the sea soon, very far away, very far, said the child, we're going to study shark behaviour, very far, very far, he repeated, Petites Cendres was listening to their sweet chatter when he saw three policemen get out of their cruiser and seize the child's father, cuffing him and forcing his head down, they're illegals, said one of the officers to Petites Cendres, what are you doing there with your stupid balloons, let us through, you can't do anything for them, it's a fair arrest, do you think we have a choice, we're just following orders, they were taking the father away, they were roughing him up, a female officer appeared and stood between the father and son, don't worry, she said, he'll be placed in foster care, we take good care of the kids who are born in this country, where will his father go, asked Petites Cendres, back home to Guatemala, said the woman, we told you, we're just following orders, it's not something we like doing, I'm a mother, I'm doing this against my instinct, if this wasn't my job, but what do you want us to do about it, it's just the way it is, can you let us through, sir, please, the balloons are in our way, and Petites Cendres just stood there, he couldn't let them through to the cruiser, the woman clutched the little boy's hand, he was calling out to his father, Papá, Papá, where are you going, Papá, don't leave me alone, Papá, the cry of a father whose child is being taken away was a pitiful thing and before he knew it tears were running down Petites Cendres's face, the cry of a father torn from his son reminded Petites Cendres of Lena, Angel's mother, a cry as guttural and abrupt, despair restrained but so deep Petites Cendres would never forget it nor hear its like again, at each loss, the abductions he would witness in the future, children, women, men, they were scooping up illegal immigrants, wherever they were, they would be abandoned, Lena wailing before her son's ashes as they were scattered in the ocean among the orchids, the white roses, and the flowers they call birds of paradise because they look like wings, that sudden silent cry, still in the sea air, when the pelicans resumed their diligent flight, seeing that Petites Cendres was crying the woman said, thank you for letting us through, believe me, I know how you feel, I know we'll feel bad about this, who can do something like this, it's disgusting, I know, I know, I'm a mother and if anyone tried to separate me from my son, believe me, I would kill them, I can't imagine doing anything else, having said those words, she disappeared with the child into the police car and the street was silent once more, as if the moment had only been some passing scene in a nightmare, thought Petites Cendres, maybe that was all it was, and his tears would dry soon, he couldn't feel them anymore in the parched wind. As for the red hibiscus flowers, the garden would be overflowing with them for many seasons, through the summer, fall, and winter, Mélanie thought, with their heavy summertime corollas the hibiscus seemed more vigorous in the fall and winter, they sprang from the light, from the sun, their successive blossoms were always such a surprise, luminous red bunches with a delicate perfume, and then they're gone, they burst into bloom on a rainy day, red pearls of water, of wind, fickle flowers, Mélanie thought, and since that day, the droplet of plutonium that fell on the fields of Ukraine had spread like a slick for miles across the world and those in charge had decided it was better not to talk about it, there was no point in causing panic so they alone kept the secret, whether they were competent or not, whether they were tyrants or respected leaders, they alone guarded the secret of the plutonium, which now was referred to in sterile code, it was fair to say that we were all living in a vault of hidden strategic missiles whose great and unacknowledged propulsive power those men knew would mean millions of deaths, those men, with the complicity of the women in their service, they knew it would mean the end of an entire civilization, strategic missiles, tactical missiles, missile guidance, the words were manoeuvring their way into us, Mélanie thought, and we weren't even taking the time to reflect, our perception of them had been rendered abstract, those words, Mélanie thought, she would say that at her lectures, she wondered if anyone would come to hear her, to listen, her son Augustino had inspired her, and Daniel too, Augustino's indignation, his revolt, his absence was a sign of his refusal to give in, it was as if he had shouted to his parents, I will not come back to you until the world is at peace, not a war zone stoked by the appalling indifference of grown-ups, yes, that was it, yes, perhaps, Mélanie thought, that was why he had left, he wanted his writing to be active, a movement, and his life as well, he wanted it to be sublime, never dull, wasn't that why he had left, Mélanie thought, that was why he had written in his first book, already I am bidding farewell to children with no tomorrow who have not had the presence of mind to stop this madness, who are passive like their parents and who tomorrow in their obliviousness will be the first victims of the most despicable enterprise of all, nuclear powers guiding missiles toward them, they pretend to doze off so that they won't hear anything, their phones glued to their ears, just as they hear the drone of the weapons, they don't make a sound as they kill, it occurred to Mélanie that without Augustino she might never have understood the urgency that often kept her awake at night, to speak up, to speak out, she talked about it with Mai more than with Samuel and Vincent because Mai was the vessel of a future in the making, or she was on the brink of that future, whether it was a cliff or an unhoped-for cosmic renewal, she was ready for anything, although sometimes she seemed so carefree, she was ready especially for friendship and affection from her friends, for parties and get togethers, wasn't that what mattered most at her age after all, Mélanie knew she had to step back, that was Mai's world for the time being, she was surrounded by friends of whom Mélanie knew nothing, as if Mai hadn't invited her to cross the threshold of the mysterious forest of friendships that were hers and hers alone, Mélanie knew that there was also depth and seriousness in Mai's soul even though the loam in which Mai's qualities grew was still uncultivated, however precocious that depth and seriousness were, and however clumsy she still was in expressing them, that was the depth that bound Mai to Mélanie, they shared the same fears and hopes, though they couldn't always tell each other, Mélanie knew that women could be extraordinarily strong together when their thoughts were linked, and Mélanie remembered that on that festive evening, or rather on those four festive nights celebrating Vincent's birth, Mère had noticed Renata's arrival, her sister came through the front door, Mère adjusted her glasses and said, why is she so late, Renata always shows up late, Mère said in a jealous whisper, is it because she's transcendentally beautiful, did Mère feel any jealousy that night toward the younger sister she saw too seldom, Mélanie wondered, how could Mère compete with Renata's three marriages and numerous affairs, she was disconcerted by Renata's arrival, showing up at the front door like that while guests came in through the garden gate, because Renata seemed too free a woman, her shoulders were bare beneath her satin jacket, or perhaps Mère had begun to feel that Mélanie was getting too close to Renata, a licentious woman, a woman who left no urge unconstrained, and who was extremely successful as a lawyer, perhaps she was worried that Renata would have too much influence on her daughter, whereas any beneficial moral influence should have fallen to Esther only, to Mélanie's mother, Mélanie whom Mère sometimes loved like a sister or a confidante, although Mère was modest when she spoke to her daughter or confided in her, but Mélanie saw her mother's face tense slightly, almost as a reproach that the woman she described as transcendentally beautiful, the sister who was nearly a stranger to her should suddenly appear at the front door of the house, and that it was Renata, who according to Esther was too free with her bare shoulders under her satin jacket, who would subtly influence her daughter and, who knows, perhaps even transform her, already their relationship was far from warm, that was Mère's role, it was Mère whose daughter would be a leader, she had been preparing her for her vocation since childhood, Mère had expressed her reticence to Mélanie differently, she never spoke of what actually bothered her about the relationship between Mélanie and Renata, wasn't it worrisome, she told Mélanie, that Renata still hadn't quit smoking, after major surgery and despite warnings from her doctor, it was obvious, Renata seemed to revel in the scent of her cigarettes, was it pride, recklessness, she smoked even as it was banned almost everywhere now, yet another way for her to assert her freedom, Mère thought, breathing in the scent of Renata's cigarettes, the scent that Renata herself was exhaling, she couldn't just dismiss the sight of Renata smoking like that when she had been warned not to, Renata reaching for the quick flick of the lighter or for her gold cigarette case, for Mère the scene was a provocation, everyone had seen Renata come in the front door rather than through the garden gate, an incitement to desire for all the men who were there, the young musicians, singers, accordionists, and violinists who followed her around in the cloud of smoke and jasmine, intoxicatingly sensual puffs of hot air, or were they all drunk at her side, holding out their glasses of wine or champagne, intoxicated by her proud presence, a stunning goddess of flesh and bone to be contemplated as if she were the source not only of pleasures promised but of eternity. Mère heard Mélanie's voice, the joyful sounds of her welcoming Renata, come, Renata, with all your friends, welcome to our home, Renata, the young men trailing after her with their bubbly, discordant music, and Mère rose as she watched them all coming toward her, noisy and laughing, thinking that later she would have liked to hear Renata talk about the cases she was working on, she was defending rape victims in Israel, young women, students on a university campus, she could have learned a lot from Renata, she could have listened, yes, she had never been able to understand her sister, she was an intellectual, she was worldly, yet Renata only ever managed to shock Mère for reasons Mère couldn't quite put her finger on, that was how it was, inexplicable and absurd, and her daughter Mélanie absorbed Renata's complexity, she cleaved to her so naturally, which seemed incomprehensible to Esther, it was irritating, perhaps also because Renata was a creature no one could control, her autonomy was so casual that she could escape even the watchful eye of her new husband, Claude, a young New York judge, with whom she disagreed diametrically about the death penalty, Claude felt that it was necessary sometimes, so Renata was often seen alone, even though she was smitten with her husband, is it possible to be in love with someone and so at odds with them, Mère wondered, how can you give in to passion when everything seems to rise up against the other person, Mère thought as she watched Renata arrive through the front door of the house, Mélanie remembered telling Renata that Vincent was her strongest baby and taking Renata with her to the bedroom where the child slept in the half light, the two of them leaned over the sleeping child, Mélanie stroked the brown down of Vincent's hair, Jenny and Marie-Sylvie de la Toussaint ran over and said, you see, Mélanie, his breathing is steady now, this was at the time when refugees who came by sea could still be saved, Jenny and Marie-Sylvie, they were taken in by families on the island, Mélanie had told Renata how devoted the young women were to her, constantly looking after Vincent and the others, how grateful she was to have them close by, but they would always hold the pain of separation from their country, the desolation of exile, a sharp, indescribable pain, Mélanie said, Mélanie knew she had lied to Renata by telling her that her newborn was in good health, she knew he never would be, some harm would come to him, was it the drop of plutonium over the fields of Ukraine that would mar Vincent's breath every day, it had no name, other than some invisible misfortune striking the family, at this moment Mélanie felt such disappointment at Vincent's birth, his survival or else his demise because of a drop of plutonium sweeping from black cloud to cloud, not just over the fields of Ukraine but everywhere else, constricting the breath of millions of children unborn or already breathing, was that when Renata had said to Mélanie, we women are creatures of doubt but one day that will no longer be true, we will be strongest because we are capable of compassion, it seemed as if Renata were admitting her weakness with her husband while at the same time she fought him, or at least his ideas, which she didn't share, otherwise she and the young New York judge were fulfilled, a sensual couple, people thought they were happy, like Daniel and Mélanie, radiant with the splendour of their youth, but whose joy had been tarnished by Vincent's rasping breath, all happiness is precarious, Renata laughed, as she came back down the stairs to the party in the living room, Mélanie close to her, wrapping her arm around her, what a beautiful child, she said, Vincent carries the future of the world in his eyes, don't worry so much, my dear Mélanie, the child has your resilience, he will grow up to embody your passion for life, Renata alone had been able to reassure her that Vincent would make it, Mélanie thought, but she was still so worried, there had been reports, investigations by newspapers, compromising compilations, Renata had said, all the rapes, thousands of rapes, not just on that campus in Israel, but thousands of rapes in the former Yugoslavia by soldiers from every region, and we still don't have the courts to judge the guilty parties, the justice system won't commit to defending these women, though I believe the young women who are in law school now will be the standard bearers for those judgments, it must be done, it cannot go unpunished, Renata said, unaware then that a day would come when those men would be judged, punished, though too few, it's always been like this, Mélanie thought, mutilated girls, so many of them now women, would hide the collective wound together, never leaving their homes, forever overlooked, while the rapists remained at large, soldiers raping and murdering, Mélanie, thinking of her son who was breathing more easily now, said to Renata, you'll see, Renata, the young women who are studying law will create these tribunals, the truth will come out, everything that is hidden in the vast archives of crimes against women, everything will be exposed, it's true, Mélanie thought among her flowers, her hibiscus, the scent of the lemon and orange trees, it's true, as Renata sensed back then, that women's compassion for one another led to a zeal for justice, although we're still only at the beginning of the struggle, Mélanie thought, the bouquet was ready and all she had to do was hand it to Mai when she landed, what a perfect day to welcome Mai. I've known happy couples, Daniel said to Uncle Isaac as he walked along the water beside the old man shuffling the pebbles with his cane, I was thirty then, I admired them from afar, they were emotionally mature and I wasn't, I was still unsure about my marriage to Mélanie, I told myself she didn't deserve an oddball like me, a young writer already burdened by the brutal legacy of my great-uncle Samuel, by what happened to him, shot by the Nazis in Poland, sometimes I used to think that, because all of them were dead, those who had killed and the one who had succumbed to the bullets in the bloodstained snow, I often think of his tears, his face covered with ice, his eyes, the eyelids letting the salt seep through, the cold, the frost, even before he fell into the snow, his coat torn to shreds from the bullets and blows, that's how I see him in my dreams, yes, dear Uncle Isaac, you escaped such violence, you weren't in Poland that day, you weren't the rabbi praying to heaven to spare him, I used to think that all the dead, shooters and victim, my great-uncle Samuel, must have met in what we with our paltry words call the infinite or the afterlife, there each person finds themselves suddenly with their enemy as with their brother, and how would they speak to each other, I often wonder, do villains recognize their crimes, old Uncle Isaac, without answering Daniel's question, said, dear nephew, I thought you wanted to talk about happy couples, I can remind you of some of my friends, Caroline and Jean-Mathieu, Suzanne and Adrien, Charles and Frédéric, before they broke up, that's always the risk, we believe couplehood means both people will be satisfied their whole lives, but that's not always consistent or true, there's a whole universe around a couple and the universe is designed to divide, both by its seduction and by the immensity yet to be conquered, too many of us want to be loved, dear Daniel, I can see them still, Suzanne and Adrien, going to the tennis court every morning, hand in hand, of course, that was in the beautiful years when they were young, they would walk by here, nearby, my hotel was simple, there was the tennis court and a single swimming pool, now look at the three pools, iridescent in the setting sun, the grandiose new architecture, endless green paths, streams and fountains, there are even bonfires near the ocean so guests can warm up after a cold swim on a winter day, it's too much luxury, I shouldn't have let this happen, but that's what rich men are like, extravagant people who love pageantry, and I among them in this kingdom of lust, I had to return to the Island No One Owns, to my island, to return, yes, to the silence at the top of my tower, although the tower's not an easy climb for a man who's almost a hundred, but my cane helps, what was I saying, even Caroline and Jean-Mathieu, the closest couple, they even wrote books together, Caroline was a wealthy woman and Jean-Mathieu had been a deckhand on the Atlantic, he hated money and profit and she was so different, she calculated everything so cautiously, watched too closely over a fortune she ended up losing, that's how many lives unfold, old Isaac said, listen to the singing of the waves, Daniel, a far more pleasant sound than my old voice dredging up bygones, but Daniel liked the old man's halting voice, the slight tremor in it, as he listened he thought about Jean-Mathieu's last visit before he left for Italy, he'd been writing a biography of Stendhal, how damp the pension in Venice was, before Jean-Mathieu's fatal, definitive departure, that visit from the man who was still in love with Caroline, he couldn't get through by phone but he told himself that he might finally see her that morning, perhaps he had been indelicate somehow, what could he have done to offend her, she had an assistant, a woman who also served as her chauffeur, but was that a reason for her not to see him anymore, for her not to come have lunch with him on the patio by the sea, they had been so loving, so connected, as much by their professional literary interests as by their mutual affection, always so solid and unshakeable, and they loved their friends as they loved themselves, Suzanne, Adrien, Charles, and Frédéric, they had so many friends among the English poets Caroline had photographed, even if several of them had come to tragic ends, how many of them are still with us, Jean-Mathieu thought, as Charles had written, you would see a poet sitting on a green bench smiling at Caroline as she took their picture and then all at once there was no one there, the green bench was empty, Charles's observations were often sombre, too pessimistic, Jean-Mathieu slid a letter in the sticky mailbox beneath the oleanders in front of Caroline's cottage, slipping it in with one hand, it seemed careless, but his heart was beating, would he see her again, would she answer his letter before he left for Italy, he'd had a premonition that his time in Venice would be beautiful, unless it was too humid, which was often the case near water, but, Daniel thought, why hadn't Jean-Mathieu been bold enough to knock, perhaps he had come a little closer and fled under the oleanders when he heard laughter, he was a discreet, composed man who liked peace and quiet, he was a serene meditator, a peaceful soul, what was the point of tormenting Caroline with his presence if she didn't want to see him, in the letter he told her how much he missed her, could they even live without each other, he said it all, he loved her and admired her, although they had different political ideas, it was better not to say or write anything about that, was that what had driven them apart, or was Caroline too elegant for him, too rich, Jean-Mathieu had long been just a sailor on a boat out of Halifax, he had been poor and moved around a lot, when he was fifteen years old he'd had to be the man of the house, no father or mother, in those shameful days Caroline had Black servants in her parents' house, he had written his letter in careful calligraphy, the letters leaning right, so solidly shaped that Caroline would have seen no sign of Jean-Mathieu's trembling fingers, she would not have seen anything if she had taken the time to read Jean-Mathieu's letter, but she'd never read the letter because Charly had grabbed it and burned it, Daniel thought, lighting it with her cigarillo, didn't Charly realize how twisted that was, but she had no choice, Caroline and Jean-Mathieu's long relationship had to end, that was Charly's decision, she would be the pivot in Caroline's life now, a total upheaval, that was the way it was, everything was upside down, as if the moon had come to graze the earth, muddled, night would turn to day and day would be as dark as night, that was Charly's will, she was a Jamaican girl whose father had been a white soldier, a deserter, perhaps, she didn't know, no, Charly had to take revenge on the treacherous white race that had depleted her Black blood, she had to, that old man,

Jean-Mathieu, dreamed of vacationing in the Venetian countryside with Caroline but he would dream in vain, Charly was a dream-slayer, he would go to Italy alone, after burning his letter with her cigarillo out over the waves, Charly came back to Caroline, satisfied, she distracted her a little, coaxing her out, she would lie naked by the pool and ask Caroline to rub sunscreen on her muscular back, long and lean, and Caroline thought, what a seductive, baffling being, that mystery is what lingers, it's like she cast a spell on me, I do feel like that sometimes, like she could cast a spell on me, I've taken too much of the meds she gives me for my migraines, it's like I'm drunk or I've been poisoned, it's like, yes, Caroline couldn't get her thoughts to line up, as she got up she felt uneasy, she felt like a pushover and she didn't like it, she was serving Charly when it was her, it was Caroline who should be obeyed like their servants did when she was a child in her parents' house, they obeyed, but in her own house, that miscreant, Charly, Charlotte was her given name, she had left home, left her mother, it was Charly who commanded, she demanded, until Caroline found herself signing cheques, Caroline felt strange, uneasy, she had brought this on herself by submitting to Charly, disclosing her finances, she had basically given Charly her soul, money for Caroline was precious, an ancestral family possession, it was sacred, dear friend, Jean-Mathieu had written, can we have dinner together this evening, can we, dear friend, your home seems closed to me, what did I do to displease you, I await your reply, call me, we'll go to one of those wellness resorts you like so much in Italy, we'll go, we'll do, the words faded little by little against the burning ash of the cigarillo and floated over the waves with a watery hush, Jean-Mathieu's final words, don't you know, my dear Caroline, how much

I respect and admire you, we worked together for years with all those English poets, you and I were the first to work against segregation, through our art, your photographs and my writing, we were pioneers, activists, even if your principles and mine were often notched by difference, nuance, and incompatibility, weren't we friends, lovers, yes, tied to each other forever, inseparable, what's going on, dear friend, after Charly stole the letter there was only Caroline's silence, before the wound that Charly stepped into, Jean-Mathieu and Caroline were a happy couple, Daniel thought, lining up the facts, the past, in his mind so that his book *Strange Years* would reconstruct each person's existence, because nothing of us ever really disappeared, he thought, no, we were the whole universe, a composition in flesh and blood that nothing could dent or diminish, we had to believe it, the happy couple, Jean-Mathieu and Caroline, had seen their fascination with each other fade, the seduction wane, but it had been the impact that did them in, incidents, accidents they hadn't been able to control and which they might have avoided, when Charly swooped down on them like a bird of prey, a star that struck them down, that could have been avoided, Daniel thought as he walked beside old Uncle Isaac, Daniel was looking far away, elsewhere, toward scenes on the pier that old Isaac's eyes could not see, not least because Isaac suddenly seemed lost in thought, the day was still warm and the birds opened their wings, the parakeets with their masters on the pier, their wings were open so wide it seemed they might break, once, twice, saluting the majesty of the sea, of the sky, tonight the acrobats would come out with their rings of fire, swimmers played in the waves and all the dogs on the beach barked together, and Mai, as she did each day, wrote to people she knew online, friends from around the world, as if the oceans, the seas, the continents were nothing but passages of air to carry her words, her wishes, her desires, especially the terrifying yearning to step into the unknown, where some otherness could join her, regardless of who the other person was, they only knew each other through their messages, from Japan to America, everywhere letters written on air, selfishly, often, sought an answer, a word, a friendly reply, and so the word love was spoken, written, linked now to the image of a head, a face, and always in that fertile exploration, forever renewed, traded in exchange for a letter written to roam across the clouds, the sky, and the seas without end, that's how it was, yes, Daniel thought, Mai lived online, it shaped how she thought and how she behaved, she didn't read very many books, unfortunately, not enough, it was all about the flurry of messaging, would she even read her father's books, Jean-Mathieu's poems, would she, Daniel also saw a sailboat in the distance about to head out to sea, its flags flapping in the wind, the young captain was saying goodbye to his friends, perhaps he would come back in the fall, it would depend on the wind, Bermuda first, he was saying, then back through Cape Cod, it always depends on the wind, I'm heading out solo, just me and my dog, who knows what's in store with those cyclones, the winds can pick up quickly in the middle of the ocean, we're ready for anything, for adventure, just me and him, who will find us if we drown between the ocean, the sky, and the squalls, drowned and devoured by sharks, but in the meantime, we're heading toward adventure, the sharks and dolphins by our side will rattle our home on the water, hooray for freedom, goodbye, goodbye, the captain saying, a little drunk on his own words and a bit of whisky, goodbye, goodbye, I'll see you in the fall God willing, but is God willing, I'll do anything for a thrill, for adventure, for the journey, there's nothing more delicious than utter freedom, there's nothing to weigh me down, no one to tell me what to do, in that call to adventure Daniel remembered how Jean-Mathieu had been when he was young, a hard life at sea, in nature, the rookie captain saying goodbye to his friends on the pier, that was how Jean-Mathieu would set sail too, following in the footsteps of Henry David Thoreau on the Concord and Merrimack Rivers, or so he thought at the time, a deckhand and a sailor, the American essayist's treatise on civil disobedience was still read today, between the trepidation of the water and the glimmering stars at night, he would have his logbook, though what radar would guide him, he had his dog at his feet, his words would land him in prison, who knows, perhaps that was how Jean-Mathieu left too when he was young, toward far-off continents, admiring Thoreau's prophetic path, he'd been a poet too, like Jean-Mathieu, that was the ideal, the departure toward his dreams, a nameless adventure, the goal of which was a search for something ascetic, yes, spiritual, Jean-Mathieu had been like that, but for Daniel the quest rang hollow, when he was Mai's age, seventeen or eighteen, he thought drugs had ruined his body, his brain was a jumble, what was a young man from a good family doing wasting his life, everyone around him said so, Daniel felt that he had to push his limits to the edge of his self, even at the risk of losing himself, like the captain, who still stood on the pier saying goodbye to his friends before he went back out to sea, every person went through a dark night without stars, Daniel remembered being curled up against some building or other, lying there, he thought he might be dead, he was barely breathing, before the ambulance got there, he was lying there in his fancy clothes, was it by a bank, the owners were friends of his parents, he never showed up at a party where they were waiting for him, he curled up somewhere in the streets of New York until the ambulance came, you have to stand up, sir, a paramedic told him, what are you doing there, lying there in a coat like that, it's full of mud and snow, what were you thinking, what's wrong with you, you're lying in the street, sir, you're not at home in your apartment, it's so cold tonight, come on, come on, try to get up by yourself, we know you're a proud young man, your parents are important people in the city, it's just an accident, an accident, tomorrow you'll go back to college as usual, Daniel remembered thinking he had fallen into blankness, no one could understand him, he was as alone as a young captain with his dog in the middle of the furious ocean, or worse, he would be nothing at all, drowned in nothingness like so many others, he would never write any books, he would never have a family, in a brief moment of euphoria, a moment of rest in the vision-besieged addiction, he could see himself flying over the world, over endless lush green fields, his feet barely touched the ground, in the floating ship of his delirious brain he had no idea how to make landfall, how to lie down in that green, was it a cradle of seaweed or grass, the vision fulfilled none of his wishes and was replaced immediately by voices, macabre screams, bodies tortured and howling, since 1945, one of the terrifying, cynical voices cried, long before you were born, we stood trial, we were judged, yet we were just following orders, ethnic cleansing, they said, nothing more, we were men and women unemployed and languishing and at last someone offered to set us free, to release us from misery and poverty, we were offered work, all we had to do was follow orders and we would get our wages, do you think we even asked ourselves the question, was it good, was it evil, was it moral or not, although our hands ran red with blood, all we could think about was not dying of hunger and thirst and when we saw our persecutors marching toward us with their judges, we escaped, we ran into the woods, we left Germany, everywhere along the way we looked for those we had hanged or gunned down, by the hundreds, the thousands, the Roma, they were hanged from trees, children with their skulls smashed in, that was our doing, the pillage, and our judges or persecutors chased us down and brought us back one by one to the scene of the crime, and there one by one we were executed by firing squad, our face hidden under a mask, or hanged, one by one, in the very spot where we had committed what you call our crimes, we were just obeying orders, obeying the greater order of things, after that vision of hell, after everything he'd heard about that infernal gathering of unrepentant souls, Daniel woke up in the snow, he couldn't move, like the damned souls he dreamed of, would he be granted a last chance to escape, was he as innocent as he wanted to believe, a man laid his hand on Daniel's forehead, the paramedic, sir, the man said, sir, get up, you fell asleep in the snow, can you hear me, say something, I want to hear your voice, sir, please, stand up, it's getting colder and colder, and in the old-model car, the expensive convertible that El Toque had probably stolen, Mama complained, two thieves, as if one wasn't enough, she grumbled, you and El Toque, he hobbles around on one leg, when he was small, Pastor Jeremy, his father, had to carry him out to the school bus and now after everything his father did for him El Toque is stealing cars, here's proof, we're sitting in one, this antique convertible, Mama kept mumbling, and all the passersby were watching on Bahama Street, on Esmeralda Street, sit up straight, Carlos, everybody knows you were in detention, I always said I didn't know where you were, except to Lazaro's mother, she knew all of it, Mama doesn't know and never will, thought Carlos, about the guard in charge of Group C, Group A was for the real murderers, they were kids, twelve or thirteen, there was a brother and sister who'd killed their parents in Dallas, at fifteen they would be transferred to adult facilities and tried as adults, when they were asked if they were sorry that they had killed their father and their mother, they said as one, no, no regrets, we would do it again, they answered, in the meantime they were in Group A, while the rest of us, for involuntary manslaughter, we were in Group C, I wouldn't have wanted to be in Group A, no, Perdue Baltimore, the lawyer, she said I could be rehabilitated, I was fit to be reintegrated into society, in Group C I would be sheltered from the fate they had in store for the murderers, Group A was for teenagers, baby assassins, twelve or thirteen, the brother and sister awaiting trial or a transfer to adult incarceration, the hardest places in the country, people said they were monsters but to look at them I didn't know, you could hardly see their faces under their thick hair, Mama would never know that the Group C head guard one morning shouted us awake at dawn, he was walking along between the rows of beds in our dormitory, we were still sleeping, get up, he shouted, today you're going to learn the first lesson of juvie, we're going to show you what will happen to you if you keep going from felony to felony, everybody out in the yard, on the double, and let me hear you sing, yes, when I whistle, call out with each step you take, all the way, the convoy of the dead, you'll go sit by the graves, we'll take you to the mass graves and you'll have to dig a hole for each burial, be careful, until we get there you'll be chained at the ankles, you'll see pretty clearly where your nonsense will lead you, no, Mama would never know about the chains on our ankles, our shackled steps, there we were with the dead and the graves, a great convoy, it reeked and many of us were crying, we had to dig with our shovels as soon as the chains were taken off, we dug for a long time in the sun until a bulldozer from the town came to haul out the soil and widen the holes into pits, and the dirt and the stones tumbled down into the holes, that's how you'll end up, the guard said, if you head to jail from juvie, no one will remember you, you'll get sick and no one will look after you and you'll die and no one will come visit, you'll be all alone, what you see around you today could well be where you end up, think hard so that this doesn't become your future, a future in a mass grave, with no friends, no parents, those men and women sometimes stay with us as long as sixty years, in these institutions, they're forgotten and now see where they end up, is that what you want, and many of us were snivelling, we didn't want to be there in the convoy with the dead, and, scarier still, digging holes to bury the bodies of strangers, many of us were crying, our hands in the soil, with our shovels, no, Mama will never know about that day with the Group C head guard, Perdue Baltimore said later that it was against the law to expose children to that and threaten them like the guard had done, and she would request his removal from Group C, though he stayed, Mama will never know, what's everyone doing around the car, looking at us, on Bahama Street, Esmeralda Street, it's an old car, a classic, maybe they're jealous, thought Carlos, I don't know if Polly had the courage to wait for me, I was gone so long, but Polly knows she only belongs to me, I will carry her into the waves, in my arms, then she'll remember, I can still hear the roosters here on the lawns, their hostile crowing, I can hear them, I see them as we go by, Mama will never know and it's better she doesn't, her hair has gone white, she'll say it's my fault she's aged so quickly, all my fault, yes, I wonder if Polly remembers me, I stole her and the basket, I kept it all, the basket and the puppy, the yellow bicycle, like my yellow T-shirt that day, I had to take everything otherwise I would've lost it all, was there a fire, at first I thought it was for me, like when they all came out in front of Trinity College saying I shot Lazaro, it wasn't true, the gun wasn't loaded, or if it was true, I was set up, I barely grazed his knee, though it bled a lot, it was so red, I ran away, they caught me quickly, they grabbed the hem of the yellow T-shirt sticking out of my jeans, they arrested me, it was like my life was over that day, I was only fourteen, and besides Lazaro had stolen my watch, and from that day on, Mélanie thought, the drop of plutonium over the fields of Ukraine got stronger, bigger, now it dripped through giant, toxic, chemical drains, onto the heads and faces of Syrian children, it poured during air raids that the United Nations barely bothered to speak out against, war had become a habit, how could we condemn it now, we had lost our moral ground, it dripped, it poured, those little bodies, just like Vincent, Mélanie thought, they were racked with convulsions, and we rushed to cover their little faces with gas masks for all the good that did, many of them died, Mélanie wrote it all down for her lecture but would anyone come, thinking that before, yes, who knows whether Vincent hadn't been a victim of the radiation, as far away as it had been, and how many were still sick, how many still had convulsions every day, the drop of plutonium was getting bigger and bigger, those chemical, toxic substances, beneath the air raids, how long would it all go on, her grandson Rudie, Samuel and Veronica's son, would he suffer too, he seems so healthy, smiling, a child who seems to know nothing yet of the hardships that surrounded him, perhaps he was coddled, perhaps they loved him too much, it was true what Renata had told Mélanie that night when they had gathered to celebrate Vincent's birth and Mélanie wondered how Vincent could survive when he could barely breathe, Vincent, Vincent, she thought only of him, so it was true, as Renata said, but women carried doubt and clawed back compassion, was Renata thinking of her own past with Franz and his children, her sentimental, passionate past, which Mélanie couldn't imagine then, she was still young, she admired Renata, the lives of other women, that day she was only thinking of Vincent, her failure, perhaps, the failure of her flesh, how she wished the torment would pass, the obsession, Vincent would live, other than his lungs he was so strong, Renata's first husband, Franz, was a conductor and a well-known composer, we were heading toward Brest, toward the port, a storm had come up on the ocean but we were fearless, we laughed in the face of danger, Mélanie could still hear Renata's voice and her sorrows and torments surged, Renata was trying to distract her with tales of their adventures, her madness perhaps, she adored Franz though that love was devastating in the end, would the rolling waves over the boat take me first, would I go first, Franz had written an oratorio for Christmas in a cathedral in England, on the boat with Franz's children, Franz thought of nothing but his oratorio, Franz had forgotten me, would I be first, yes, as soon as the lighthouse beam shone over the rocky outcroppings at Brest I would feel that consolation, that joy, Franz's son cried, Vati, the light, see the light on the sea, the rocks, the waves are getting closer on the deck, I thought Franz had grown tired of me, he was surrounded by other women who loved him better than I did, I didn't even feel the need to be faithful to him because the music was more than enough for him, it was the most complete love, he was a very sensual lover with me but I felt that I couldn't truly inhabit his soul and mine was foreign to him as well, she had wanted so much to be understood by that remarkable man who could do anything he wanted, he was the embodiment of freedom, and I was incomplete, I was an imperfect stand-in, a caricature, Mélanie listened to Renata, they were by the pool, it was late, although even then the music of Renata's young retinue still played, there were flowers everywhere, or maybe they were down by the misty sea before the break of day, Renata's voice was low and gravelly, the smoke from her cigarettes whorled into the night, I don't want to bother you, Renata was saying, I want to reassure you, your little boy will be fine, he'll be better tomorrow, yes, I can feel it, and she went on, telling Mélanie the rest of the story to try to distract her from her concern for her newborn, there are no fair afflictions, she said, she wished she could spare her all the sorrows, all Mélanie could feel was the weight of her pain and the night air against her neck, on her arms, everything seemed so heavy in the damp night, if her son died tomorrow, even if the worry that plagued her was tempered by Renata's voice, at times convincing, at times broken, Mélanie thought, there was always and ever a doubt, the fear of the breach Renata had spoken of, Franz's oratorio would be performed in a small church in the Finistère region, Renata was saying, another hazy night like this one wrapped around us, a composition for a soprano, one of the Psalms, sung in Hebrew, the soprano was a child, that voice was a herald of plagues and curses, yes, it burst with such lightness, clear and strong, the divine shepherd would guide us through the storm, the child soprano was so confident and I remember thinking, where is that divine shepherd, I was a woman who doubted everything yet what I remember most about that oratorio was the lightness and the joy in the voice, the triumph of sensuality, of life, even though the boy who sang the soprano part was too young to have experienced anything like it, who knows, perhaps there was a divine message in that boy's cry in the oratorio Franz had composed, it was bigger than us, that thrill of joy, of gladness, and in spite of ourselves it filled us, Renata laughed as if she wanted to shake off the seriousness of the story or it might have been the opposite, some things always seem too light to be spoken, Mélanie thought there was a mocking on Renata's lips, tender or sharp, those lips drawn expressly for the pleasures of life, and she thought again of Vincent, no, she would never have access to joy again, no joy would come to her, Renata's words only increased her pain, Mélanie thought, and old Uncle Isaac repeated to Daniel that he had seen them so often walking by here, beneath these same silver palms, Suzanne and Adrien, they would go say hello to Adrien, who was writing and dozing, his computer on his lap, on the shore, contending with the ocean waves, in the deck chair Simon always saved for him, Simon the waiter, his faithful friend, he always looked after Adrien, the boy was a bright light for the future of the Grand Hotel, he attracted a younger, quirkier clientele, Uncle Isaac said appreciatively as he wedged his cane in the sand, Adrien is forever starting the same poem over and over again, he's always looking for perfection in purely mathematical verse though I don't know anything about it, my dear nephew, why can't he just publish his poems the way they are in the first comprehensible draft, for a man like me, a classical reader, a regular reader, my sister is more cultivated than I am, she's the only one who can understand Adrien's poems, I'm too primitive, old Uncle Isaac told Daniel, let's go say hello, he could probably use the distraction, we should congratulate him for the latest prize he got, for his body of work, he is astoundingly intelligent, Adrien, and as old Uncle Isaac dragged Daniel across the sand toward the spot where Adrien was writing or drowsing in the solitude of the late afternoon by the sea, Daniel very much doubted that Adrien wanted to see them, he was always so grumpy when he saw Daniel, or perhaps there was something else, a kind of sullen jealousy, some envy or wariness in the poet, who was almost a century old, was he jealous of Daniel, a writer whose own trajectory still stretched far ahead, he was at the top of his game, he heard again the captain's voice still saying goodbye, see you, to his friends on the pier, the boat's flags snapping in the wind, at the top of the mast there was a wooden owl, its head turning left to right to show which way the winds were blowing, the gales, there were also three flute-like objects on the mast and the wind whistled through them, the calmer breeze of dawn, the moment of departure drew near, but the captain seemed to be postponing it, he told his buddies he wanted to have a last drink with them, my friends, let's go over to Adrien, though who knows if he'll feel like talking to us, old Uncle Isaac said, when he's writing he doesn't see anyone or anything, he's a hermit, a monk deep in contemplation, it's a good thing his maid, Dorothea, looks after him, when he comes home at night, always chauffeured by Charly, the girl spoils him, she has him bewitched, they say, she drives him everywhere, even to his Sunday strolls to the tennis court where he remembers Suzanne, his graceful wife, she was a poet too, but overlooked, old Uncle Isaac mumbled as if he could read Daniel's mind about Suzanne, of those two great literary voices, Daniel replied, we'll only ever hear one, the man's voice, Adrien's, immediately he regretted having spoken so bluntly, he remembered having lunch with Suzanne on the terrace by the sea on cold, clear February days, back then Daniel was still silent and shy around her, and as for her work as a poet, she thought it was unpublishable, although she had published books, she wouldn't write anymore, she explained to Daniel, no, my Daniel, she said, I leave the writing to Adrien, he writes better than I do, and during the memorable hours they spent together, Daniel and Suzanne having lunch on the terrace by the sea, life ticked by, one second at a time, Daniel thought, he knew that he would never again be able to cry, of course you're right again, taking Suzanne's hands in his, you'll never stop writing, he was only a young man then, he venerated the maturity in Suzanne's work, and the charming, voluptuous nature of this woman who was older than he was and wiser, at the time he was writing his first book and she was like a guardian angel, her presence, while Adrien, Suzanne's husband, was gearing up to tear into Daniel's first book, a harsh, terse review, Adrien would chew him up and spit him out, he was fearsome, oh, I still write in my journal, Suzanne said humbly, behind the paper screen, by myself, and especially I write to my daughters, I tell them that one day Dalet will rise before me, the door, the gateway, Dalet, it looks like a closed door, and I will be granted passage, behind the door there will be light, a blaze of light, utterly transparent, without a shred of darkness, no, a sheer runnel of light, Dalet, I will tell them not to be afraid, I will be happy there, and I will tell them how much I love them, Dalet is the door, Daniel could almost hear Suzanne's voice again, or perhaps her voice was within him now, she was no longer suffering, she was at peace, that's how it was, Daniel thought, there was no way around it, never again would he have lunch with Suzanne in the blinding noon sunlight off the ocean, while Adrien was still alive, writing every day in his deck chair, his face healthy and hale, barely wrinkled beneath his white hat, the conclusion of an imponderable injustice, Daniel thought, holding old Isaac by the elbow, the old man had almost fallen as he bent to pick up a seashell, old Uncle Isaac was already snapping that he didn't need anyone to hold him up, especially not you, my dear nephew, he murmured, especially not you, but I wonder sometimes if I hear as well as I used to, that's the cooing of a mourning dove I hear, isn't it, sometimes it sings at dawn, it's a little sad, that aching modulation, yes, I can hear it as soon as I wake up, and then the pigeons cluster on the beach, that's when I come down out of my tower, that's when my day begins, in the splendour of contemplation, every day I am moved by everything I see, I wonder if my Florida panther will give birth today, today or tomorrow, do I have any foxes, and old Uncle Isaac seemed lost in thought, back in time, racing up the river of his memories back to Suzanne and Adrien striding to the tennis court, they walked by here, along this path, you see, Daniel, in their tennis whites, of course, as the years go by, none of us can know what will happen to us, we don't know, it's the deepest mystery, Daniel could still hear Suzanne's voice, she was always so happy, it was so beautiful in those days, by the sea, Suzanne declaring she would not write again but that every second of her life would be all that much more intense and precious for it, dear little Daniel, believe me, the intensity of living well, why shouldn't I have that, I'm a woman, it's the pinnacle of freedom, of my refusal to live in servitude, for the past few months I've had the feeling that I'm writing in my husband's shadow, there's nothing in it for me personally, it's almost like Adrien is laughing at me somehow, you're the only one I can say this to, even though it might not seem like it to anyone else, but everything was so different when we were twenty years old, there was no shadow at all back then, we were just two young poets, apprenticing, equals, and then suddenly Adrien got successful, and what was I doing there by myself writing behind the paper screen that stood between me and his workspace, the screen had a drawing of a white lotus on it, Buddhist philosophy had already taught me to relinquish, but when women are sensitive and talented they always relinquish too soon, that's what I've just written to my daughters, there are so many contradictions, don't you think, I know they won't give in that easily, it was too easy for me to choose happiness because writing was a shadow on our happiness, Adrien's and mine, and all I wanted was to be happy, I didn't want the lacerations of being a writer, I didn't want to be torn apart, I suppose I was selfish, don't feel sorry for me, my dear Daniel, I am a woman and much loved, too much perhaps, in a way that is almost contrary to how I imagined it would be when I was young, but I'll say it again, everything I'm saying to you today seems so contradictory, one day, later, you'll write this all down, Suzanne wasn't wrong, Daniel thought, sublime friend, a mature companion guiding his first literary steps, she read his first book with such a nuanced critical eye, Suzanne was already part of his soul and the soul of his books, he was forever writing her as a character, untangling the knot of contradictions of who she was and how she was, the depths of her passions, writing and love, love or writing, and now there was that word, Dalet, the word had lost all its poetry, the substance of dream, the loftiness, the reaching toward another world, natural or supernatural, by becoming what had horrified the poet Adrien, he was still in love with his wife, the horror of it, medical assistance in dying, there in Zurich, for the longest time Suzanne had said nothing about the cancer, it was so aggressive, so fast, perhaps Adrien had only found out that last long night in a clinic in Zurich as Suzanne said goodbye, no tears, she was smiling as if she felt sorry for the man she loved, still and always, although by now she knew all his faults, and when he thought about that sleepless night in a cold clinic, a cold room, the effluvium of cold was a harbinger of death, Suzanne had loved the heat, the warm embrace of love, cozy summer mornings as she hurried to the tennis court or the pool at the Grand Hotel, and after tennis, after lunch with Adrien, she would go right behind the paper screen, she was by herself, writing out the words of a poem, a story, the words that inhabited her, she had told Daniel once that she couldn't live without writing, that if it had been otherwise, she would have lived for nothing, she would have wasted her life, when he thought back to Suzanne's last night and the cold prison of her death he understood the sorrow of a man left behind at the doorstep, unable to cross over, how abandoned Adrien must have felt when his wife was leaving him, they always walked off the tennis courts together, hand in hand, had there been music playing or only silence, just like Suzanne, Daniel felt sorry for Adrien, and now he determined to be friendly, to let go of his anger, yes, Daniel thought, he would try to be compassionate with the old man, his face pink in the summer sun beneath his hat, the way Adrien himself wasn't remotely friendly, he always sat up so straight, he didn't even seem like an old man, no more than Uncle Isaac did, just now he looked like a tourist reading messages on his computer, without pretension, this was no longer the pretentious poet critiquing other writers' books or pontificating at a university podium, just a solitary figure sitting beneath a palm tree, writing, reading, or dozing, at that moment Daniel remembered a mountaintop in Scotland, the way the mind flies off in every direction, landing nowhere, that's the astounding thing about memory, Daniel thought, it absorbs everything at once, present, past, sometimes it foretells our future and we don't even know it, he remembered the international festival of writers for peace in Scotland, one afternoon he had been signing books at a table set up beneath an arch of pine and fir, the air smelled good, he had gone for a walk to relax before the conference, the whole event was very troubling, how could they talk about peace during wartime, you couldn't even say the word peace anymore, only to refer to our bellicose era, to talk about the massacre of entire peoples, the slow, collective agony of humanity imperilled each day, threatened by loathsome nuclear decrees on top of the daily struggle for precarious survival, during his walk he came across wide green fields, so green they seemed to shimmer in the setting sun after the rain, that was where Daniel had met Eddy's five friends, Eddy the waiter, the five women rushed toward him, saying, write us something, just a word, something about how much you love Scotland, that you love us, silly girls, we danced all night with Eddy at the Mer du Nord pub, we promise we'll buy your books, they laughed together, one of them, her name was Daphnée, told Daniel that he blushed when people talked to him, was he afraid of silly girls in the countryside, girls had to have fun while they were still young, Daphnée said, she was the one who was getting married the next day, to Peter, the wedding would bring more parties and dancing to the Mer du Nord pub, was she too young to get married, Daniel wondered, and Daniel lingered with them for so long he almost forgot about the conference, the gravity of all of that, he was probably frivolous too, silly, he liked to laugh, he liked everything that was human and alive, he couldn't resist, just like he could never resist Suzanne, she was so full of joy, when she called him to join her on the terrace by the sea, dear Daniel, so full of happiness, I'm so glad to see you today, she would tell him, kissing him innocently, as if he were her son, a particularly favoured child, the chosen one, but Daniel saw the exchange from one writer to another, lunch with a beautiful woman, there was no denying her sensuality, most of all what he loved was the wonder of spending time with that beauty, the balance of heart and spirit in a single being, she was a friend, not a mother, love, the feeling of love could hold so many variations, he thought, although what he feared most was that Suzanne's face, like Mère's, would fade, melt into a black abyss where everything is lost, spreading like waves of an ocean to the black night beneath the surface, he could still hear Daphnée's laughter, Suzanne's laughter as if they were close by and he remembered that he thought he had seen Augustino on one of the mountain paths, but it was an illusion, two young poets chatting on a bench beneath the pines, as he walked up to them through the dense trees, at the end of the day, seeing them from behind, Daniel was struck by the sight of their necks, so like Augustino's, one of them had dark hair and the other was blond and their hair curled against their shirt collars, the two of them were arguing, they were talking about a great poet from London, a writer Daniel admired, a bohemian man, a bard, the two of them were happily debating how best to pay homage to such a writer, and they were sad, too, because he was no longer with them, the red-haired poet, his three red-haired daughters, and as they spoke, their animated conversation about the poet who had died that year, all Daniel could see was their necks, the hair curling against the collar, he told himself Augustino didn't look like them, no, his son was scruffier and his long hair was neither blond nor brown, what colour was his hair, everything suddenly seemed nebulous, he had really believed it was him there talking to a friend, why wouldn't he have been attending a peace conference, he was an activist, like so many writers of his generation, the program suggested he might come but Daniel knew he wouldn't, the two young men on the bench were still talking, the great thing about that London poet was how ironic he was, they said, he wrote that we were all merely hybrid, we're just floating in God's mind, we are less than fish in the sea, yet take comfort, we don't have to make any decisions, the beginning and the end are predetermined, we are caught on a hook and released into the sea just as we are taken out of it, the two were happy again and Daniel wasn't trying to find Augustino anymore, he was exhausted, bone-tired suddenly, he had to get back to the hotel to read over his text for that night, who knew, perhaps that faithlessly ironic poet was right, and even during the literary festival, Daniel remembered so clearly the evil, the sickening, shameful facts and deeds, he had written about it in his book *Strange Years*, he remembered it like it was yesterday, the man they called the angel of death, the doctor of all agonies, Dr. Mengele in his laboratory at Birkenau throwing a little girl into the air, catapulting her six-year-old body, and during that dance, as he broke her bones and as his ugly fingers dismembered her neck, her throat, the screams he no longer heard, he had dismantled so many skulls and necks, the still-living, panting bodies of little girls, he liked it even better when they were twins, the moans and screams resounding like distant thunder, he no longer heard any of it, all he could think about was his research, all without anaesthetic of course, it didn't bother him in the least to work like that, he was nothing but a scientific robot manipulating flesh puppets, their screams and moans, what did it matter, he was a doctor, honoured by his peers, he had accomplices too, he remembered as he was breaking their necks, the twin necks, the boys and girls, with the cold competence of his foul fingers as he sliced through nerve and severed ligaments, but you had to see it, those children just waltzing through the air in Dr. Mengele's laboratory, you had to see it, all of them waltzing, how masterfully he made them all dance, waltzing, yes, the screams were unbearable for a man as sensitive as he was but he didn't even hear them anymore, they were just a distant roll of thunder far away behind the forest, was that it, was it his fault he had become God, he wielded such power, such unfathomable sadism, he was omnipotent, his power was a treasure, that power meticulously acquired, did he remember, the doctor of all agonies, as a young man he had studied philosophy, how have you become so denatured so fast, did he ever ask himself that, he had been a popular student, studying philosophy in Munich, rich, charming, generous even with his friends, he thought he would always have friends, rather than chucking them into the ovens, the Romani children, since they didn't have any parents anymore anyway, that matter had been settled by the central bureau so why not experiment, a few castrations or an injection of some chemical concoction into their veins, or would it be better to practise first on the mentally deficient, society doesn't know what to do with them, kind Uncle Mengele tempted them with chocolates, with warm clothes, he drew them to his car or to a car he said belonged to the Red Cross, to his laboratory, oh so gently, without frightening them, even the children would later say, he was a kind uncle, a kind man, he invited them so gently to come be minced and mangled in the laboratory's dim light, don't be afraid, he would say, I won't do you any harm, the thought of touching them at all was revolting, they were lousy and they all had typhus, later, when all that was left of them were carcasses sullied by his own hands, he said take away this filth, I don't want to see them, his disgust befitted a man of his class, the lice and the typhus, is there anything filthier, he thought, sometimes at the end of the day he held his cane in a gloved hand and smacked the vanquished backs of his patients, they had come to the end, hadn't they, they were just cadavers now, that was all, sometimes he stopped, bored of his bloody fanaticism, bored with everything, he thought perhaps he should leave, he knew his parents would help him, he could go to Paraguay, shortly before the end of the war, he had to get out, Plato and Hegel, he'd always had excellent taste as a student, that was before the apocalypse, it was, it was, and through the window, through the shadows, he could see the snow falling, men, officers and guards struggling to haul a cart full of them, the detritus of humanity, women, men, children piled as the snow fell, covering them, how hard the officers and the guards worked for them, Mengele thought, only those men were his brothers, those guards, those officers, his concern for them was like his concern for himself, but what would happen to them when it was all over, it was getting late and he no longer thought of victory, what will happen to us, the doctor of all agonies thought, and though it was late and his patients were sleeping, were they asleep, he didn't know anymore, he had to be parsimonious in these hard times, you couldn't just give them a sedative to ease their suffering, and then there was no longer any screaming, only silence in the endless snow over the camp, the fields, the forest, and after the slaughter he saw one more as he peered through the window, through the shadows and the frost, him, a butcher of little children, but he was a learned man, a philosopher, a physician, a decorated captain, he saw one he had forgotten, a miserable, spidery-legged creature, probably from the day's batch, it must have escaped the ovens, the mother had just been shot, her body tossed in a cart by an officer who hadn't noticed, everywhere there were screams that night with the snow in the storm over the field, the shape squirmed next to the cart, it must have been calling Mama, Mama, thought the doctor, a man decorated for his conduct once, it was obvious that the guards and officers who worked so hard to haul the cart of corpses had overlooked that quivering thing, squirming and crying Mama, Mama, the cry of a child rejected, forgotten, calling its mother, the officers and guards couldn't hear because of the wind, the doctor thought, stock-still at the window as it frosted over slowly, the doctor saw too that the mother had dressed the child warmly before leaving, in a hooded sweater, and he thought it was touching, surely they were from a good family, and he said nothing about the boy, alone in the uproar, though in any case the child would not be saved, he would die forsaken in the snow during the night with his hooded sweater and his spidery legs, he looked barely old enough to walk, he was tiny, just one bastard fewer, but the doctor didn't go outside, saying, see, there, why don't you shoot him, he said nothing, the wretched child ran on, a shape dancing in his feverish head, he had caught something, it was debilitating to have to attend to them like that, with their lice and their typhus, he had grown weak, perhaps it was only a cold after all, he would feel better tomorrow with a new load of boys and girls, he would rally, and the small figure with the spidery legs, the child running after his murdered mother, that touching image would stay with him as he worked, stopping his hand for an instant as it reached for the scalpel, though his white coat was splattered with blood, how disgusting, viscera everywhere, the rotten smell all around him, all day long, he was only doing his duty as a researcher, all that eviscerated flesh, still seething with life, the war was ending, if there was an uprising, if the foreign soldiers came, he had to think of getting out, Argentina or Brazil, his parents would help, they were unspeakably wealthy, he had been a model student, he'd had so many friends, he'd had a great youth, he had flourished, back when he was only a man among others, not yet a prince of darkness, the lord of the dead before whom the carts and convoys paraded to the crematoriums, master of the abyss, he could have gone out into the night in his imposing military uniform, he could have said to the child, would you like to come warm up little boy, come into my lab, come, I have a blanket and chocolates for you here, you'll be safe with me here, I'm your friend, your kindly uncle, I'll wipe your tears, you'll see your mama again, yes, you'll see her again, I'll do everything in my power to help you find her, and the child would have huddled against him, he loved it when they did that, so trusting, babies, they were adorable, little boys and girls fresh off the trains, they always looked frightened, their charming faces marred for the first time by fears, the faces they turned to him as he repeated, I love you, don't be afraid, that was before every one of his gestures became a rape, a deflowering, he laid his hand on the child's thigh and with his fingers opened the barely budding flower, let's see, are you a girl or a boy, you see, I'm a doctor, and I'm conducting scientific research, you have nothing to fear, I am your kind uncle, your friend, let me touch you a little, be a good little patient, the spidery-legged one, the boy spoiled by his mother, the child in the hooded sweater, what a delight it would've been to preserve him like a jewel, to rock him in his arms as he thought of the sons he would have himself one day, he would rock them like that, and the little boy would have stopped crying, every day he would have loved him more and more, always dreaming of his own future family, a son of his own, and he would tell that son that he had been decorated in Ukraine for having saved men from a burning tank, yes, that was true, he had done that, he would tell his son, I am not what they believe me to be, I had the courage to risk my life to drag them from the flames, one by one, my men, I was even injured, quite badly, between two battles they sent me back to convalesce in Germany, I'm telling you, son, whatever they say about me someday don't believe them, your father was a hero in Ukraine, I was seriously injured, I had time to think, that was when the fevers started, they consume me now, every night at the same time, when my charges, my little experiments, have finally fallen asleep without so much as a sigh and I am alone at the window, it's snowing and the officers and the guards are struggling to drag them back, that carrion, those bastards, the Roma and the Jews, and soon thanks to my work and to the courage of these men a new race of men will be born, a superior race, immaculate, nary an ethnic blemish, you will be the fruit of that new race, my son, my future child, I did a first doctorate in anthropology at the University of Munich and a second in medicine, already I was writing about the odious influence of ethnic and racial shortcomings, that's when they offered me the laboratory, don't believe what they say, my son, I was only doing my duty as a researcher, without humanity's recognition, only persecution, yes, yes, as he walked along the path toward the top of the mountain Daniel could hear the voice of the cursed doctor of all agonies mingled with the voices of those who had forced his great-uncle Samuel to kneel in the snow, before the massacre of the rabbis, if ever the doctor had felt the slightest inkling of remorse as he fled terrified from one country to the next, he believed that until his injury in Ukraine he had been an honest man, perhaps the trouble was that bullet to the head, and then came the fevers and the delirium, and so his conscience was clean, he had been injured, he had only lost his mind, the ambitious prey of a political party whose mission was to debase men, demean them, he wasn't responsible for any of it, he had only been a feverish, delirious convalescent, in his experiments, as he systematically shredded child after child, the hapless flesh he operated on, there was another reason for his madness, when he went back to Germany, in those long days and nights in his hospital bed, the former philosophy student, the rational, exceptionally intelligent man understood that he would be allowed everything, every excess, life is so short and all flesh is mortal, so what do good and evil mean, he would free himself from those shackles and his slightly sadistic imagination would be free too, nothing could be more important than satisfying his insane desires, for purely scientific ends, of course, he would be the greatest researcher, he would experiment on living flesh, would as much as the shadow of a regret ever graze his conscience, Daniel wondered, could there be any redemption for the souls of the damned, his cluttered mind had quieted, as he walked he heard Daphne and her friends again, so, are you going to come back and see us in Scotland, Daniel, are you going to come back, who knows when, by then we'll all be married with a pile of kids but in the meantime we're having fun, come have a drink with us, Daniel, no, it was with old Uncle Isaac he was walking in the enchanting gardens by the Grand Hotel a few hours before Mai's birthday, he had chronicled the actions of the unholy Dr. Mengele in his book *Strange Years*, among so many other details just as heinous, a story that must not be forgotten, he felt like his book was getting heavier and heavier, this wasn't about some ancient, secular era, this was our time, thick with cruelty, cruelty without end, and in her sunny garden Mélanie was remembering a dream of Renata telling her about the trials she was working on, as if she had walked into the dream triumphantly through the front door like that night as they were celebrating Vincent's birth, yes, she would win her cases, the trials, it was early yet, justice for women was slow to come, in so many countries, everything was slow but there was hope, and Mélanie hoped everything would change, peacefully and fairly, and when she woke up from her dream, the doves cooing on the roof of the house, Mélanie thought, I have to find her, I have to find Renata, she came to me in a dream, it was so real, she was warm and kind, just like that day I saw her come in the front door, she was so glamorous and I was small and dark, so worried about Vincent's breathing, his little body gasping, where was she in the dream, with Renata, in the countryside with her husband, their dogs and horses, where was it, she had an email from Vincent telling her he might be a bit late for Mai's birthday but he would be there, Mélanie had a premonition he would be late, he always was when he came to visit his mother, my colleagues and I are extremely optimistic about the research we're doing, he told her, they were also quite concerned about climate change and its effects on their young patients, it's our own fault, there's so much respiratory disease in young children in Los Angeles, he would come, he would be there soon, Mélanie thought, she was excited at the thought, he would always be her little boy, even now, as research director at the hospital, he was so grown up, yet he'd remained a simple man, she could still get through to him, why did she constantly worry about him, like before, every time she thought of him, he shouldn't accept his friend's invitation to go to Jordan on the humanitarian mission, he couldn't just say yes to everything, he had such compassion, he made himself available to everyone, she didn't want that for him, she had almost lost her son, what was she worried about, Vincent was just delayed at the hospital, she was fretting for nothing, soon they would all be together, except Augustino, though thinking of him was unfair to her other children, today, soon, very soon, they would all be together by the sea, gathered around Mai in the magnificent gardens, Mélanie would have all her children with her at last. Venus had often held her daughter's hand as they walked through the streets toward the Coral City Temple, that evening Rebecca would be singing for her mother's graduation, after working so hard in the hotel during the day and going to school at night her mother had finally earned her diploma, we'll be late for your recital if you keep walking so slow, Venus told Rebecca again, stop daydreaming, what's wrong, Rebecca, don't you want to sing the Psalms at the recital, your grandfather, Pastor Jeremy, would be disappointed to see you dragging your feet like that, they had to walk faster, that was what her mother would have said, my own mother Venus could be as temperamental as Pastor Jeremy, she firmly believed there would be no forgiveness, even in the afterlife we will never be forgiven, and recently they were insulting their Black president, mocking him viciously, do you think that can be forgiven beyond what we've already suffered, do you believe that, Rebecca, Rebecca listened to her mother wondering who she was talking about, who are you talking about, dear Maman, later she would call her Venus, they never stopped trying to talk to each other, Venus and her constant, sanctimonious anger, and Rebecca girding her hope for the future, her innocence, she was still so young, what was her mother talking about, segregation, Rebecca went to a mixed school, they could talk about anything, mutual understanding and social and cultural progress, Rebecca deliberately kept herself at a distance from what life was like today, things were evolving, thought Rebecca, maybe because Mama held such a grudge against white people, she said so herself, she would never forgive them, that was an old idea and Rebecca didn't like it, she didn't see a way through except with love, we had to forget about the notion of an enemy race, not so much to forgive, but to allow them to forgive themselves, to do better, to repair, Rebecca believed the world was evolving every day, every hour even and they had to let go of that ancient hatred to give way to a new world, who knows, Rebecca's world and her friends', it would be like her class at school, people from everywhere, every colour of skin, refugees too, Rebecca was still a child but she wanted a world to be a solid house with solid foundations, she wanted all her friends, no matter where they came from or what the colour of their skin was, to be happy, it was so simple, why couldn't things just be like that? You had to pray a lot too, Rebecca often sang in church, her mother said she was too pious, like Mama and Pastor Jeremy, Venus didn't believe in the prayers of men, or women, and especially not white people's prayers, all the hypocritical requests we make of God, said Venus, Rebecca loved singing as much as praying and if prayer was a song that was sweeter still, God surely would be happy, but Venus had never known or seemed not to know what Rebecca was really worried about, she thought she wasn't Trevor's daughter, her little brother, Trevor Junior, was, but Rebecca, yes, Venus had never known the uncertainty that ate at her daughter's heart, she was too busy being angry at white people, Rebecca wondered if she was really the Jamaican musician's daughter, the man who'd been living with his mother for years, so whose child was she, why didn't she know, why had they lied to her about her birth and all the trouble around it, at that time, why did Venus start crying when someone brought up her disappeared husband, Captain Williams, that white man she'd loved so much and who'd been lost at sea, murdered by a rival gang, was there some traitor who had abused her mother, what happened before Rebecca was born, and why did the captain disappear, Venus's husband, why do they have so many enemies, what kind of job did he do, with Venus as his accomplice, Mama said it was dirty work, but what was it, Rebecca was heading to the Coral City Temple where she would sing that night, just a few years before her mother would have been holding her hand, telling her to hurry along, they were going to be late, and tonight Rebecca would sing for her mother and for all the students, real students, thought Rebecca, even though they were adults who had gone back to school later in life, including her mother, she had worked so hard during the day while taking night classes, her mother Venus would be among them and Rebecca was so proud, she only had one mother, despite her anger, despite the secrecy surrounding her past, how mysterious she was, but still she was her mother, Venus, a woman who in her daughter's eyes was always beautiful even when she was angry, always, yes, the clink of jewellery at her ankles and her wrists, her head held high, rebellious, she loved Venus, her mother, so often Rebecca had asked Venus, is Trevor really my father, and Venus told her to shut up, don't ask questions, Rebecca was Trevor's daughter, no doubt about it, hadn't Rebecca ever noticed her father's lighter skin, same as hers, how light their skin was, barely even brown, both of them, you are Trevor's daughter and we will not speak of it again, Mama had said, now they were across the bay, they could see the lighthouse where Rebecca used to come to watch the boat races at Christmas, her mother would tell her not to wander too far, stay close, now Rebecca went everywhere alone, even out to the bay, tonight she would sing at the Coral City Temple like her mother used to do before she turned to more secular tunes at Uncle Cornelius's mixed club, Mama and Pastor Jeremy, Rebecca's grandparents, spoke poorly of their daughter Venus, Rebecca didn't like hearing them accusing her like that, she was a pagan, dissolute, she wished they would stop, Mama was more tolerant than the pastor, she was almost tender with her daughter, a kind of austere tenderness, there is nothing harder than the life of a young Black woman, said Mama, surely we can make some allowances here and there, Venus's heart was honest and decent, Rebecca's grandmother would say, it's just that there's too much temptation around her, with men, it's the same thing for Deandra and Tiffany, the twins, and Pastor Jeremy and I can't do a thing about it, you have to remember that although Pastor Jeremy and I are good Christians, we were young once too, we weren't always perfect, the pastor and I, Mama brooded, Venus had at least given her Rebecca and Trevor Junior, the little one, their father Trevor was a musician, a double-bassist Venus had met hanging out with jazz and rock and roll bands, Mama has never liked all that noise, it wasn't holy music, it wasn't music that rose up to God, but at least the Jamaican man had made her forget the captain, Trevor, the double-bassist, with all that music around him, in the bars and often outdoors, by the sea, in the amphitheatre or out in the street on hot nights, Venus had forgotten the husband who was lost at sea, the looming dubious past of their marriage, what was the captain doing on his sailboat, it's going to end badly,

Mama would say, the sailboat bobbing back alone through the mangroves flying a black flag, all of it, she saw it coming, she'd told Venus not to marry a man twice her age, a drunkard maybe and worst of all a white man, how could Venus love a white man, did she even love him that much, all that wealth, everything he had was tainted, why, and Venus would tell her mother it was nothing she could explain, that's how it was, she had to be an honest woman, otherwise she would be an escort all her life, that was no life, Venus liked pretty dresses and jewellery, she was tired of her parents' little patch of earth, Venus said, the roosters and chickens running around the parched lawn, the icebox always out in the yard, nothing has moved in a hundred years here, Venus said, I want to be a rich woman and I will be, that man is a good man and he loves me, he will be my beloved and my liberation, and you and the pastor don't get it, he's always got to be right, doesn't he, you don't understand anything about it, you love only what is lawful and deferential, you're stuck in such a rut and I am going to be who I want to be, that was before, before Rebecca was born, Venus used to talk that way, but why had Rebecca been born, how, who was her father, why has no one ever been willing to tell her, wondered Rebecca, that was the real worry, it ate away at her and then she could never admit it to her mother, she didn't want her mother to feel guilty, she loved her too much, if she felt attacked she would be even more wary, and so angry, no, Rebecca didn't want that, the boat races every year were such a great show, thought Rebecca, Venus always did her daughter's hair, taking out her braids, now Rebecca did her own hair or didn't do it at all, she wore her hair as a mass of tight curls, Venus said you couldn't even see her face anymore, but she was growing up fast, she already went to school and to church by herself, Rebecca had to be careful, like the twins Deandra and Tiffany, said Venus, tall, thin girls, they wore tiny shorts when it was hot and loose camisoles open over their flat chests, they were tantalizing, they were quarry, they had to be careful, said Venus, at the Coral City Temple, Pastor Jeremy recommended that everyone read the gospel according to Saint Matthew, over the years his voice had lost some of its strength, said Mama, Mama was waiting for Carlos to come home, they would have a meal in the yard to celebrate Uncle Carlos's return, she would make beans, Rebecca visited him on Sundays with Venus in the juvenile detention centre where Rebecca spoke to Carlos by phone, there was a pane of glass between them, they couldn't hug or anything, Carlos told them that his lawyer, Perdue Baltimore, was doing good work, I'll be out soon Rebecca and we'll go to the beach with Polly, Polly, my dog, she's waiting for me, and Rebecca would say, no, Uncle Carlos, they're on a third Polly waiting for you, you've been gone for years, dear Uncle Carlos, even I'm not the same anymore, Venus was studying law thanks to her friendship with Perdue Baltimore, one day too, she told Rebecca, she would stand up for young Black men, kids like Carlos, they shouldn't be in jail, they were defenceless, they shouldn't have criminal records, she went to school at night while working days, she was always tired, she got angry when she didn't understand, but I said that things are going to change and things are going to change, yes, said Venus, and Mama told the pastor, my husband, you can see that Venus is a good girl, why are you so hard on her, and the pastor replied, she married a thief, a cheater, that Captain Williams and his contraband, they lived on the wages of sin, the glut of dirty money all over everything like seaweed in the mangroves, do you think that's a good thing, my wife, but Mama always answered back, she's our daughter, it's our duty to love her, whether she's married to the captain or not, dirty money or not, she's our daughter, she didn't want a mediocre life, she's always been ambitious, beautiful girls are like that, we can't do anything about it, we're only their parents, yes, thought Rebecca, Mama and the pastor always thought about Venus, about her past, they fought about Deandra and Tiffany too, the twins had started going out every night and the pastor was annoyed, they're going to end up like Venus, Deandra is already so vain, the twins' clothes smelled like weed and they were staying out too late, I didn't want to see poor people's clothing drying out on ladders anymore, said Venus and the twins heard Venus's voice, like Rebecca they worshipped Venus, Venus warned them, white bikers attacked schoolgirls near schools and in vacant lots, make sure you don't play with them, Rebecca thought her mother had seen too much violence, was that the story of her birth, wondered Rebecca, Venus had often alluded to an employee of her husband's, though she never really said what had happened, as if she was ashamed, she was so scared of him she couldn't sleep at night without a gun under her pillow, no, why did Captain Williams, her husband, spend so much time out at sea, Venus had her animals, her dachshund and her birds, the hummingbirds and sparrows, it was a paradise, but a paradise full of poisonous things, said Mama, Venus was still afraid of the white stranger who would swoop in and take over, it just goes to prove that we can never have a moment's peace, said Mama, we think we're safe but we're not, we live under the illusion that we're respected, but no, no, said Mama, not everyone can see that things are evolving in order to crack the past open, thought Rebecca, so that we can't see it anymore, so that we can step into the future, though it's true, she thought, from here you can see the whole congregation of colourful boats, it was so beautiful, every year. They'll have a party for me in the yard and good food to celebrate my return from juvie, the commuted sentence Perdue Baltimore managed to work out, thought Carlos, sitting next to Mama in the vintage car as Mama drove down Bahama Street, Esmeralda Street, as if she were announcing to everyone, look at my son, he's free now, no more chains on his wrists or ankles from now on, every time he was called to the warden's office he was cuffed, they all were, they couldn't be trusted and had to have their hands bound in case they turned violent, the young inmates in dormitories one, two, and three, Carlos told me all about it, thought Mama, his fear and his despair, my son told me everything, the next wing over was for the men, for dangerous criminals, the younger ones heard about their crimes, they had committed adult crimes, serious ones, Carlos told me all about it when I visited on Sundays though I knew he wasn't telling me everything, maybe he was shy or he didn't want to offend his mother, thought Mama, but he said that many of the younger inmates were shocked by the abominations, some of the crimes took place in the prison itself, in the basement, and the warden, who was strong, a colossus, had the basements converted into cells so that there would be fewer dark corners for people to be murdered in, Carlos told me all about it, Mama seemed to be saying to the neighbours on their porches, take a good look at my son Carlos, a mother always loves her son, even when he acts like a hooligan, he's back, respect him as he is, and you're all just camped out on your balconies smoking hash, you will respect my son, my child, Carlos, more than once he lost his way but from now on he's going to stay on the straight and narrow, the whole family will help him be good, even Pastor Jeremy, Mama was an opulent princess in her purple dress, a devoted mother, though she seemed stony on the outside, what did she really think about Carlos, was she disappointed in her children, especially Carlos, her delinquent son, not to mention the other one, El Toque, who had probably stolen the vintage convertible, what Mama didn't know, thought Carlos, was that in the adult wing gangs were killing each other as they did in the streets of Chicago and Detroit, guys with tattoos on their faces could gang up to kill a man they didn't like, there was nothing reassuring about being in jail, it had its own pecking order and it all ended in bloodshed, you could smell the stench of those crimes all the way to juvie, the smell of it, thought Carlos, right next door, close by, behind the black gates, horrible events that terrified us all, we weren't used to living so close to hell like that, grown men and their collective, consensual murders, we were still green, we might have a shot at a future, a glimmer of a future, if we got out of there, they told us again and again, all was not lost, that's how the guards talked to us, we must never become like them, they explained, those killers, they're headed straight to the gallows, believe us, the saddest thing I heard was about a sexual predator who was murdered by a bunch of men in the prison basement, the laundry was down there, the guys on good behaviour worked there, they tortured him first and just before the end one of them said, don't finish him off, let him live, we've tortured him enough, yet that same guy couldn't keep from strangling him, he said later that he regretted it, the feeling of his hands around the man's neck, it felt so low that he couldn't help but regret it, those stories wafted up to us like an eddy of filth, of corruption, and it made us even more miserable, thought Carlos, we too had sunk so low, so far underground in such vague depravity, it terrified us though we couldn't describe it, yes, that's how we felt, thought Carlos, it was better if Mama didn't know anything, she's so far removed from that world, she's incorruptible, just like Pastor Jeremy, my father, seeing Polly again would make me so happy, it would be so nice, thought Carlos, we'll run to the water together, we'll never leave each other again, no, never, thought Carlos, I'll become a mechanic like my brothers, my cousins, and Polly and I will never leave each other again, no, never, thought Carlos, and Kim held her baby in her arms and thought, this is where I used to come sit in the street with Fleur, where that poor girl is, all her bags scattered around her, now I walk around like a lady, if I sat there and let Pearl Saved from the Waters play with my phone I'd see all sorts of pictures pop up, a whole safari, elephants, zebras, she'd constantly be asking me questions, what's that Mama, and I'd say, look, that's a flower called the night cactus, it's a Peruvian flower that opens its white corollas only at night, and that's Orange, your budgie, Orange, Orange, Pearl Saved from the Waters chirping in Kim's ears, when she thought of Fleur, when they used to panhandle together, Kim was tempted to go sit next to the poor girl, the temptation was so strong it was almost physical, holding out her hand just like she used to do with Fleur when he tucked his head under his hood or turned slightly away from Kim to play his flute for passersby so that it was her, it was Kim who had to hold out her hand to beg, the temptation was so physically irresistible even though she wasn't hungry or thirsty like she used to be, even though it was very hot, all she could do was give in and she let herself slide along the poor woman's back, among her bags, the scattered suitcases that had almost nothing inside, it was right here, they had been so close, so connected, in front of the smoke shop that sold Cuban cigars and in the street Kim could breathe in their dry, acrid smell, what are you doing, the woman growled, this is my turf, you've got a man who feeds you, I've seen him around, Rafael, the Mexican, he's rich, he's a craftsman, he pampers you even though he has a bunch of wives, go away, you and your kid, she's too clean, she's even got a phone in her hand, did your man steal it, he probably did, we're going to leave soon, we're going to go away on a boat, said Kim, we don't get to leave, said the girl, everywhere it's the same thing, poor people, rich people, everywhere it's the same, do you know that I have a family, I can't support them, I'm divorced, alone on the street, I don't even know how I ended up like this, I don't drink, I don't even touch drugs and they won't let me in at the women's shelter, they say I'm crazy, whatever, I don't want to think about it, where are your kids, asked Kim coolly, thinking only of him, Fleur, he used to sit up against her, against her back, in the evening as the sun set over the city, summertime was like a howling fanfare, said Fleur, could you hear them, Jérôme's drums, would he have his dog with him tonight, did he even know how to take care of it, asked Fleur, they're with their father, I don't know when I'm going to see them again, answered the girl, you'll see, even if you leave with your man, everywhere that's all there is, rich and poor, the powerful and the weak, I'm not crazy, I have too much time to think, Kim asked her if she was thirsty, was she hungry, but the girl only shook her head, nothing, I don't feel anything anymore, not even the sun beating down, it's like I'm made of steel, get out of here, I already told you this is my turf, take your brat and get out, we're getting out of here, said Kim, this island is stifling, and suddenly he was there, Rafael, telling her to get up, grabbing Pearl Saved from the Waters out of her mother's arms, what are you doing here begging, what are you doing in the street, I gave you a place to live, come with me, are you still mooning over him, he left everybody behind to go chase after his fame, no, everyone worships him, he was nothing but a beggar, and Kim suddenly saw that Rafael would be capable of violence, he was so jealous of her love for Fleur, Orange, Orange, babbled Pearl Saved from the Waters, let's go see Orange, Orange, Rafael was dragging Kim, Kim and the baby, to the loft, far from the store with the acrid smell, they were heading for the loft, to safety, thought Kim, at the same time she couldn't stand up to him, Rafael was irresistible, his hair down to his waist, out in the street with Fleur, his flute, soon dusk would turn to darkness over the city, soon, thought Kim, she would forget Fleur, and old Uncle Isaac took Daniel by the arm as he walked along the water and proudly told his nephew that soon there would be a whole forest of new Australian pines here, new silver palms to replace those torn out by the cyclones, is it true, dear Daniel, that it's still summer, the oceans are already bringing hurricane winds, oh, I hate this time of year, the old man complained, his cane rubbing in the sand, shuffling the seashells, even though it looks like a huge fury from the top of my tower, it's very impressive, but soon I won't be able to climb that high anymore, and that divine fury will fling me to the ground, the ocean is God, they say, you can't fight against it, or can we, can we try, what do you think, dear Daniel, and Daniel thought it must have been comforting and so debilitating too in a way to be like Uncle Isaac, a master of the world because he had money, the whole illusory fortress could crumble with him, his stone tower overlooking the ocean, the gulf, tonight or tomorrow, even if his health seems to promise an extraordinarily long life, old Uncle Isaac wouldn't be able to escape the term limits that had been fixed for him far beyond countries and oceans, which in an instant would rob him of all his assets, even the majestic Grand Hotel, the gardens and swimming pools, a great crashing wave sweeping away everything in its path like the hurricanes Uncle Isaac had spoken of, not without fear as it got closer, and even through the exquisite summer light, those days of interminable dusk, he had a feeling, he almost knew, with his faith in life forever restored Uncle Isaac kept inventing new architectural universes, new projects glinting on the horizon, in fact, he said, I could add another floor to the tower to be able to put up more poets, and on my island, the Island No One Owns, that's what I promised Jean-Mathieu before he left us, Daniel was watching the green light of the swimming pools in the distance, the wind, still soft, lulling the palms and the flowering flame trees, the voice of Uncle Isaac held an echo of hope, full of energy, his stride too, though he walked with a cane, Daniel again in spite of himself was mulling over his book *Strange Years*, he decided there would be no forgiveness, no restitution, even the bullet to Mengele's brain was no excuse, no redemption, he had drowned in Brazil, not even drowned, actually, since a heart attack had caused the drowning, he hadn't had the same death of those he tortured, by what Dantean mercy had he been spared, or perhaps he thought he was guilty of everything but that, they may have acted on his orders but a whole group of doctors had insisted on carrying out the experiment, they wanted to be able to save the lives of soldiers, too many of them were dying of cold, too many, yes, they said the experiment would be humane, when the heart attack hit and his heart stopped beating as he struggled in the clear water of a lake, was he by himself or was his son with him, he had a new family, he had managed to get away, in exile, yes, at that instant, faced with the inevitable dart of water that would cut the thread of his existence, however vile, it was a life nonetheless, the life of a man on earth, something out of nothing, or perhaps an infernal growth, until that moment he had known nothing, had he ever seen them again, the people he used as lab rats, they had been lab rats for the whole lot of them, strong young people, Russians and Jews, they were submerged in tanks, in cisterns, in tubs of near-freezing water, every detail has been carefully determined, the goal was to study the effect of frigid temperatures until loss of consciousness, so close to the freezing mark, would they still be alive at all, and their power lay in resuscitation, in starting life back up again, yes, they were bringing back the dead, they were mad enough to believe that they could, they took out the half-frozen bodies and shone a bright sun lamp on them, burning the stiff white skin, how long would those bodies resist, how long, but they were no longer breathing, did the doctor of all agonies remember those beautiful young people, the carnage of cold, in tubs and cisterns, did he remember those tanks full of hardened cadavers revived by lamplight, he would have a son as handsome as the one he had imagined at the laboratory window when the spidery-legged child wriggled in the snow and, compassionately, he did not kill him that night, perhaps he was tired, the good surgeon had worked long into the night, in any case, he thought, the poor thing would die of cold during the night, his own son would be pure, an Aryan with blond hair and blue eyes, hidden under a different name, or changing names, perhaps he was many men, a veterinarian one day and the next a farmer and healer, a doctor with multiple personalities all as false as they were good, cloaked in his fraudulence, he seemed like a man like all the others, he was good at healing animals while he was a veterinarian, he meticulously cared for women as a gynecologist or small-town doctor, and hearing that he was wanted once more he would disappear farther still, in the hills of a tiny slum in Brazil, setting up house with two guard dogs, all he had in his shack was a bed, a table, a chair, he became a frightened man, his health was fragile and his digestion was poor, there was so much evil lodged in the grotto of his body and he couldn't get it out, his son came to visit him in his humble abode, a hovel at the bottom of the hill in the favela, he only saw him twice, but during the visit he gave him his own bed and slept on the ground, the son he had dreamed of when he was working without anaesthetic in the camp was there, he bravely came and said I want to know why, even though you're my father, why, why, and the fugitive physician broke down, crying and shouting, I lengthened their lives, I did the best I could, they were all condemned anyway, I don't regret anything, what do I have to regret, thanks to me so many twins were born, all blue-eyed and blond-haired, that was the fruit of my research, a pure, blue-eyed Aryan race, and I was banished, even my family disowned me, and here you are, more valiant than the rest, dear son, you've come to me, please, come into my humble home, do you see how sparely I live, your persecuted, rejected father, can you not love me just a little, I see it, I recognize you, yes, you are my son, and the aggrieved son saw a man hunched and old before his time, poor father, he said, poor father, he seems so small while in old photos he was always tall, handsome and fit, as he was tracked around the world by the investigators, they hated him, he'd been forsworn, the son thought, as if the future lawyer in him had already pleaded his father's case, he is my father, I owe him respect, I have to see him, and before his son, a rare pure soul, the damned father, the humiliated doctor thought, I regret nothing, I had no other choice, perhaps he alone will love me a little, but the son thought there was no forgiveness, no redemption for those actions, craven monstrosities, nothing will be forgiven, yet he kissed his father as he left, he smiled at him, and the father felt a gentle shroud passing over him, repeating as he left, my dear son, I will leave you my poems, my notebooks, no one can understand how alone I am, perhaps you will understand, and later the son wept over those school notebooks where the father had written, I hear a bird answering the voice of another bird, a friend answering another friend, today I read Goethe, I listened to a concerto, a friend's voice answered another friend's voice, but no one could know how alone that son's father was, and the son knew he would never save his damned, lost father, he was just a sad old man now, he had nothing, his intestines were blocked and hurting, he was a tormented man who had tormented men, women, and children, the son left Brazil and never saw the father again, Daniel wrote in *Strange Years*, there with old Uncle Isaac, Daniel realized they were heading over to Adrien, Isaac felt it was only proper to go say hello, Adrien was on his third round of edits to his manuscript of *Faust*, what dedication, Uncle Isaac said, he's here every day in his deck chair or at the table his loyal waiter Simon sets up before him just out of reach of the waves, he's been doing this for years, editing and writing, the constant humidity isn't good for your computer, Simon warned him, and you shouldn't get your feet wet in those sandals, Monsieur Adrien, let me move the table a little, and your chair, all these material concerns that seem not to bother you at all, Monsieur Adrien, you're so distracted when you're writing, oh no, it's not a distraction, don't you see, Simon, how focused I am, here, I just spotted another mistake, and another one I didn't see when I read through the first time, good God, so much hassle before it becomes a book, but then when the book is published you're never happy either, Simon replied, and they chatted like this day in, day out, Isaac told Daniel, but Daniel wasn't thinking about Adrien roasting in the sun in his pointy hat, about Simon handing out delicious cocktails shortly after five o'clock, there was a story behind this comfortable man, a poet and translator, the author of a *Faust* brought into the present by his own personal story, his personal chauffeur Charly was always around, with all her suggestions to entertain him, wasn't that how she had seduced Caroline, Isaac said, just like Caroline, was it the sun or had he lost weight, Adrien seemed younger, or perhaps Charly's brash youth was wearing off on him, his pink forehead under his hat made him look for all the world the very picture of a kindly poet and literary critic who had laconically eviscerated Daniel's first book, the first volume of his *Strange Years* series, it still bothered him, how could he wander over to greet this man, the review still stung, he would probably write that Daniel's new book was much the same, *A Ship of Fools*, a parade of unsettling, harrowing human fauna, and once more, just as the author in his first book had absolved Hitler's dog, the children forced to die by suicide in a bunker by their Goebbels relatives, he now added to the list of the innocent the son of an evil, insanely cruel doctor, having never lived through the events he described, having never witnessed any of them, was Daniel appropriating the silent, deliberately censored memory of his parents, his grandparents, or was he instead possessed of some gift of prescience, some insight into memories before his own time that whispered to him all the horrible events he wrote about in his books, which everybody would rather forget, Daniel could almost hear Adrien's words, meanwhile Uncle Isaac was going on about how lucky he was to live in this paradise with eaglets flying around, great blue herons, as soon as he woke at dawn he saw his big cats coming toward him, his Florida panthers, there was a pond for alligators too and other creatures, Daniel thought he should be kinder to Adrien, yet what he felt as he walked toward the old man was not gratuitous benevolence, he's one of those people who will always make us doubt ourselves, he's one of those men, yes, Kim woke up in the middle of the night tangled up in Rafael's dark hair, black as a raven's wings, the smell of hash and incense in his hair and his clothes, the floor-length embroidered tunics he wore as if he were Kim's guru, a dizzyingly sensual lover, though she only ever thought about Fleur, she saw her little daughter nearby, Pearl Saved from the Waters was twittering at her budgie Orange, she thought the child had been asleep between them, Kim asked Pearl Saved from the Waters where her phone was, if she lost the phone it would be like losing Fleur again even though he never answered her calls or her emails, the photos she sent of Pearl Saved from the Waters, as if the child had been his and not Rafael's, look at her growing up, Fleur, isn't she beautiful, this is Pearl Saved from the Waters with her budgie, Orange, on her head, she's still such a wild child, I'm sending you this photo, I'm thinking of you, and other, more intimate images flicked past on the phone's magic screen, Fleur whose name was now Andrew Adam, what a cold name, Andrew, he was Fleur no more, he was conducting an orchestra in a city in Germany, he was introduced as a musician, composer, and pianist in another city in Italy, or was it on TV, in a documentary she had recorded celebrating the young virtuoso, no, he was no longer the same Fleur from the streets, he was Andrew Adam, a different man in a different life far away, thought Kim, so sophisticated in his tuxedo, she didn't recognize him anymore, if the phone was lost it would mean the end of how Kim saw herself against Fleur, the end of Kim loving Fleur, Pearl Saved from the Waters chatted away without answering Kim, tell me, darling, where is it, tell me, this is Orange, Orange, chirped Pearl Saved from the Waters, petting the bird's green wings, Orange the budgie, and Kim fell back asleep as her daughter chatted away until she fell asleep too, curled against her mother's warm body, maybe it was only a bad dream, thought Kim, not being able to have access to the phone anymore, in her troubled half sleep she saw Fleur's red lips, the delicate hands he looked after so carefully, he washed them in the showers on the beach, warmed them under hot water in winter, Kim had watched those habits of his for a long time, Fleur took such care of his hands before picking up the flute, though he cared not at all about the rest of his appearance, his feet were often bare, but my hands have to be supple, he used to say, to play that Telemann, listen to this, it's a Carl Philipp

Emanuel Bach sonata, he was Bach's most proficient son, his father admired him but how sad when the son doesn't deserve the admiration of a father, how distressing, sighed Fleur, was Kim listening to Fleur, could she hear his abandon in that melody, a happy dance in the night, she should forget about him, Fleur was much too delicate for her, whereas Rafael's strong body was a comfort even though she wasn't really attracted to him, all those perfumes, the incense in the house everywhere in the loft and in Rafael's hair, even once the boat was fixed, even in the middle of the ocean, won't the coast guard always be around, patrolling all over the place with their guns and their lamps, Fleur's red lips burning with fever on Kim's forehead, sleep, you have to sleep, he said on their bed on the shore, the white sand beach, the noisy flight of a last egret over the waves, sleep, we have to sleep, said Fleur, he smelled like the sea, he had just gone swimming almost completely naked and his skin was salty, Paul came by with his band calling before nightfall, music is meant for joy, hey, Fleur, why don't you come with us, Paul the trumpeter marched out front, you're dreaming of concert halls, Fleur, but we're just playing together outside, out in the parks, come with us, this is the music revolution, follow me, Fleur, I promise you joy, we are made only for joy, good night kids, we have to go play, they're waiting for us, music everywhere, everywhere it can make people dream, good night, kids, said Paul the trumpeter, the waves are creeping up and the heron has flown, music is progress, said Paul, and Geisha told Yinn as they put the finishing touches on Robbie's bar before the opening, Yinn, listen, it was a hostile message, I'm telling you, not even a signature, just a scratch, some obscure, unrecognizable sign, who would want to hurt us, I'll guard the bar, said Yinn, I will stand watch, believe me, Yinn, you're too trusting, anybody could just walk in here, I'll be at the door, I'll be looking out, I may look like just a girl but I am a karate champion, I've got tennis arms, I'm as strong as Victoire even now that she's a woman, and she's still a soldier, with all that combat knowledge, she remembers the fire at the UpStairs Lounge that killed thirty-two of us in New Orleans, said Geisha, that was no fire, said Yinn, that was a murder, on a summer night like this one, everyone feels so sultry, so ready for pleasure, for those connections that warm us up even hotter, summer always has something so sensual and delirious about it, they were dancing just like us, on the top floor, it was a private room, they could hear the sound of the pianist going nuts downstairs, all those fabulous queens strutting around, there was a huge crowd, then someone downstairs rang, had anyone called for a taxi, no, no one, go answer anyway, they never saw who the fake driver was, only the bomb, the blast, the flames pushing through the whole bar, some people climbed up to the windows but they were sealed and they died there against the bars on the windows, the roof was on fire, they died like that, trapped, they were twenty years old, in the staircase, at the door, bodies lying everywhere, torched, that was no fire, said Yinn, it was a massacre of poor innocents, on a June night as beautiful as this one, said Geisha, when all you want to do is give in to pleasure of every kind, melt into every embrace, the Community Church performed the service, Reverend Ézéchielle inviting the crowd to prayer, the Community Church saved our honour, said Geisha, the reverend began her sermon by saying that we are all equal before God, let us pray for our unfortunate brothers to whom God will offer a feast of joy for what is destroyed by hate is saved by love, for what is destroyed, a massacre, massacre, repeated Yinn, my heart is bleeding, it is, you see, replied Geisha, at moments like this, whatever Reverend Ézéchielle thinks, at moments like this, there is no God, it's an illusion, there is no good news, it's false, a supreme, universal failure, it is, and Geisha fell silent, suddenly crushed, and Mabel came to kneel on Merlin's grave, kneeling ever lower, closer, the grave under the roses, it looked like she was rocking herself, her knees in the soil, the roses, she always came to bring roses, these were fresh and still damp with dew, there's nothing as expensive as roses, she said on Merlin's grave, and you're worth every single flower, my beautiful Brazilian bird, I sold lots of lemonade and ginger ale on the pier today so I thought I should go say a prayer for my dear Merlin, dear Merlin, repeated Jerry, grasping Mabel's shoulder and pecking at her neck, beautiful bird of the tropics, repeated Mabel, my beauty, my comfort, it rained on my roses, a downpour, but here they are, I will leave them on your bed of sand, beauty, comfort, repeated Jerry gutturally, you know, Jerry, all I have left is you since Angel left for more celestial planes, all I have is you and you know it, don't you, said Mabel to her parrot Jerry, and look at you all cocky, puffing out your chest, aren't you feeling grand, you're just a humble little bird, even though that sinner Petites Cendres and I have doves, he's a sinner, that's why I don't stop praying for him, all I have left is you, Jerry, all the doves want to do is fly away, they refuse to be tamed, while you, you're willing, Jerry, though you do grumble a bit, they can hear you across town, we were there all together, mourning him, the little one and his dog Misha, Brilliant had him on the leash, Brilliant who was going to marry Lucia, even though I was scandalized, can you imagine, two completely different generations, I said to myself, but so be it, I hope they're happy, as for me, chuck the husbands to the curb, I wouldn't want that, I wouldn't want another man, I have to go see my daughter, she's pregnant again, the reverend said not to worry, she'll pay for my plane ticket, but all I can think is here comes another Black child who'll get killed by the police, one more, yes, he'll be heading out of the house to go play football and bang, shot by a cop, just like you Merlin, that kid was laughing when he threw the rock at you, but he'll regret it, I'll find him and drag him to the police, yes, he's going to regret it, spiteful lout, it would be her fifth child, and her husband doesn't have a job, Reverend Ézéchielle told me not to worry, but no, five pregnancies is too much, my daughter is young, she needs freedom, five pregnancies and him on unemployment, it's too much, the reverend said let us welcome him into our hearts and in the hearts of the world but it's too much, or else he'll be afraid of stepping out of the house, in Chicago, in Detroit, it's too much, yet for our little Angel, even though we were all crying, even Misha, it was a celebration, thanks to Brilliant, his upcoming wedding to Lucia, though nobody quite believed it, Lucia was an old woman, with that boy, it made us laugh, the Black Ancestral Choir sang "Sleep at Jesus's Feet," Eureka was singing, welcome to heaven, Angel, and all of us were listening to the hymns when Brilliant said let's pop the champagne, fly to the light, Angel, and come back to us each evening as the sun sets, no goodbyes, Angel, and Misha, Brilliant had him all riled up, the dog started running all over Pelican Beach, barking, he was calling Angel, Angel, and we could only laugh at the idea of Brilliant and Lucia getting married, I can tell you now, it's like Angel was with us, urging us to sing with

Eureka and the Black Ancestral Choir, as if he had been there, not the sick boy he had been but another version of himself, yes, it was wonderful to feel him running with his dog, he wasn't pale anymore, Eureka said, no, he was dark and healthy, and Eureka said those who go are always with us, it wouldn't take much, the way we were calling, singing, the way I know my Angel, he would have wanted to be back among us right then and there, those who are truly alive are like that, they always come back, look at the waves, look how they keep coming back, they never wear out, well, that's how my little Angel will come back too, and you too, Merlin, who knows, it'll be a long trip, believe you me, to go see my daughter in Indiana, but Reverend Ézéchielle told me not to worry, she took up a collection for me in her church, a fifth child, a fifth pregnancy, it's too much, too much, said Jerry, where is Merlin, where is Merlin, and as the wind rose over the water Mabel felt some relief from the heat, her tears had dried, she wasn't sure anymore if she was crying for Angel, his ashes among the orchids dispersing on underwater paths in the ocean along the Coral Coast, they were just bubbles now, swallowed by the fish, the sharks swimming by without even seeing them, bubbles of air and water, nothing more, my little boy, thought Mabel, kneeling in the soil on Merlin's tomb among the pink and red roses she had bought that morning, or whether she was crying for Merlin, her beautiful tropical bird, her companion and Jerry's for so long, her sorrow for both of them was so heavy, and especially she wanted them to never be forgotten, neither Angel nor Merlin, no, to forget is to erase and we have to pray for all the souls, Mabel told Jerry, we can't forget a single one, single one, repeated Jerry, hey where is Merlin, asked Jerry, his eyes round as he watched the sky clouding over, and that's the way it is, thought Martha, Fleur was scattered all over the house, sheet music in the dresser drawer, that was when he still came to his mother's house, she would wash him, bathe him before he went back out on the street with Kim and their dogs, to those beaches foggy in the night, to that transient, mortifying life, yes, she thought, there were notes everywhere for a new piece, an electronic composition with voice, and sometimes something she didn't quite appreciate, like Gian Carlo Menotti who wrote in a notebook stained with black ink, when I was thirteen without my mother's support I wrote an opera for the little girls of Hiroshima, they were heading to school on the morning of August sixth when suddenly, suddenly, were they singing on the way to school, that song, how can I transcribe that, two violins here, Martha could read her son's hesitations, his reticence, the notebook had been tossed in a corner of the room, cast off, headphones and videos of Fleur, she had given him everything he wanted, her spendthrift son, she had so little, then there was his father, they were divorced, the grandparents on their drought-withered land, in Atlanta, everybody supported Fleur and he' d spurned them, hadn't he, she knew so little about him, he never wrote to her, he never answered her though she begged, a mother's supplications, is that how a son acts with his mother, it broke her heart, his silence was devastating, she wanted to tell him about bravery, Father Alfonso's courage as he welcomed undocumented migrants into his chapel, and her own too, his mother offering them her own home, wasn't he proud of his mother for doing that, of how boldly she broke the law, wasn't she a little like him too in that way, it was better to do good than to obey, especially in those days, when homes and families were ransacked and shipped off on buses and planes to Colombia, Honduras, countries where people risked torture and death, they would all be gulped up by gangs and murderers, wouldn't he be proud of his mother, of her, Martha, always ready to defend the weak, she would have liked to lose a little weight, to be like before when Fleur was little in the flowered dresses she sewed herself with Fleur dressed in the same fabric too, toddling around barefoot to the piano, his friends from the Cajun band, Lizzie and Seamus, wanted him to come back too, they were simple kids, the band was just like it used to be, Fleur shaking up the audience on the piano with them, when will he come back, they asked, we're still waiting, no one draws a crowd like Fleur, he was the star, what's he doing so far away from his island, so far away from us, Martha worked late into the night in her pub, the captains and sailors never left early, she wrote to Fleur, her disloyal son, did Fleur remember that a few steps away from the pub, overlooking the sea, the Gulf of Mexico, there was a theatre, The Ocean, where he'd been welcomed so warmly by the actors, the theatre gleamed like a lighthouse, the actors came to the pub to have a drink, the theatre mostly put on satirical plays, we get it, the actors told Martha, we see you, we put them up too, these undocumented people, on Sundays there's always a meal ready for them, for all the families, we're not going to say anything, we're not going to rat you out or Father Alfonso for sheltering illegals in the archipelago, we're on your side, it's a crime what's going on, but we've got to tell you, Martha, we've gotten threats, we've always put on our plays freely, my dear son, I wanted to write you about all of it, but if I were younger, fitter, running from one end of the pub to the other with plates and beers, I wouldn't be as exhausted, when you were here

I felt like I was more elegant, lighter, now I have no one to help me but if you were here things would be different, I wouldn't be the same, it's so beautiful here, you can hear the waves at night through the pub windows, the birds sing late in the summer and the wind is cool after the day's heat, and with Lizzie and Seamus's Cajun band nearby the place seems like heaven for the nighthawks, when there's no sheriff around people can stay late into the night, I tell the families to come dance, let off some steam, they call them illegals, they dance so well, they waltz the night away, just the other day one of your good-for-nothing friends was talking about you, your friend Marius, you know he has no teeth or hair left, it's the coke, he told me, the crack, but he doesn't smoke anymore except weed, he always has big bags in his trailer, he's still living in a trailer, not on the street, I felt sorry for him and I thought if that was you, Fleur, if I saw you in the street like that it would kill me, it could be a blessing, that's what Father Alfonso says, it's a blessing that you aren't like your friend Marius, he's only smoking weed now, and who knows what else, Marius surely has a mother of his own, it must be hard for her, Alfonso is always so offended by how priests behave in the Catholic church, sometimes I wonder why he doesn't leave the Church and he just tells me that his place is right where he is and he's going to keep on denouncing what he sees, writing about the scandals and talking about them, he's a dutiful man, and he says that you're right where you should be too even though I can't believe it but I listen to him, he's a wise man, a good man, it's late, I have to get back to the pub, I'll be thinking of you, dear son, in my pub under the stars with the ocean nearby I always think of you, I tell myself what a blessing that Fleur is no longer on the streets like Marius, Marius with his coke and his crack and what all else, no teeth in his head and no hair, and I tell myself maybe it's better that you're far away, maybe it's better that way, yes, tugging along the pink balloons blowing above them in the sky, Portia and Porsha headed toward Petites Cendres and Geisha, laughing, we wanted to be the first here to celebrate the opening of Robbie's bar, we brought balloons to add to the decorations, said Porsha, you look like such a nice flamingo couple, said Geisha, come on over, yes, so we are, Porsha's wife said shyly, all we need are the feathers and the wings, although we do have pink skirts and pink tops, and even our pink berets, even though it's so hot out, and it's my Porsha's birthday tonight, isn't he the loveliest bird, so tall, with that long neck and his nose, it looks a bit like a flamingo's peaked beak, today should be a day to celebrate flamingos so that they don't go extinct like so many other birds in the archipelago, I know it's a bit early but could we have a pink drink, asked Porsha, I'll go make some, said Petites Cendres happily, you're pretty tall, Porsha, you're a tall man even in that cute pink outfit, you can be the male flamingo, I can be whatever I want, just ask Portia, my darling wife understands me so well, one day I can be a man, I'm working on the farm, and the next, if we go out in town, Portia likes me as a woman, pink from head to toe, her girl, so then I become a flamingo, the walk and all, everything in moderation, I do what my wife Portia wants, yes, that's my Porsha, that's how I love him, I love him however he wants to be, whatever strikes his fancy, said Porsha's shy wife, he's no less my man in overalls and playing with our piglets, working on the farm, we do what we can to prevent cruelty to animals, we're vegetarian, we work to keep a balance in nature, she was so shy her cheeks were pink under her tan, they loved each other so much, thought Petites Cendres, it seemed surreal though they were quite real, for all their spontaneity and courage, they fought against prejudice simply by being who they were, their double identity, double and distinct, just like flamingos, they protect each other, Petites Cendres envied them, he thought, it wasn't healthy to be so alone in life, he thought, despite Yinn's affection, those old steadfast, distant feelings, we may well be the last flamingos, the last of our species, said Porsha, what with everything that's disappearing these days, everything is going extinct, said Porsha, soon the marshes will be empty, and Uncle Isaac was still speaking to Daniel, a little breathless now, do you remember back when I used to go out with my architecture students and with biologist friends to look at wolves in the wild, we would leave at dawn with our binoculars and our cameras to head out to the national parks, to Yellowstone Park, we waited until nightfall for the grey wolf packs, we seldom saw them, they travelled in groups through the cold, we waited for them on snowy hillsides, it took several parks for the species to be saved, grey wolves have clear yellow eyes with wide black pupils, their ears are like black and grey velvet, they're endangered, even in the parks where they're supposed to be protected, they would hunt deer and rest, sated, beneath the pines by a lake, the last one I saw was alone by a river, the wolf lifted its head and looked at me with his yellow eyes, as if to say, will you come by helicopter to shoot us down, they had opened up the wolf hunt again, even in the parks, or will you let me drink from the river in peace, I looked at the animal silently, thinking of my grandnephews and grandnieces, I was thinking about Mai, I wondered if she would ever see a pack of grey wolves, how many would there be and for how long, would she get to see brown bears and their cubs, I was thinking about my wealthy friends locked in the enclave of their privilege, it was time to step away from all that, those habits, it was time to cut myself off on the Island No One Owns with my animals, dear nephew, you know, here, in this enclave, ninety-six percent of the population is white, privilege here is traditional and well-established, so that nothing can ever change, and it started bothering me that those people in their enormous mansions with their personal jets could get up in the morning and think that the pedicures or the champagne some enslaved Black person brought them were just among their personal pleasures, that they could canter through the waves astride a white horse, that seemed cruel to the horses, forcing them to run through the waves like that, it was too much, the waves against their legs, their legs are muscular but fragile, and I told myself that if I stayed with them in this enclave of privilege I would become just like them, corrupted by riches, money can tarnish a man, it reduces us, you may not know this but all of us can be corrupted, oh, look at those dancers, the young women in their pink and blue tutus running toward the pier, I loaned the dance school one of the rooms for their rehearsals for the summer concert, where did that young man come from, he almost shoved me into the water, he cut so close to us on his skateboard, they should be banned, dear Uncle Isaac, we can't ban skateboards or roller skates, even at your Grand Hotel, Daniel said, smiling at his uncle, that's true, old Uncle Isaac said, I'm nothing but a grumpy old landlord, if you think about it, nothing really belongs to us in this world, although the illusion of false ownership is a pleasant, imperial illusion, it's also a way to forget all those who are close to us, who for one reason or another we like dominating, that's a pleasure you can't possibly know, my dear Daniel, and it does seem a bit late for me to become less authoritarian, what do you think, Uncle Isaac remembered a fawn that had been separated from its mother, the doe had been put down by two men in a truck, he had no idea how that happened on his island, the Island No One Owns, it was an outrage, I thought I was alone with these animals and yet the cruelty of men reaches me nonetheless, they snatched a fawn, a doe, it was demoralizing, it was the end of paradise, the old uncle's scratchy voice betrayed his emotion as he shoved the tip of his cane in the sand, their underbellies are so soft, a doe, a fawn, old Uncle Isaac said, that pinkish white fur, where did those murderers come from, can you explain that, dear nephew, there are all kinds of crimes in your books, you must know that evil exists though I would rather pretend it didn't, Daniel thought of her, Dr. Herta Oberheuser, less well-known perhaps because she was a woman, the only woman doctor at Auschwitz and Ravensbrück, although she was as bloodthirsty and brutal in her experiments as the doctor of all agonies was with the children he worked on, she wasn't as famous, she barely avoided the death penalty after her trial, she was sentenced to twenty years in prison, which was commuted for good behaviour, and she went back to practising medicine, she led a second life like other Nazi doctors who had been found guilty, she fled to northern Germany and opened up a successful practice, she thought she had been forgotten, she and her crimes, did it even matter anymore, those dour days of war were over, you had to forget everything, Daniel thought, did Dr. Oberheuser sometimes think back to her own childhood, that little girl in the school uniform, her face already hardened, her upper lip set like a blade, her blue eyes honest but too direct, her tall, pensive forehead, was that cruelty's first face, had she recognized it in herself, when she was in solitary in prison, did that face appear to her in her dreams above her victims' bones or was it simply the face of an ambitious child who wanted to do right, already so rigid, that rigidity would become her insatiable yoke, righteousness and rigidity, along with sadism, which shone for the glory of the party, Herta had decided very early on that she would never be like anyone else, she would have a career, she would be noticed, she would blossom, in the party that beckoned the little girls, she would be a doctor, she would study in Bonn, dermatology, she would live a man's life, she would be respected, that little girl's face had learned early on not to smile, that sharp upper lip, how ugly, the face seemed stern and closed, she let nothing show, no emotion especially, emotions and feelings were vulgar, they said so in the party, don't feel anything, emotion is weakness, and she held herself upright, her face closed, upper lip like a blade, during university she understood that she would be a doctor and the party would need her, her knowledge, she would be unrivalled, what an honour for the party, it was such an extraordinary political party, the glory of her country and her race, she rejoiced when the bombs rained down, when she was hungry she vowed she would be stronger than hunger, her face grew hollow, her upper lip softened, she was almost beautiful later on, but people noticed not her beauty but her intelligence, this was war, she was hungry but she had learned not to feel anything, she was inscrutable, as heroic as the soldiers, she would have a future, a spectacular career, sometimes in the throes of hunger she wavered, and the face of the austere child she had been, the child denied and hungry, the exhaustion of her studies, that face haunted Herta Oberheuser the war criminal during the tedious hours in jail when the world had condemned her as a monster but they would forget, you could forget anything with time, there, alone, in confinement, did she see that little girl, the child whose youth had been stolen and denied by the party, the party she had adored, idolized, was it all in vain, would it always be in vain, adulation had trampled the child, the little girl whose face showed nothing, that upper lip at the time already looked like a blade, her features drawn and severe, her gaze direct and penetrating, she was born like that, she thought, she couldn't do anything about it, if she had been able to choose her own fate everything would've been different, she would never have worked at Auschwitz and Ravensbrück, she would never have been part of the League of German Girls, those virginal teens, a bouquet of life so quickly wilted, her sisters, her friends, though Herta was a loner, all of them devoted to their great leader, they lived only for him, if anyone had offered her a different destiny, a more banal life, though that was never what she wanted for herself, she was proud, she believes she was destined for what she called a unique experience, everything would be special for her, the signature of the infinite projected into another, less intransigent fate, she never would have met Dr. Karl Gebhardt, the camp's head surgeon, she was his assistant, nothing that came after would have happened, her hands would have been clean, she would have lived a righteous life, a rigid life, above all she would have killed no one, it wasn't clear how that had happened, the head surgeon imposed his will, Dr. Gebhardt said, think of our troops, we want to assess their tolerance to pain and how to ease the pain and to that end we must operate on human flesh which we have here in endless supply, know that if not for us they would all end up in smoke and ashes so what is there to lose, tell me, you're young, you'll learn quickly not to feel anything, about life or death, nothing, I know it's hard to hear them moaning, crying, screaming, but then all at once there is nothing, you don't hear them anymore, you had to yield to the coldness of the soul, Dr. Oberheuser thought, that was what it was, she would get there, bit by bit, or so the head surgeon promised, the master of fear, to feel nothing, to be nothing more than a machine, her supreme austerity loved order, cleanliness, she could go further than the other doctors, the adults allowed her to infect their wounds, to transplant their nerves, these surgeries were the renaissance of medicine, far beyond human capacity, as for the children, that would be harder, she would have liked to have children one day, she manipulated them with her skilled, cold fingers, sometimes she caressed them awkwardly, their hair, she injected them with a fatal substance then treated them, removing their vital organs, that part she didn't enjoy, for a few moments they were conscious between the injection and death and suddenly the tiny eyes watched her operate, helpless and frightened, in that agonizing struggle, they were so young and their gaze weighed heavily on her but she had to remind herself that she felt nothing, it was merely flesh condemned in advance and in the end in her cold trance she thought she was doing them a favour, if she kept working like this she could be head surgeon one day, it seemed like a reasonable ambition after so much work, she thought of the suffering of the German soldiers and pushed on, always going beyond, if she placed a piece of wood or a nail clipping in the open wounds of the poor damaged bodies, already slipping into a coma, how long would they survive, like soldiers on the battlefield, their flesh blasted open by the shells and shrapnel, what was the resistance of the still-living bodies of these children, their limbs hacked and torn, the men and women, how long would life hang on, and at last came the supreme honour she had been waiting for, she was the first woman head of surgery in the camps, the pinnacle of distinction, she was special, it was a recognition of her heroism as a doctor, it was always unpleasant, even as head surgeon, that the children were so affected by what seemed to her to be only the care the troops needed to survive, they had to survive everything, her exhausting labour carving young flesh was to serve them, later on at her trial when they noted the number of her victims, she thought to herself I was just a physician, caring and operating to help the soldiers survive, they were still dying each day, she had only ever thought of them, that was how she pleaded her case, for the fatherland, I only did it for the fatherland, I am innocent, I'm innocent of all charges, while her friends in the gigantic conspiracy were hanged or executed by firing squad, it made her shiver with horror, how could this be, after serving the country and the party, working for the triumph of the Aryan race, and all those women too, still young, she had shipped them off sternly to the operating room, she explain later at the Nuremberg doctors' trial, yes, you had to be ruthless, the girls were Polish political prisoners, when they were called to the operating room, they knew they wouldn't be executed that same day, they could avoid the firing squad already gathering in the snowy yard, her surgeries had protected them, she had cared for them afterwards with her nurses, accomplices of her pity, bent over the pale bodies, they had lost so much blood, they came out of the operating room grafted, limping with pain, you could see their leg bones through the open wounds, she was hard on them and refused to let them sit or lie down, they were only political prisoners, nothing more, they had to be punished, yes, she said at her trial, and as for the children, it was unfortunate to see them pass out, slip off her lap, in spite of her scruples, since one day, who knew, she wanted to have a family too, it would be nice, she would be a strict mother, she would insist on order and cleanliness, and she learned not to see them anymore, their cries made it hard to operate and even keeping them alive for yet another experimental operation was bothersome but she didn't have a choice as she explained later to the judges at the Nuremberg doctors' trial, a tall woman in a grey suit, her once-smiling face changed, her blue eyes pale, the eyes had lost that overly direct arrogance, it had been appropriate when she was a medical student, now they seemed sad and disappointed, her eyelids heavy, and her mouth, although it was harder now, the upper lip still a blade, her mouth was tired, you could see her bitterness and her suffering, as if her whole face had lost the will to live, so jaded, disenchanted, she was defiant before the judges, she dropped her eyes, yes, defiant, between two guards, their helmets pushed down over their foreheads, no, she said, she said no to those judges, to the whole courtroom judging her, another time she wore a black coat and beneath the coat a black dress buttoned to the neck, a white ribbon at her neck looked like a noose, she left the ribbon undone, fifteen of her colleagues had been hanged but she thought that wouldn't happen to her, she was a woman after all, research into the human body was only in its infancy, she thought, and one day that research, cruel as it may seem, would be part of our shared experience and the healthy women, men, and children she had destroyed with her knowing, rubber-gloved hands, her hands, the gloves stiff with cold, they were only objects, they weren't men or women or children, they were only objects of scientific use, which was as it would be in the future, Dr. Oberheuser believed that sincerely, she was relieved when she heard the judge's decision, only twenty years in jail, so little, already voices rose in protest, that's not enough, kill her, kill her, but she couldn't hear them anymore, she would be downright monastic, a model prisoner, she would earn everyone's approval, they would applaud her rigidity, her austerity, her absolute striving for everything to be clean, loyal, the vengeful voices would fall silent, she would be freed, free to resume practising medicine, far away, in West Germany, it didn't matter where, a small town, a village, she would work as a doctor and they would forget her, no one would see her, she would be honourable, she would heal and dress wounds and injuries, proud of knowing how to heal and treat and they would notice how attentive she was as a healer with little children, people would trust her again, they didn't know who she was or where she came from, her past was clean, spotless, no one would remember her, she was a woman without a past, just a respected healer, a doctor, fifteen scientists and doctors had been hanged or executed by firing squad, those were the sentences, and she would outlive them all, a distant, anonymous life somewhere, it was a big country, though it had been devastated, she had survived, she, Herta, the girl now named as a war criminal, it was inconceivable, no, she was an honest woman, she had integrity, they saw wrong, she didn't deserve twenty years in jail, no, who were all those people who thought they could judge her actions when all she did was her duty as a researcher, as a scientist, who did they think they were, during the interminable trial one of her victims appeared, showing the scars on her arms and legs, stigmata, why had she let that one live, now here she was testifying against her, it was unfair, it would always be unfair, and then finally she was able to practise medicine in peace in some lost little town, Germany was a big country, though torn and destroyed, in Dr. Oberheuser's mind, her sentence has been commuted, only five years, she served only five years of a twenty-year sentence because of her behaviour, her righteousness, rigidity, and silence, when she was released she practised medicine with the same righteousness and rigidity, her patients respected and admired her, yet it always came back, they always reappeared, the ghosts of camps, they had survived, with their lost limbs, their scars and stigmata, and they said, all of them, that's her, take away her licence, put her back in jail, the judges and judgments were endless, they kept accusing her, she couldn't sleep, in her little house beneath the trees she had finally found some measure of comfort and now she couldn't sleep, they harassed her in her dreams, her nightmares, why hadn't the judge sentenced her to be hanged like her colleagues, why, what was she doing there, alive and caring for patients, she even had a house and good food, she, Dr. Herta Oberheuser, one of the greatest war criminals in the world, by what false pardon was she still breathing, living, and then those women, the victims of her transplants and dislocations all through their once-healthy bodies, the survivors weren't just ghosts, they were standing up to her like a wall of hatred, she thought, the women who had been treated like human trash in the camps were now calling for her licence to be revoked, one of them from Ravensbrück recognized her, she lost her licence in 1958, she was a friend, a family physician, that was her strength, reassuring families, comforting children, healing them, caring, the ultimate duty even if her soul had succumbed to the cold, to the frozen touch of death, everything was ice, even her hands, her fingers were always cold, it was because of the winter, the steel-grey sky, as if the world were stuck in a perpetual season of war, she was forever caught in mourning, Daniel thought, what were her final hours like, she had wanted so much to be special, she wanted a spectacular destiny, Daniel thought, Uncle Isaac was showing him cooing doves nearby, what a nostalgic cry, a bit of Mozart in the sky, that's how my old musician friend Franz, with good-humoured nostalgia, used to describe the mourning doves that wake us up at dawn, and good old Adrien, they were walking toward him, always still writing despite the heat, the sun, it takes courage, it does, Uncle Isaac said, Daniel was preoccupied with Dr. Oberheuser's final hours, had they been filled with illness, with some sense of defeat, had she raged against herself, rage and hatred, perhaps, like the rage of her victims, or was she challenged by regret, though without remorse about her party, those at the helm of her vanquishing, did she think that she too had been tortured like those human objects she had used for science, she too had been pressed and compressed and oppressed under the torture of a party that exploited its youth and all adult life, she too had been held in the grip of the empire of torture, she was a victim overlooked, she didn't speak, didn't confide in anyone, was she dying of cold like those victims in the Nazi laboratories, the cold that slowly numbed her limbs, her hands, her frostbitten fingers, cold was an evil that could kill, did she think that she might be a victim too, she had denied everything at Nuremberg and would deny it to the end, that wasn't me, that wasn't me, there was no God, no heaven or hell, we were alone, she was more alone than others, all this time she had only been a woman whose only fault was her ambition, her own advancement, nothing else, so why all this hatred all around her, perhaps until the last seconds of her life, even when she was no longer breathing, she could hear the accusations of that hatred that seemed until the end so unjustified, so unreasonable, she would have liked her scientific merit to be recognized without judgment, her devotion, the irresistible passion that had led her somewhat astray from her austere, strict principles, it had changed nothing in the honesty of her objectives, she would have liked her death not to be as cold as her life had been, she would have liked to have someone nearby, there would have been a bed where she would have lain feeling her body slowly go numb in the cold, she hated the cold, she would have been in the hospital or at home, perhaps there was no one with her, was that not what she dreaded most, she didn't always want to be faced with that wall of hatred, spelling out her crimes and calamities, when you were an executioner could you even die with dignity, was that what she would ask herself at the end, she hated thinking about the others, the colleagues and friends who had been executed, each one so brave, she hadn't had the courage, and the lower-class women who had been executed, lowly kapos following their husbands' orders or faithful to the Nazis, sadistically whipping and ravaging the miserable camp prisoners at Ravensbrück and Auschwitz not for science but for pleasure, she pitied them, Dr. Oberheuser thought they were inferior, brutes, those women were so sad as they marched to the scaffold or crawled to the execution chamber, blindfolded or wearing white caps over their heads, hands bound behind their backs, one of them, they called her the hyena of Auschwitz, she had been hired by the party to torture prisoners, she was convinced she had accomplished her fastidious task, quickly, she said before her execution, she wanted the noose to tighten quickly, it was true, the reel of her crimes named at the trial, in Auschwitz and Bergen-Belsen, she seemed bored as she listened to the list and the description, she was executed at the age of twenty-two, the youngest of the accused under English law, at the trial Herta could see the faces of the accused, the poor daughters of working-class parents, their mothers dead by suicide, at home they were beaten and they left school at fourteen to join the League of German Girls and later they were molested in school, they were poor and ugly and no one cared if they were humiliated, they were just dirty worthless girls and they would get their own back, they wanted revenge against the mothers who had swallowed hydrochloric acid, the nasty brothers, the grimy lives that could not be redeemed by the party's open arms, by the League of German Girls, they would take revenge against their classmates' derision on the innocents in the camps, barely teenagers, without any education or training, the larger-than-life figure of the greatest leader would push open all the borders, come to me, he said to the girls, they were seventeen, come to me, they would become nursing assistants, they could go back to school, hope was so close at hand, and they volunteered for an initiation into brutality, yes, wholeheartedly, these children, they wanted to please their masters and they were promoted quickly to guards, they supervised those who were pouring in every day, one of them rose through the ranks so quickly that she was in charge of the gas chambers and their passion for brutality became an instinct, madness, a desire, a sexual rage that could never be fulfilled, you always had to hit harder, make them bleed more, even the victims, the pain of seeing torture inflicted became all-consuming, unbearable, one day you discovered you could actually walk all over them with your boots, you could rip the skin off, you could nail their flesh, was there any fulfillment after all that relentless violence, thought Dr. Oberheuser, the torments and the tormented marching to the scaffold with those girls, the same funeral march, when they heard the sentence pronounced and the night before they were hanged they sang Nazi songs, until dawn they sang, they heard the footsteps on the stairs, the guards coming to their cells, high up in their prison, the warden was waiting, they heard their names called, come, come here, the bars were open, the guard said follow me, that's an order, was it morning, nine thirty, only hours before they'd still been singing, a choir of three young girls or a recitative for two voices, three voices, an angry plaint, they were not resigned, they refused, there was a trap door beneath their feet, where did the bodies go at the end of the rope, they wore a ridiculous white cap so they couldn't see anything, not to make them more afraid, then a doctor would come, saying, no, they are not breathing, and so, Dr. Oberheuser thought, the verdict was straight and sincere, those torturers, she wasn't one of them, she had only worked for science, she thought, they were guilty of the deaths of five hundred thousand prisoners, most of them women and children, children taken from their mothers, it irritated her, it annoyed her, how could they have acted that way, how power-hungry could they be, they wanted to outdo the men, everyone saw it at the trial, like Dr. Oberheuser herself, it was so cumbersome, humiliating, the large placard around their necks with their names written in black letters, it was odious to be treated like this, humiliated, debased as they themselves had humiliated their prisoners, trampling them, robbing them of their dignity, and now the horrible placard, she was so proud, Herta, her first name, her name, as if her profession and who she was had been forgotten, she was a doctor, the first woman doctor named to a research position on human subjects, in the camps women were never treated fairly, even when they were marched to the scaffold they were stripped of their dignity, it was unfair, they had to drive them through the mud, they were just guards from small towns, Maria and the others, often they had gone through the very things they were putting others through, they weren't like Herta, she was from a different class altogether, a different social group, those girls had known where they were headed, blindly devoted to the party and to their great leader, it was a time of mad adulation, how could they have known, they were ignorant girls, nothing more, they were born in Bavaria or in Hungary, like Herta, they had parents, one of them was born in January and died in January, quivering on the scaffold, the few steps up to the noose, she had a hard time walking up, it was January, it was snowing, fine, powdery snow, maybe she would see her fall one last time before she died, she would tell them all, do you think I feel nothing, do you really believe that, that final cry on her frozen bed, she thought, feeling nothing, those cold hours at the end of her life, all those guards felt nothing as they chose them, those women, the millions of women, men, children, no, they had felt nothing, Maria, Joanna, and their sisters, torturers all, quickly, come on, up against the crematorium, the oven walls, quick, get out of here, we don't want to see you, Joanna had explained at the trial that she had joined the army to make a bit of money, the judges saw a poor girl, she was only looking for a job, like so many people, she was hungry, all she wanted was to live, to survive, Maria meanwhile had explained that she was good at music, and she had a chance to form an orchestra, the women's orchestra, yes, and the sweet music, all compassion and sweetness, it helped the prisoners who were selected, women especially, Maria had complete control over thousands of prisoners, women and children, their resettlement, I knew what that meant, resettlement, but, Maria said, I was the one who had the idea to make the executions a little kinder, my orchestra, the women's orchestra, music could accompany them where they were going, I knew what the place was, of course, there was lots of smoke, I never dared get very close, I knew, yes, but you have to understand I created that orchestra for all of them, for each one, so that they would be a little less unhappy, I wanted to make their fate a little lighter, they told her she would be executed on December 13, 1945, in their cells, two of the women had asked to be pardoned, their requests were turned down, was the musician torturer one of them, did she hope for pardon too, she received no answer, only that her execution was still scheduled for December 13, on that day she would feel something, the rope around her neck, she would suddenly be alive, suddenly she would ask herself, what have I done with my life, today, on this terrible day, this execution I can't appeal, I'm only thirty-six, what is this nightmare that's brought me here, they've even refused to pardon me, Herta kept coming back to the innocence of those torturers, one day they were born, beautiful babies, adorable little girls, they had parents who loved them like Herta herself had been loved, admired, nothing suggested that they would be hanged to death one day, their backs broken by the jolt, there was nothing to suggest such a fate for those babies, the little girls they had been, there was some mistake, thought Herta, they had played with their dogs, run through fields of flowers, swum in rivers and lakes, they had climbed mountains with their guides, they loved the mountains and the rivers of their country, their village, their town, very young they had learned to sing little songs that seemed strange, Nazi songs, but what did any of it mean to their ears, just a tune they could skip rope to, laugh and play, they were children, in school they had to learn other songs, other words, heavier, worrisome, it was just a part of what they had to learn, she thought, that was where everything started, little ditties and games in the village square, words full of joy and laughter, who could have thought that twenty or thirty years later they would be subjected to such an egregious trial, that those little girls would be the shame of the nation, she felt so sorry for those stupid, lost little girls, criminals that they were, from the age of ten she has been a member of the League of German Girls, singing and laughing, still so carefree in their uniforms, the dark blue skirt, the white blouse, the loose, feminine black necktie, the rough walking shoes, all the badges, they were thrilled, delighted as only children can be to be a part of all that playful pageantry, to offer themselves up lightheartedly to the fatherland in new costumes in which they could escape their families, their poor families where they always ate the same beets and potatoes, where the father and the older brothers hit them, the thing to do now was to rise through the ranks, get as many badges and honours as possible, the first flight from misery and poverty, that was how they came to be, she thought, by escaping, by fleeing, and when the fatal knot tightened around their necks, choking them, what would they see, one of them, surprisingly, remembered a sleigh ride with her parents on a mountain path, they had stopped near a snowy peak and she heard Christmas carols, she saw a nativity scene in the village church with shepherds and sheep, they had them too down where she lived with her brothers and sisters, they used to go for walks in the woods, they would race through the valley, there were crystal-clear blue lakes where the children swam, that might be the last thing she saw, the Christmas carols, sleigh tracks in the snow, the horses pulling them, the mountain peaks in the sparkling snow, and then the end, silence, another one, who took longer to die, she was dropping into a bottomless well, she could feel the rope slide along her ribs, her throat, all the way to her feet, she felt like she was bound, in the glimmering depths of the stagnant water she saw heads, faces with their eyes closed turned toward her, begging her not to come any farther, she would be executed by all of them once more and she would say, I asked for forgiveness, why didn't you listen, and they would reply, it was all for nothing, nothing, see what you did, see what you made of us, and then she heard nothing more, as for Emma, the torturer, there was only silence, the heaviest night. Yes, near them, right near the beach, under the palm fronds bowing in the warm wind, they could hear the mourning doves and the white rock pigeons cooing, Uncle Isaac was telling Daniel, his voice broken by the effort of walking, sometimes he stopped to take his nephew's arm, no, slowly, please, I get tired faster than you do, dear Daniel, and I can feel that you're distracted, you're in your writing head, why bother listening to me, I'm an old man, and the uncle went on, recounting his adventures, his extravagant past, as if Daniel had been listening distractedly and patiently smiling his approval, yes, this was in Timbuktu, I was staying in a yurt on the river, they called it the Dog Cabin, it was so comfortable in the tent there on the shores of the Niger, there were even pictures hung up on the canvas walls, and muslin mosquito netting, you could see the migrating birds go by, in Nepal, in my comfortable jungle hideaway, I saw rhinoceroses, elephants, even Bengal tigers, those might have been the last tigers you could see, at what price, and what about those places in the Himalayas, it's breathtaking seeing the snow leopards, I was a fearless traveller, I wanted to hurry up and see everything before it was too late, I travelled from India to Siberia, there were only four hundred Siberian tigers left, I can still see those cabins, we lit oil lamps in the evenings in the jungle, it's unfortunate that not everyone can take that kind of trip, it's too bad, yes, I saw blue butterflies in Costa Rica, the most beautiful parakeets in South America, Uncle Isaac remembered, he had seized the world around him, he had discovered the beauty of the universe from the vantage of privilege, everything sumptuously enlarged for the needs of an independent, wealthy man, which wasn't to diminish his personal qualities, it wasn't a flaw, he couldn't have acted any other way, his own privilege had increased while others' waned, Daniel thought, he felt guilty for inheriting Uncle Isaac's privilege, no matter how distantly, and his parents' too, gone were the days when Daniel would have liked to know old Uncle Isaac better, that was already far away, in his parents' time, his great uncles', they called them my writers, my artists, my dear Tennessee, my dear

Truman, oh my dear heart, that was how Jean-Mathieu referred to his writer friends and Uncle Isaac did the same, gone were the days when Uncle Isaac was young and humble, building a majestic home for his writers, his artists, his dear hearts, that was his first hotel, on the island, the same hotel, painted white, overlooking an emerald sea, with time and with Uncle Isaac's financial conquests the modest writers' mansion got bigger, sturdier, a palace with adjacent swimming pools and canals, a marble path down to the water and bonfires at night, it became the Grand Hotel, imposing and majestic, Jean-Mathieu's dear hearts passed on and he followed, gone with the voices reciting poems until the break of day in the old hotel by the emerald sea, though Uncle Isaac could hear them still and sometimes he said to Daniel, you know, Tennessee, Truman, those dear hearts, they're still here, reciting their poems until dawn, when I go out by myself to the Island No One Owns I can hear them at night in the canoe on the ocean, you'll see, we've got it all wrong, nothing really ever changes, no, Uncle Isaac, Daniel broke in, you know the world isn't the same without them in it, they left us alone, but Uncle Isaac, who was listening to the song of the birds, didn't seem to hear. Across the way there was the bay and the lighthouse, thought Rebecca, she would be singing tonight at the Coral City Temple, boats drifted by on the water in the gentle wind, sailboats, soon they'll turn their green lights on, they look like pearls in the night, the leaning masts in the dark, when would her mother's brother be home, when will Carlos come home, why have they been ignoring him, why did they send him so far away, what did he do, Mama said they lock up Black boys in juvenile detention for no reason, the slightest stupid thing gets them thrown in jail, cuffed and shackled, was it because the weather was so mild, there were no thunderstorms, the sky was quiet, Rebecca remembered Pastor Jeremy rocking her in the yard on Sundays before she learned to walk, or had she been walking already, running around, she'd always been a little girl to him, enough of a baby for him to give her a bottle of lemonade, he said, that was during Sunday dinner after Pastor Jeremy's prayers and sermons, her grandfather, they were all together in the yard with the chickens and the roosters, Pastor Jeremy's thundering voice proclaimed that Sunday was a day of rest, after Mama served a good meal, that was the tradition, he said, rocking Rebecca on his lap, one day she'd be too big, like her mother Venus, and we won't be able to do it anymore, God knows what happens to girls, just look at Venus, she's always done exactly as she pleases and see how unruly she is, Pastor Jeremy carefully rocked Rebecca on his lap in the creaking chair on the yellow lawn, I've been telling you, Venus said to her parents, that chair is busted, and why is that icebox still sitting on the grass, everything around here is all busted up, time stands still here with this old furniture, old chairs, the old icebox parked here with the roosters and the chickens and the grass keeps growing and growing, although Venus always made her resentment apparent Pastor Jeremy rocked her carefully, thought Rebecca, she just a child, the pastor fed her the bottle of lemonade so slowly, watchfully, Rebecca doubted that Trevor was her father but she had never felt unloved, who was her father anyway, some thief who broke into Venus's room while the captain was at sea, she couldn't imagine what had happened that day, it was like when you're out on a rough sea and you don't really know what's happening but you keep watching the waves until you're dizzy and all kinds of odds and ends wash up on the beach, shoes and ripped clothes, glass bottles deformed and remade by the swell into sculptures, shattered and sharp, that's how it was, Venus was often resentful while Rebecca allowed herself be rocked by the pastor, sipping her lemonade, Venus stormed around the lawn with her bangles clinking around her ankles, ranting, why hadn't her parents ever come to visit when she was rich, when she was married to the captain, at her mansion, the estate where hummingbirds foraged in the roses, because it was a house of sin, replied the pastor as he rocked Rebecca, the pastor's words fell heavy in the humid air, he sounded like he was preaching even when he was talking to his family, he only ever spoke softly to Rebecca, almost whispering, may the Lord always protect the head of this beautiful child, her eyes, her mouth, may the Lord, the pastor's prayer as he held his granddaughter annoyed Venus and she shouted, what about Uncle Cornelius, I sang with him at his club from the time I was fifteen, he had a medal from the Korean War, he was a hero, they said, and look at how he ended up after playing the blues in every club in town, he could only play his guitar or bass at night, he came home to his trailer at dawn, he was so tired sometimes he couldn't get up in the morning and his musical instruments started rotting along with him, he had a lousy army pension, he was broke, he didn't have a clean shirt to go out in, he was rotting away in his trailer like a fly in a web, I can still see him with that red beret pulled down over his forehead, singing and playing all night long, the regimental medal of honour, he used to say that would be it, the end of segregation, all those thousands of Black soldiers and their Puerto Rican brothers-in-arms, war would be the end of prejudice, that's what he had served for, all the freedmen and the enslaved men who had come before and who got sent to work camps, forced labour, said Uncle Cornelius, we were cannon fodder, but then I got a good regiment, I rose to commander after I saved men outside Seoul, but it stopped when I was wounded, October 1953, I don't remember anything after that, there was a nurse next to me during the transport from Korea to Japan and coast guards from some mission, six hundred thousand men served, yes, what happened to them all, Venus asked the pastor, did they all end up living in trailers like Uncle Cornelius, that would be the end of segregation in the army, said Uncle Cornelius and he probably believed it, the end of segregation everywhere, and as Rebecca watched the luxurious sailboats and all the other, regular boats, little boats that left for other islets every evening carrying workers who came back out early each morning, it occurred to her that her mother always talked only about the past, the present did exist, Rebecca was a reminder of that, and the future was nothing like the past because the future wasn't as shadowy, the future belonged to the children who were born today, how wonderful that they could all be born so different and from all over the place, from Asia, Europe, the island where Rebecca lived with her mother, her mother Venus, her father Trevor, her little brother Trevor Junior, it was wonderful, and Rebecca thought about the future, she could imagine the first Black woman astronauts heading to space soon, they would sail out over oceans, countries, planets, space belonged to everybody, they would be engineers, doctors, and scientists, there they were, you could already see them blasting off in their orange spacesuits, barely visible and so mysterious in those shiny black helmets, space meant freedom, it meant the heavens had been brought a little closer to earth, maybe all the angels in the Bible were out there too, making sure nothing and no one lost their balance, space was perfect, a place where every beautiful thing gathered among the stars, it was true, Pastor Jeremy rocked Rebecca every Sunday, she was loved, maybe she didn't need a father, maybe she didn't need the man who had made her mother so sad, and worse, maybe her father was that violent caretaker Venus spoke of in anger, Rebecca didn't know but she had her doubts that Trevor, Jamaican Trevor, was her real father, Trevor loved Venus, he would pull her to him and kiss her, she sang to his music, swinging her hips, they loved each other and that should have been enough for Rebecca, she was loved too, more than many of the Black kids in the neighbourhood, yes, much loved, as her mother kept telling her, but they argued a lot too in the yard on Sundays, even though Pastor Jeremy never stopped rocking Rebecca, Pastor Jeremy said Uncle Cornelius loved women too much, no harm in that, said Mama, no harm in that, she said, sometimes prostitutes, and sometimes they were even white, said Pastor Jeremy, preaching again, he thought segregation ended after the Korean War, said Mama, he liked alcohol and women too much, repeated Pastor Jeremy, we must pray for his poor soul, said Pastor Jeremy, and they argued like that in the beating sun, the chair where the pastor rocked Rebecca creaked more every day, she could have bought new chairs, said Venus, a new icebox for the yard, and even a new bicycle for Carlos and dresses for the twins, anything they wanted, she'd been rich once when she was married to the captain, she was so happy with him, she used to model for him back when he was still painting, before he got in with those other sailors who dragged him into all kinds of sketchy deals, they weren't sketchy, said

Mama, your husband's business was downright shady, why couldn't you see it, Venus, you were blinded by love, that's why you couldn't see anything, and now here you are, all alone, without a husband, but I still believe, Venus, that your husband wasn't a bad man, and now you have Trevor, Rebecca's father, God bless your husband who died at sea, his boat sailing back to you empty through the mangroves, flying a black flag, may God in his goodness bless him, yes, said Mama, Mama was wearing her white Sunday shoes and her purple dress and she patted Rebecca's head kindly, Rebecca knew how much she was loved, even without a father, Rebecca was very much loved, more than other Black kids in the neighbourhood, said Mama, and Kim woke with a start, she could feel the cold of the phone under her back, along with her daughter's toys, she saw that the screen had gone brown, it was dead, and when she held it up under a lamp and plugged it back in, waking it from its apathetic slumber, Kim saw the screen was streaked with cracks, as if her daughter had knocked the phone against the wall or dropped it in the pool's chlorinated water, a sad sign that Kim would never again see Fleur's face or his body standing there as he conducted an orchestra during one of his concerts in Europe, the picture was cracked, broken in her mind, the phone was symbolic proof that she would never see Fleur again, he had left her forever, that was the final blow of an irremediable separation, she and Rafael and their child and their animals would be leaving soon, sailing out to sea; she didn't yet know where but Rafael said people were waiting for him in port cities, he had a serious mission, they had to get back to a more natural, pure state, they would live primitive lives on some lost island, that alone was salvation, said Rafael, he didn't want Pearl Saved from the Waters to have to go to school when she grew up, he didn't want any of those futile obligations, they had to get away from the decadence of civilization where lakes and oceans were polluted, all the world was wreck and waste, get away from the wars governments waged, away from any corruption that might have affected Pearl Saved from the Waters, their beloved child, they would bring all of Rafael's other children, all different races, so that they could escape stupid rules and the powers they would have to bend to, and as for money, there would always be money, Rafael's imagination was boundless, he said, and Kim listened to him, thinking, that may well be true, but I've never had a home so why do I have to leave this one to go live between the sea and the sky, at the whim of the wind, why, I guess we'll live on Rafael's questionable business dealings and one day the coast guard will come arrest us, why, but no, said Rafael, we'll be happy and carefree, we'll live under giant palm trees by the sea, you've got to believe me, Kim, I always land on my feet, they would head to Bermuda, Rafael's friends were waiting, the sky was always blue there, everything was blue and green but Kim could only think of her gloomy, sordid day, the poor woman against the lamppost that morning a reminder of her past with Fleur, when they were homeless out on the main street like that with Jérôme the African and his droning drums, they still loved each other back then, they were so close, proud and panhandling, they slept together on the beach, that same day they saw a white parrot, smart and bright-eyed, they used to see the bird out on its master's shoulder, there it was next to a second parrot with red and blue wings, a child passing through town with his parents had teased the bird mercilessly, scratching its wings with his vicious fingers, and the white parrot flew off, they saw it fly into the Cuban cigar shop and fly out again, into the street where it was hit by a car, its master ran up and cradled the throbbing mess of bloody feathers under his shirt against his bare chest, can't you see you've killed my bird, he shouted, can't you see, we've been together for almost twenty years, can't you see what you've done, I hate you all, he carried the bird to his truck while another man dragged along the open cage, and the parrot's master sat on the bumper with the other bird on his shoulder and the white parrot huddled under his shirt, caressing it with his big hands, kissing it, under his shirt, like he was saying goodbye, Kim went up to them, she thought she had wept along with the man but maybe she had choked back her sobs, she was usually impervious to that kind of street drama, she remembered Mabel, the same crime was being repeated here, the death of Mabel's magnificent parrot Merlin, just as white and beautiful as the dying bird, never again would Merlin's voice ring out, croaking in the street, seducing all the tourists with that raspy call, Mabel was still heartbroken, and Jerry too, Jerry had lost a brother, said Mabel, those were disastrous hours, and now the cracked phone, disfiguring Fleur's face and body, that was how this dismal day would end, that was the way it was, thought Kim, just as the bird had vanished so Fleur disappeared too, Kim knew she would never see him again, and Mélanie remembered that winter she'd called a nurse because Augustino had an earache, she'd thought she heard the nurse tell her they had too many activists over at their house and who were these refugees they so gladly took in, the two of them, Mélanie and Daniel, wasn't it illegal, exactly how many did they have living with them, whose idea had it been to take them in without telling the mayor, did they think they could simply put people up just like that, they'd jumped off a boat that had been adrift forever, from Cuba or Haiti, as if they were our own people, they were just foreigners, perhaps even criminals, you didn't know a thing about them, the nurse had said in a scratchy voice, Mélanie thought, no, it's only Olivier, his wife Tchouan, their son Jermaine, was it Olivier's fearless journalism that bothered her so much, it troubled her, it was true, in an article Olivier had accused the KKK of the bombing in Birmingham that targeted Black leaders in May 1963, some people were saying that Olivier's articles had incited the massive non-violent demonstration that turned into a riot, all those young Black activists out in the streets, that tragic month of May, Olivier started to doubt if it would be peaceful at all, he was an activist himself at the time, committed to defending his people against an old, never-ending injustice, you could still feel the violence coursing through communities and families, the effects lasted a lifetime, Olivier had sided with Rosa Parks, the dauntless woman they called the first lady of Black civil rights, she was a young woman then, humble but resilient, she'd refused to obey a bus driver who demanded she give up her seat in the coloured section for a white passenger and they went after her for civil disobedience because she had violated Alabama's segregation laws, that tiny icon of huge victories against segregation, Olivier admired her, he'd written about her, he called her an icon of resistance against racial segregation, he had always written, he had never stayed silent, and now he was in a wheelchair but he still protested and spoke out just as he had when the KKK bombed Birmingham, it was the story of his life, there were no accidents, Mélanie thought, from an activist down in the streets to the first Black senator, until he retired, exhausted, to be with his wife and son, to write in solitude, Olivier had led a risky life, his life was his own, a hero's life, though he didn't think of himself as being at all remarkable, as Augustino was, a young writer leaping in to help in the wake of disasters, for some time now Mélanie had been seeing him everywhere, among the poor in India, those who were considered untouchables under the old caste system, washing and feeding them, he must be there, even as a child he had promised to help them one day, or perhaps he was doing relief work after that earthquake in Italy, wherever human suffering was Augustino would be there too, for him writing was leaping into the fray to catch the world's last breath, you could see it in his books, yes, Mélanie thought, her son constantly grappling with danger, child of a global world, he had returned to the same font from which he refuted the dehumanization of a disintegrating humanity, wasn't that what it was, Mélanie wondered, the absurd memory of those earaches of his, like his first rebellious outbursts as a teenager, that had set him on a journey that drew him ever farther until one day, without a word, he ran away, as if he had told his parents, you'll see how well I can manage on my own without you, you'll see, as soon as he could walk, running around the house in his superhero cape, he had noticed the White Riders going by on the other side of the fence, he'd heard Julio telling his mother, there they are, they're right there, they tagged your boat with their red mark, or was that just a nightmare that drifted sporadically through Mélanie's nights, shouldn't she have been thinking of the present, Mai would be there soon, Mélanie would be at the airport soon handing her daughter flowers, shouldn't she allow herself to feel the happiness of seeing her again, and although Uncle Isaac kept rambling on about his exploits, the time those monkeys had followed him into a museum or a church in Thailand, it was incredible, seeing brown bears in Alaska in a preserve, he said, he believed in parks and protected areas, all Daniel could do was lose himself in his words, *Strange Years*, his thoughts swarming amid the sound of the waves and the flight of doves and pigeons in the hot sky plummeting toward the cooling sea, in spite of himself Daniel let himself be tugged toward the visions of hell he described in his book *Strange Years, like a Descent of Christ into Limbo* by the Spanish artist Bermejo, he wasn't anything like the pious painter's Christ figure, Daniel gazed through furrowing embers at those damned souls blessed by Christ, the holy golden halo above his head, in the red, scarlet colours of the flames, Daniel looked within himself for some merciful shelter where those shackled souls might have found rest, those souls were the sisters and brothers of the executioners who had shot his great-uncle Samuel and the rabbis in the snow that unforgettable winter day in Poland, they were the ghosts of a distant past and of a present that was still contaminated by them, Daniel thought, Daniel replaced the flames in that Bermejo painting with nuclear warheads that trapped Christ among the damned, held captive by the warheads and those who would fire missiles toward humans, their countries, their cities, that was the Christ Daniel strove to modernize, the one who with a wave of his hand could prevent the conflagrations of hell from descending on entire populations, lost in the depths of Great-Uncle Samuel's past, Daniel saw Dr. Oberheuser again on her bed, was she at home in the last apartment where she had lived in Germany or in a clinic far from the city, she knew she would die in a place that was as cold as her experiments had been when she had given the order to immerse healthy young people in ice baths, the cold scalding them like fire as the temperature dropped lower and she would feel the same icy cold beneath the hospital gown or her nightdress on her limbs, on her skin, it suddenly seemed dry and sterile, she had been abandoned by everyone in a stiff, inhospitable body, without access to any medical care, there was no other way, she couldn't even cry because everything inside her was frozen, as if she had been entombed in ice or frost, and perhaps while she was still lucid she wondered, how could I have committed all those murders, but then, no, she decided, she hadn't murdered anyone, her passion for science could never have been described as murderous, never mind her wartime heroism, but life was absurd, wasn't it, it was useless, all of it just dragging you toward that sterile cold, she wasn't that different from anyone else after all, her pride wouldn't die with her, she was just like those senior guards at the camps, proud that her authority was respected, proud, she would be proud to the end, the guards had been following orders and suddenly they were all being humiliated at some ignominious trial, they had to wear numbers, front and back, as if they were animals, cardboard placards marked one, two, three, four, five, and so on, it was appalling, they were older and no one helped them sit down or get up, the soldiers watched them, laughing silently as they trailed out of a row of black vans, shuffling awkwardly, one held out her hand to another prisoner because all that was left was infinitesimal acts of charity before they all faced the same fate, the one took the other's hand and said, you are my friend, have faith in me, the English soldiers, the officers, the guards, everyone despised them, like them Dr. Oberheuser had been despised, they hissed at her and insulted her even though she was of a higher class, in her status she would have wanted to be as nameless as the male scientists, as they walked to the scaffold the men looked at each other blankly, blind to what lay ahead, their expressionless eyes, there was only the absence of emotion, as their numbers were called in the din of the military tribunals a helmeted guard shoved them toward the back, the antechamber of death, number one, number two, number three, the executions would take place one after another on a September morning, while the women looked frightened, they hopped down off the truck's high steps clumsily and walked together to the courtroom where the photographers circled them with their flashes, oh, don't feel sorry for them, look at this one with her hair neatly combed, this other one in her fur coat, war makes you rich, she won't be wearing it for long, believe me, the women suddenly looked frightened, so like the faces of their victims they could have been mistaken for each other in a crowd and now the crowd was judging them, everyone was hungry to see them die, one after the other, as if they were going to unleash dogs they had starved so they would bite or even devour the prisoners, as if those dogs trained for pure destruction had escaped straight from the camps to come here, the crowd was gathered and watching with their fangs out, whether they were wearing fur coats or rags, Herta felt them all quaking with fear, and now, here, parked in the grey courtroom with their judges, almost all the judges were men, and their accusers, they had no whips or guns as they had had when they strolled among the rows of prisoners, when they were guards, if they felt like it, if they felt like being a bit sadistic, now they could no longer shove white poisonous powder in a prisoner's mouth to hasten their end, the guns and whips and kill-trained dogs, tools so cruel were turned against them, she thought, at least that's what they all feared as the sentences were read out, that the hell they had sanctioned would be turned against them, and not all vanity was futile, the fur coats and beautiful hairdos, the perfumes, the piles of corpses had made some of them wealthy, the bodies they had stripped, or on occasion they were gifts from husbands or lovers during that reign of plunder across Europe, the fur coats and beautiful hairdos would blow away in the wind and the smell of smoke, how little deference they warranted now, a few seconds before their execution they would remember their childhood games, hands clasped together in a circle, round and round in the forest, and one would say to the other, no, this isn't how it was supposed to end, we wanted rainbows, a scramble of girls in the snow like in the old days when we were still in the League of German Girls and we loved playing together, it was summer or springtime, before every season became the season of death, we were still so young, we were children, let's take care of each other, let us love each other, these men have no pity, goodbye my sister, goodbye my friend, goodbye, friendship's flower wilted so quickly, how had they gone from childish games and pushing each other in the snow to learning to kill, now their turn had come, they would die by hanging or firing squad, broken, I'll think of you tomorrow, and I will think of you, replied the other, let's meet again somewhere, they say there's such a thing as the soul, we will meet again, they sang songs until dawn from one cell to the next, recitatives and hymns, it didn't matter what the words were, they were shaking with fear, these were their farewell songs to the earth, to the clouds in the sky, to the snow that tomorrow would sweep into drifts in the prison yard, one of them died by suicide in her cell, she was the worst one, the barracks commander, she had enjoyed seeing her prisoners shivering in the cold, naked in the square, one night, two, a disciplinarian, her husband was a brute who dominated her, one was a mother, she held her child in her arms and kissed him in the castle on a lake where she lived, a poor girl who at fifteen had been working in a shoe factory, she was spared and decided her own end, she had fulfilled her dream of wealth and aristocracy and hanged herself with her bedsheet on the day of her release, leaving a scrawled, illiterate note, she had no choice, she said, being released would have brought her nothing but unhappiness, she was a pariah, where was the son she loved so dearly, how had he gotten through those years when his parents would come home in the evening covered in a sheen of sweat from the arduous labour of slaughter, they played with their son by the lavish house on the lake, did the little boy smell smoke as he took his first steps on the lawn neatly trimmed by servants, the maids showered him with affection, the boy would become a man, cursed just as his mother was, or pitied, an innocent standout in a house haunted by such sinister omens, yes, people would pity him, or else the child would pity the mother, she was hysterical, he could never judge her for her crimes, he loved her, he remembered every kindness, he was stuffed with food while people were dying of starvation out there, far from the castle on the lake with the servants and the maids, it actually wasn't that far at all, just down the road he had been forbidden to explore, where plumes of smoke poured into the relentlessly snowy, gloomy winter sky, no, he stayed away, he listened to his mother, she told him he was the most beautiful child, she loved him most of all, and it was true, he had only ever known that version of his mother, the woman who was accused of horrible things yet she was also his mother, he understood better about his father, his father was an officer, a cruel man, he was tyrannical with the child, he didn't have the mother's patience, his mother said to him, when you grow up, I want you to love beautiful things, works of art, everything that is beautiful, there were priceless paintings and sculptures in the house, when I was young, she told him, I had nothing, I didn't even have bread, I worked myself to death in a shoe factory, where the paintings came from he didn't know, or if they had belonged to others, he was growing up in a castle and outside screams rang out, the howls of war, though he no longer heard them, he waited for his parents to come home every night, his parents had friends and they all liked to get together, there was so much food in the cellar, they had years of supplies, and so many bottles of wine and champagne, they had parties and the little boy liked parties and he liked seeing his parents happy and carefree, but they said don't go where there are dark shadows on the trees, don't go there, stay close to the servants, what was there to be afraid of, his mother had had a fitness centre built in the house just for her, who were those emaciated men building her gym out of wood, they seemed so ragged and weak, while the little boy, the castle's young master, was always warmly dressed, the winters were so cold, sometimes he asked questions, why them, why me, but they didn't answer except to say, aren't you happy, we're doing all of this for you, for your future, what he wanted most was not to suffer in that future, it seemed so dark, so hopeless, although his parents seemed so convinced of the dazzling victory they talked so much about, but the little boy wasn't sure at all, he was tempted to go see what was happening over there on the side of the road where the trees wore ashy shadows, where the fog off the lake smelled like sulphur in winter and summer alike but they kept telling him not to go and play on the other side, everything would change in an instant, he would understand, he would see everything, he would be a man, he would watch the trials and see his parents convicted, their names splayed up across movie screens, I'm on the side of those who convicted them, the boy said, but please have mercy on my mother, she was always so good to me, she was just another link in a twisted chain, she was paid to be a link, have mercy on our errant fates, yet he would hear too the screams of those calling, no, forgive them nothing, it could happen again, the mass slaughter, a stone age of hatred, and the boy barely a man made himself look and see his heritage unspooling like a film, through the shreds of his newly awakened conscience, sharpened by the torture inflicted on others, when his parents were still alive, he wondered whether his father would be hanged, what would happen to his mother, during the trials, or were his parents dead, he had become their father, a father out of time, thinking about them hurt him, they were a wound, they were everywhere, he couldn't stop seeing those images, they were SS guards forced to bury the prisoners they had shot the day before, before the liberation, he saw them dragging the corpses, hundreds and thousands of bodies to the carts like sandbags on their backs, they stepped over the dead, they smelled the smell of their putrefying bodies and tossed them away with hatred, always the same hatred as when those women, those men, those children were alive, the same pent-up rage, a rage suddenly deflated, they tossed them toward the cart, there was a photograph of his father standing in front of a cart heaped with skeletons, skeletons and faces grinning stiffly, eyes wide open, the children's eyes, the children who had such beautiful hair tumbling over their cheeks, it was as if the children had tripped and fallen by accident, some of them were so young, they understood nothing of that misery, there was still a glimmer of hope in their eyes but it was only the reflection of the dreary sun glinting over the barracks, after the burial, they had to use a bulldozer to remove all those bodies, bones had broken through the skin, the son of the woman who had been good to him, who had raised him right, the son of the tyrannical father, he wondered what those men burying the dead might have felt during that humiliating labour, now they were being judged, they were humiliated and beaten, they had never even imagined the possibility of failure, they buried the people they had killed at Bergen-Belsen, the son could feet their humiliation though they perhaps had felt nothing in that systematic dehumanization, it was part of them now, part of their character, they had always denied the suffering they inflicted upon others, as if they had grown numb from the repetition, killing was so easy, all you had to do was pop your gun out of its holster, that was the solution to every problem, murder was merely ordinary, a necessary part of the day, the place was teeming with bodies and beyond the overflowing carts piled high with corpses lay green grassy hills, streams and ponds, a whole silent town, people praying in church on Sundays, schoolchildren walking to school every morning, and birds chirped from afar in the perpetually grey, sunless sky, what did his parents feel, the son wondered, and those SS guards, what they might have been most afraid of was the risk of typhus or tuberculosis, several women who were camp guards had already fallen, they were charged too but they would not stand trial, the guards were worried about typhus and tuberculosis, with good reason, the contagion bilging from the carts, those women never appeared in court, their faces would never be seen, although they were among the executioners, they died of the diseases they caught from those they had tortured, the war criminals' son knew all this and slowly he came to understand that he was not alone, a whole generation crawled out of the shadows, the architects of the final solution had had many sons and daughters, grandchildren too, broken by shame some of them asked to be sterilized to disown their parents' blood for good, others fled into exile, while others, like the son of those terrible war criminals, worked to redeem their innocence by fighting tirelessly against the Nazi pestilence long after the end of the war, because the son knew that strains of Nazism would be passed on, like typhus and tuberculosis, expressed differently but with the same virulence, he knew it would spread, sometimes covertly, cynically, on television screens and eventually even on the screen of his cell phone he saw again and again the arrival of the Allied soldiers offering gaunt prisoners so weak that they could barely stand a first meal, a bowl of soup, some broth they didn't even have the strength to swallow because their stomachs had shrunk to nothing from deprivation, even water, they couldn't eat a crust of bread or drink a sip of water, they knew they might die and some did, they died on the day they were freed from hell, the son of the war criminals saw that the contamination was lodged permanently in some of the Nazis' children, great criminals like his parents had been, and they boasted about their parents, they had some false sense of honour and even into old age they continued to bemoan the good Führer they had visited with their father at the Brown House in Munich to wish him a merry Christmas, women who were once little girls fondly remembered the dolls and boxes of chocolates they were given, the good Führer loved children so much, that friend of Daddy's friend they had visited each year, one of them had a father so brave that he swallowed his suicide capsule to avoid the dishonour of punishment, the woman had believed to her dying day that her father and his friends and accomplices in the death camps had been misjudged, they weren't guilty of the crimes they were accused of, someone had to create an organization to defend their reputations, her duty, she said, was to persecute those who had brought those men and women to justice, her father's friends, she dedicated her life to the cause, she said, helping her Nazi brethren in their persecution, she wanted to help them all, she was considered a true Aryan, that pink-skinned woman, a godmother to the extreme right, a mother, a grandmother beyond reproach, the saint of her own radical movement, she shared her fondest memories with anyone who would listen, the visits to the good Führer's house on Christmas day with Daddy, her dear daddy, she was a perfect little Nazi princess in those days, her father said so, with her blond hair done up in braids and her fiery blue eyes, how he had loved that little girl, she was so docile, so teachable, and she remembered trips out to Dachau with such delight, Daddy was always so loving with his little girl, their house was about twenty miles from the camp and sometimes her father would take her there, look, he would say, pointing to the barracks and the fields, that is land we have conquered, my child, look closely, she wrote in her school notebooks that she saw gardens, the pear tree on Daddy's land was starting to bloom, and she wrote that during those visits to the pear trees that bloomed even in winter Daddy used to call her Puppe, little doll, that memory was sweet, thought the son of the great war criminals, and the Nazi ideology had been preserved in the heart of a little girl who was still a child then, an innocent, as he had been while his parents were committing their crimes, what could he do against such unabashed monstrosity, what could he do, fight, always fight, fight the contagion, the evil, perhaps he would become a judge, one of those who kept dragging the guilty before the courts, extradite them from the refuge of exile, from Canada or the United States back to the country of their birth, their hands were stained with the blood of thousands and here those murderers would be forced to remember, ruthlessly, what a pathetic sight for the son, old men reduced to frailty appearing in a wheelchair before the judge, the son would have liked them to be forced to serve their prison sentence anyway, but there was an uneasy reluctance, those men no longer looked like the brutal guards they had been, without whips, rifles, or guns on their belts, and they didn't seem to remember anything, not the train whistles at dawn, not the moaning human cargo, the tragic freight, they only had some blurry memories, a few shouts, a few jarring sounds, children crying, they didn't know any more than that, their memory was a gaping hole, but as the judge rattled off their crimes they nodded their heads, yes, that's me, did I do that, when was that they seemed to say, some relative had seen to it that they were well dressed, a beige suit, yellow tie, wire-rimmed glasses, so that although they were feeble they had some dignity just like in the old days as they watched the trains pull in with their dogs dutifully waiting at their side, they felt nothing, the judge could describe their atrocities, this was what you did, the events related during this trial, don't you feel any regret, what do you feel, they replied that they were ninety-six years old and that it was too late, one of them, as if hoping to end all the questions, sighed, I'm sorry, I should have told my superiors what was going on, I should have, yes, but those unfortunate incidents were too frequent, they should have stopped the trains and the cargo, they should have, yes, I should have, but I had such a low rank, I did nothing, they stammered or looked at the judge guilelessly, as if to say, won't you show some mercy, those were the mistakes of youth, it was so long ago, it was hard to look at them, thought the son of two great war criminals, they reminded him of his own father, he might have looked like that in his clothes, crumpled in a wheelchair, losing his memory, but there had been a time when these old men could remember, they had applied for citizenship in another country, why, they worked at a stable job, they started families, they were questioned and they replied, yes, they had to hide, they were asylum seekers, they had taken on another name, they hid, they had assumed new identities, but what was the point of this persecution now, at the end of their lives, why shame them now, they said, they were good citizens, they had nothing to feel guilty about, they had always behaved well in the United States or Canada, their lawyers said, think of their new families, what would happen to those new families, what was the point of this shaming, from generation to generation, the son listened to the lawyers' plea for clemency, although he knew those men had never had a conscience, as for their memory, atrophied by age or disease, the son doubted that it was completely absent, he would have liked to see the old men go to sleep at night besieged by the monstrous acts they claimed to have forgotten, he would have liked them to be driven insane by the train whistles, he would have liked them all to be murdered as they got off those trains, one by one and fully aware, with the sun beating down on their anguished faces, the absence of memory was one of their crimes too, they could only be brought to consciousness if the same tortures were inflicted upon them, that would be justice, he thought, the old man in the wheelchair stammering apologies was the desperate image of his father, I didn't know, would I have known that, no, I didn't know anything, I was following orders, suddenly he felt that he could no longer judge, not this man or the others like him, the torture was that there was no way out of his sentence, there was almost no hope. Who are those two men coming toward me, Adrien wondered beneath the brim of his hat, in my repose by the water in the sun, he had just written those words on his tablet, in my repose by the water in the sun, the first thread of a poem, sometimes, he thought, he had to put aside his *Faust* and have the wisdom to pay tribute to life, the sun, the sea, all the pre-emptive beauty that pushed back the other hour on the invisible clock, the only hour other than birth that meant anything, everyone was curious about what time they were born but less about the other, all of it would be the subject of a serious poem, he was still working on a poem called "Taking Account," too, and speaking of account-keeping Charly had discreetly slipped him an enormous bill that he didn't quite know how he would manage to pay, his young chauffeur was asking too much, he thought, thinking of Charly reminded Adrien of his annual physical, she'd had to wait for hours with him at the doctor's, she had other, important clients, a rich European couple, Italian nobility, she said, she had no idea what she was talking about, all those fancy clients she was supposedly neglecting because of him, the line between a nightmare and reality was so thin, it was understandable that Adrien was confused, Dorothea had told him that morning, beware, my good friend, Mister Adrien, the girl is taking advantage of you, it might be time to start listening to Dorothea, Adrien thought, it was too bad that Charly hadn't wanted to celebrate his checkup with him, he was in excellent health, his arteries and his heart, everything was better than good, he was stooping a little, just a little, it was good to feel so strong, though as usual he did make a fuss about words, the sentences he wrote in his deck chair by the sea every day, and he missed Suzanne, his wife, the absence tore him apart, writing was an obsession but it was what kept him afloat, that and Suzanne, his angel, as far away as she might have been, in happy limbo or so deeply at peace in her nirvana, they kept him afloat above the swell in the storm against which he forever felt like he was struggling, even calmly, you have to walk straighter, Dorothea told him unceremoniously, she wasn't one for flattery, though she did tell him he was still a handsome man, and your head, Mister Adrien, hold your head up straight under your hat, that's how real men are, real men are like trees, yes, Dorothea said, trees like our palm trees, Mister Adrien, Adrien finished writing to some admiring students who had read all of his poetry, what a miracle, he thought, they haven't forgotten me, even though I've been retired for a long time, may they be blessed by the gods, from his computer he sent them a note thanking them, a line from the poem, repose by the water in the sun, the sojourn of our temporary joy, no, it was ephemeral rather than temporary, or temporal joy, he was writing, writing, exultant while Dorothea ironed his white trousers and put his underwear away in the drawers, he would have been fulfilled entirely by the sound of Suzanne's fingers striking the keyboard or typing on her typewriter on the other side of the paper screen like she used to do, yes, how it used to be when he still had his goddess with him, his love, his, and the pillows, I've got to change the pillows too, Dorothea said, it looks like you've been crying on them, me, crying, at my age, Adrien said, of course at your age, she said, and fresh sheets too, since I'm doing some housekeeping today, Dorothea would say as she took out her broom, Adrien was bound to Dorothea's world, shaking it off, he would say, I'm off to the sea now, my dear Dorothea, I'll be back in a few hours, don't stay out after dark, try to avoid having to have that young lady bring you home, I see some scheming in her, you know, Mister Adrien, you've known me my whole life, I'm never wrong, and now, the sun still bright in the too-hot sky, it must have been nearly a hundred degrees, Adrien finally had a break from Dorothea's advice, her surfeit of benevolence in caring for him and serving him, at last he was alone, and here now came these two figures toward him, one rather tall, it was the writer who was wreaking havoc on his nerves as a writer and critic, Daniel, the author of *Strange Years*, he had no end of books in him, and his Uncle Isaac, his silhouette against the sky hunched over his cane, all the same, here was a man coming toward him who was as tenaciously healthy as he was, it was hard to believe that old Isaac was almost a hundred, it gave Adrien a renewed sense of optimism, as if he and old Isaac were both on the side of the immortals, though he didn't especially want to see him right now, he was busy with his *Faust*, his poem "Taking Account," his musings on a life too fleeting, he thought of Suzanne, her good-humoured kindness, she had always stood up for Daniel, when he was young and starting out as an author, she loved him like one of the sons she was so close to, unlike him, Adrien never really thought about other people, Suzanne had never abandoned Caroline after Jean-Mathieu's death, she never stopped visiting Caroline at the centre, Caroline said it was a haven for artists of her skill and standing even though it was actually a rehabilitation centre for drug addicts, Adrien had never really known about it, she had brought her Black governess, a woman she called Harriett or Désirée, the governesses she'd had as a child in Louisiana were maybe only nurses helping her detox, Caroline told Suzanne that Charly had been mixing drugs in her migraine medication, was that true, Adrien wondered, though he suddenly had a nasty suspicion as he thought of Charly, she had seemed disappointed to learn that Adrien would likely live for many years still, he was made of steel, it was unusual for poets, Virgil must have been watching over him, or Charles and Frédéric, back in celestial form, Adrien found it hard to believe in all that, though the two of them had written so much about life after death in their house in Greece, they were probably wielding their power from beyond so that he would linger on for a long time in the deck chair by the sea where he came to write every day, their grumpy friend who was so scornful of their ideas about supraterrestrial life, about a supernatural empire, where according to Charles and Frédéric nothing ever perished, nothing could, life went on so that everyone had the right not so much to redemption as to evolution, what a gift that would be, eternal life where each person could continue to grow, they could keep developing their sensory faculties, it was clear that Charles had made all that up while he was in Greece, he was so in love with Frédéric that he had always been afraid of losing him, that was the intoxication of love and the vanity of feeling loved, how long did that last, we never knew, but it must be said, Adrien thought, that Charles had always had some perceptions of an occult world, at the centre in New England Caroline asked Suzanne where Charly was, she wasn't accusing her of the tortures she had suffered, Suzanne said, though it was torture, Suzanne replied when Adrien said it was all just slander, all the stories, if Caroline was taking drugs it was because she wanted to, wasn't she undergoing treatment there, wasn't that true, Caroline asked to go out for short walks, she held onto Suzanne's arm and went out to listen to the tits singing in the pines, my father and my grandfather were great sailors, she told Suzanne, that's why I can't live anywhere but near the ocean, like Jean-Mathieu, yes, like Jean-Mathieu, and what's become of him, my kind friend, where is he, hasn't he left Italy, isn't he coming back, and Suzanne comforted her, Adrien thought, my sweet wife, you know, dear Caroline, your photo exhibit is a huge success across Europe, your talent is finally getting the recognition it deserves, I've been able to show part of our history, Caroline said, so that we feel shame but also hope that the future will be different, we were writing books together, Jean-Mathieu and I, and he was the one who told me to go to the South, such good advice, all those portraits, it was him, it was Jean-Mathieu who guided me, he wrote by my side, first I made a photograph of my housekeeper Harriett, her features knotted and her veiny hands on her white apron, I think of everything she went through, Jean-Mathieu said, I told him that our servants were treated well, before working on your family's estate, where were they, did you think, Caroline, where were those servants, he asked me, and often I didn't know what to say, my friend Jean-Mathieu had a charitable side that seemed foreign to me, I only knew how to express myself humanely through my photographs, whites only, it said, I was the one who photographed that plaque so that we would remember, whites only, on the front of a restaurant, a Black man stopped to read the plaque, I photographed everything, Jean-Mathieu said to me, don't stop, take a picture of everything, chronicle every aspect of that deplorable era so we can all come out of it, though for a long time the shame will not leave us be, for a long time, yes, he said, they were photographs, unfiltered portraits, naked, exposing us all to repentant pain, Jean-Mathieu said, when will I get out of here, dear Harriett, my dear Suzanne, tell me, Suzanne, tell me the truth, and Suzanne spoke to Caroline honestly, my dear friend, someone you thought too highly of tried to poison your mind with drugs and here you are, but it won't be long now, you're going to get clean here, who could have done this to me, Caroline asked, denial was easier than accepting that she had fallen under Charly's spell, perhaps she was forgetting even as Suzanne spoke, for her own good, good thing I still have my Black governess with me, Caroline said, Harriett, Désirée, you know, my dear indispensable servants, we'll never leave each other, they're your nurses, Suzanne replied with the same integrity, and I'm your friend Suzanne, remember, Caroline, I was on the boat that day when we went to scatter Jean-Mathieu's ashes in the ocean, I was by your side, Suzanne said, and I still am, but only during visiting hours, most of all I wanted to come to congratulate you for the success you so richly deserve, at last the whole world is seeing the value and authenticity of your art as a photographer, Caroline heard Suzanne's words, Adrien thought, had he ever recognized Caroline's talent, he wasn't sure he had, any more than he had praised Suzanne for her poetry, he had never told Caroline how troubling he found her photographs of the South and her portraits of English poets on the verge of suicide, for a long time, unfortunately perhaps, there had been only one category, male writers, although Adrien had never known how to classify Charles, the critics said he was a metaphysical poet like Blake, he was in the category of those who were sanctified by the art of writing, Adrien didn't really see any women, not even Suzanne, his own wife, the one he should have seen before all others, and he regretted it now but it was too late, unless his still-sturdy health allowed him to make up for his neglect, and as for metaphysical Charles, where might he find a place in the sanctuary of thought where poets were the children of the flood, Adrien thought of himself as a wise man among fools, he alone was right, he alone wrote pragmatic, reasonable poetry and everyone else was wrong, even Charles, his imagination was too abstract, too cerebral, and delirious, mystical delirium was a dangerous thing, Adrien thought, and the two men were coming closer, mere steps away, Daniel and his uncle would be there soon, but Simon, his saviour, was there too, Simon asked Adrien if he wanted an iced drink, two, or even three, Adrien said, two friends are going to be joining me, he said, see, there they are, strolling along the water, daydreaming, but your driver, didn't you tell me that the young lady would be picking you up at five o'clock, no, it's okay, Adrien said, she'll probably be late, isn't she always, I'm going to ask for two more chairs, Simon said, but Monsieur Adrien should avoid the sun, he said, it can be nasty this time of year, you really can't judge people by their age anymore, Adrien said abruptly, as if Simon had been impertinent or as if he had to enforce some kind of deference from the waiter, Adrien immediately regretted having spoken to Simon like that, it was obnoxious, who was he to be insulting others, that tone of voice, all those people he hardly knew, he had nurtured his egotism for years, and especially Simon, he really loved him, Faust would have acted that way with his feigned superiority, wanting to command God or the devil, here come the cocktails, everything will be fine, Adrien thought, everything will be fine, Mick was the first to come into Le Fantasque, he sprang across the bar toward the brand-new dance floor, dancing stubbornly alone in the crimson glow of the enormous screen where Prince's face was frozen in bursts of purple and gold flowers, his colours, when his music was unleashed, thought Mick, the two princes fell asleep, the two princes forgot it was time to wake up, he repeated to himself, it looks as if a white man came to anaesthetize them on a bed of white flowers, yes, thought Mick, they offered them a potion to calm them and it was so soothing they no longer even felt the need to wake, and as they sank down through the water to the gleaming ocean floor they imagined they were adrift on a raft of white lilies, they imagined, yes, a group of boys were jostling Mick on the dance floor, they were friends from Trinity College, they said, was Mick here tonight for the opening of Le Fantasque, Robbie's bar, do you remember us, Mick, some jerk at school tied you to a fence once, a raging homophobe, the class moron, and we set you free, we saw you on TV during the big anti-hate march you organized, you see, we haven't forgotten you, we know about your sister too, they fell silent, your sister Tammy, we know, they murmured, and Mick wondered whether Tammy's death was written in big red letters on his black shirt, he could feel the letters burning into his back, she hadn't eaten for several days and one morning at the clinic she didn't wake up, my parents begged me to come back for a few days, I'm all they've got now, but hadn't they disowned you, bad parents, didn't they kick you out on the street, but Mick couldn't talk about his parents' betrayal without crying, he started dancing again, trying to imitate his idol's moonwalk, he had always worshipped him, though he didn't dress like him anymore, the flashy white glove and scarlet lips, it was all over, he had ripped off all his colours when Tammy died, he had retired all his best outfits and his hair was short now with a long blue forelock, we hardly recognized you, said one of the boys, you look like us, you're not so different now, they all started dancing around him, their affectionate hands touching his waist, Mick, Mick, you're right, it's time to dance, the grand opening is in an hour and you'll be with us, the couple of pink flamingos had joined them, where's Robbie, when is he getting here, they asked, we're on our third pink cocktail, Geisha and Yinn are on the second floor, they said, busy finishing with the balloons, there were stars everywhere along the ceiling by the stage, careful, Porsha, don't drink too much, said Porsha's wife Portia, the party's just getting started, I'm listening, darling, said Porsha, heading for the bar, it was already open, the bar at the back, not the one at the front, facing the street, that one was still closed, you'll get sleepy and miss the party, my beautiful pink flamingo, said Portia, when you fall asleep like that, I can't get you to wake up, said Portia, I won't take advantage of your patience, my darling, said Porsha, leaning against the bar to order another pink drink, we'll be getting back to the farm a bit late this evening, I hope our little piglets don't get too angry with us, I made sure to give them water this morning, our piglets are the cutest, running around freely in the fields, what an adventure it is to live surrounded by animals, isn't it, darling, said Porsha, a little drunk, we take in all the animals the farmers don't want any more, wherever we go, my wife and I, we save them, that's our mission, isn't it darling, especially not a fourth pink cocktail, said Portia, and as Mick listened to them, even though he was deep into Prince's music, with the doves and the rainbows and the electric purple splendour, the whole room swirled with him on the dance floor, Mick thought it was Tammy, it was his sister who was wrapping him in up in these warm feelings, that presence, he was dancing, dancing, he remembered skating with her a long time ago on the dance floor, she used to roller-skate on the boardwalk by the sea with her friend Mai, Tammy, Tammy, he thought, my little bubble of air who got away, and Mick remembered a dream he had dreamed, it was night and a man came out into the street shouting, look up at the sky, the nuclear torch is lit and we're going to plant it in every field, in every country in Asia, this has to be the night of the first experiment, when he woke up in his childhood bedroom, his parents' house, both his parents were writers, they had both been so indifferent for so long to his fate and to Tammy's, he saw his mother walking alone in the garden, he knew how harsh she could be and he hadn't dared leave his room and join her, but as he watched her from the window in the garden in a white nightgown, he thought, maybe in spite of everything she does remember Tammy, how she suffered for such a long time because of her, because of their mother, if his mother's face had been turned toward him in the moonlight gleaming on the roses in the garden he might have forgiven her everything she had done, how she had forgotten, and how unhappy she was to have brought children she had never loved into the world, but his mother stood motionless as if struck down by her own doggedness, and Mick, frozen too, hadn't joined his mother, and on the pier by the marina, drink in hand, the captain was still shouting to his friends that he would be leaving soon on his sailboat, he and his dog, for a long crossing, to Australia maybe, the universe is our splendour, he was singing, Daniel listened, his head lifted up to the sky, thinking about the next step in his book, the manuscript was feeling oppressive, while Uncle Isaac and Adrien drank their cocktails and chatted, their cheeks going pink beneath the brims of their hats, this step in *Strange Years*, as Herta Oberheuser thought about the past, no, she hadn't stood up against that hidden, insidious genocide, should she have done something, even the Catholic bishops of Vienna had said no, don't do that, no, not genocide against the sick and disabled, thousands of them, and people with mental illness, at the beginning it was just a morphine injection, they would float away, just a flash of light, they said, they declared that the disabled were unworthy of life, it was too costly for the state economy, defectives had to be eliminated for sake of racial purity, I remember, yes, they talked like that, I wanted to stand against them alongside the Catholic bishops in Vienna, some of my cousins, some of my family were among them, we were all German, men, women, and children, or Austrian, and the genocide touched us too, I had a cousin with schizophrenia, the project was dubbed the great psychiatric project, they would be put down by gas or injection, a massive euthanasia project, I knew all that, I worked with those doctors, the groups of psychologists and psychiatrists, I went to the meetings to study the great project, I was privy to all the classified details of Nazi medicine, I knew, I can't pretend I didn't know what it was about, I knew that, as for my cousin, when they went to what was called the showers they didn't come back, I kept thinking about my schizophrenic cousin, a brilliant young girl but so far removed from reality, she had a gift for language, her psychological disorder might have prevented her from knowing what was happening, there, in the showers, the deadly gas rushing in through her eyes wide open, she didn't understand anything, she was always somewhere else in some imaginary abyss where everything that was real to us, landscapes and voices, was contorted in a mass of terrifying hallucination or demented, unbridled joy, we thought she would be safe in the special hospital in Vienna, her parents paid for the private institution, she was about to come home, to go back to school, yet I knew, should I not have stood up against the doctors' great project, the doctors and pharmacists all working together to study what amounted to genocide, preparing first the invalids, the children and newborns who had no future, they would choose either a morphine injection or starvation, no water or food, and ultimately death, I wanted to shout, how could we do this, they were Germans, Austrians, but all they would have replied is that these people were of no more use than those in the resistance, it was going to happen, for all of them, all the youth in the resistance would be gunned down, I didn't even see them as resisting anything, they were just weak, just a scattered group of whiners, but the brothers, the sisters, Germans and Austrians, they would disappear too, by the thousands, filthy genocide, sometimes they were locked in trucks and canisters of toxic gas were lobbed into the closed, suffocating space, and I said to myself we will pay for this, we will pay, or else they were surrounded by soldiers and shot in small groups, I said, as I thought of my cousin, never, no, we will never come back from the shame, never, but my cousin was so confused inside her illness and possibly she hadn't known or understood what was happening to her, during those meetings with the psychiatric medicine consultants, I could have said no, like the bishop of Vienna had in a sermon, don't do it, my name is Dr. Herta Oberheuser and I am strongly opposed, we can't treat our own people like that, they are our family, our cousins, we are citizens of the same country, but I don't think I said anything, I listened and I was afraid, among all those men, those experts, I was just a woman, barely out of university, I was too young to stand up to those men, that only came later, in the course of my research, and the camps, I felt like it was a violation of medical principles, a complete violation, yes, it was unethical, all of it was illegal, all of it, but the party had lied and discreetly gathered all those doctors and pharmacists to work together for an experiment, a cleansing, and they had all responded so enthusiastically, my cousin Monica was anxious but brilliant, she didn't deserve it, no, she didn't deserve to be sent to those factories where all those minds were crushed, those brains, then they pried them out of the skull and picked them apart in their laboratories, she was just anxious, she had a tendency to be depressed, she had no way to defend herself there in the showers, the disinfection room, I've often thought about her, Monica, my cousin, they put her in with everyone with epilepsy and autism, would it be the showers or starvation, when the plan was developed in Berlin the doctors approved it, those people were costing the state a lot of money, and this other final solution, sleep or slow starvation, they would start by depriving them of vegetables, then water, you had to remember that those defectives were of no use at all, they took up food every day in the institutions, wouldn't it be better to give that food to the soldiers on the battlefield, those weaklings with deformed brains slept in comfortable beds, every day they were washed and fed, wasn't it better to give those beds to the soldiers, that was how they thought, we had to put the nation first, said the head physicians in those future factories, pointing out that they were only doing the nation a favour, this was merely an efficiency measure for human resources, an improvement, the elimination of the subsistence of pointlessness, they were a burden for the country, and at the same time it would support the renewal of the sought-after race, the Berlin plan terrified me at first because I was thinking of my cousin Monica, I wondered, would those SS doctors inject bacteria into her brain, they were always talking about conducting research for the future of humanity, she was so scared they had to chain her up during the experiment, they were brought in a Red Cross bus to the doctors and white lab coats waiting at the research hospital doors, Monica heard bells ringing in the distance, she saw ravens lifting out of the winter-bare trees, the doctors seemed so kind, welcoming them with open arms as they stared at the girls, Monica was a green-eyed beauty, she was selected, where was she going, she asked, to the camps in Poland, it was so hard to get rid of the dead there, there wasn't enough soil left, enough rocks to cover them, and there were chemists there too, pharmaceutical specialists in their white lab coats, she saw it all, Monica, the bells tolled ponderously in the fall air, where was she, Monica, she asked where she was going, no, it wasn't sterilization this time, she was worried about bleeding and infection, she said, she wanted to have children one day, the doctors were eminent specialists, men at the top of their fields, you had to listen to them, Monica had pretty teeth, she was afraid they would be plucked out, where were they taking her, and there, as I thought of Monica, I should have said something, like the bishop of Vienna, I still remember his sermon, please, don't do it, it will be unforgivable, they are your German and Austrian brothers, your blood, but little by little I came to believe that using human subjects for scientific research might be normal, as long as they were useless or condemned, and as long as they were neither German nor Austrian, and that those few days of research would give them a few more days to live, a few months sometimes, they would be spared the worst of the camps, as I listened to the doctors, impressive as they were, no, I couldn't quite approve, I came to believe that I could work like this for the good of humanity while increasing our party's prestige, so I said at my trial, in my defence, yes, for the good of humanity, I had delayed murders, for that I had no regret, I thought I was doing a good thing, and I also said that the words and slogans indoctrinated us bit by bit, the Berlin plan was an elimination protocol and a merciful program, we had such compassion for the wretched, we were drawn in by the words pity, mercy, clemency, and it was true that all those people in the hospices and asylums were miserable, not Monica, my cousin was from a higher class, she was being treated by a psychiatrist, a friend of her parents', but her fate was the same, all the psychiatrists entrusted their patients to the protocol, even today I can scarcely understand the extent of that professional betrayal, I would never have acted that way even if I had been able to condemn my colleagues, no, I couldn't have acted that way, we had a duty of care for our patients, and that was what I did after the war, after I was released from prison for good behaviour, I was a good family doctor, I provided impeccable care, yes, no one had a bad word to say about me, no one knew who I was, I was forgotten far in the vastness of Germany until one of my victims from the laboratory spotted me, she showed all her scars, the damage to her feet and legs, why didn't I explain to her that the surgeries had saved her life and that my experiments had helped prolong soldiers' lives, yes, I was working as part of an elimination protocol but it was so slow that there would be many survivors, I told them that I was not a torturer, no, often the doctors' injections were merciful, that was what we called them, in fact, merciful lethal injections, it was an act of compassion, the people I operated on might live a few months more, sometimes a few years, that was clemency, avoiding death, or else the mercy of a quick death, while outside on the snowy fields soldiers shot people down constantly, all you could hear was the echo of gunshots night and day, I was so tired of hearing that noise while I worked in the surgery, I was tired of everything, I couldn't sleep, I never left my patients' side, I was surrounded by the constant smell of blood, but now the cold is seeping into my veins, my bed is a cold tomb, and I can say that sometimes I was wrong, sometimes, I was tired, I may have made a few mistakes, since that was the protocol, the aptly named elimination protocol, my fingers and my hands grew numb, as they are now, yet I cannot bear to violate a patient's trust, it's unacceptable, a breach of trust like that, no, it can't be, no, this bed is so cold only my head now is free from the icy grip, please, don't drop the temperature any lower, that's what I told my employees, don't turn it down, they won't be able to breathe anymore, and now I'm barely breathing in this dreary shroud of ice from which no one will release me, I'm trying to explain my defence from beneath this leaden cold, I can still see the judges and the accusers at the trial and I know that a woman like me was nothing to them, me and the others, we were nothing, we didn't even deserve a merciful glance, never, even if we had acted inhumanly, was that a reason to treat us worse still, without the gaze of compassion no one can survive, I know that, what those judges didn't know was that one by one, we, the brides of desolation, we were their martyrs, the playthings of contempt and hate, the vise grows tighter over my temples, the icy grip, I don't have much time left and who's listening to me now, it's so cold, were those her last thoughts, Daniel wondered, Herta, as next to him Adrien raised and lowered his hat over his damp forehead, complaining about the heat, of course I will come to Mai's birthday, dear Daniel, though does that child need an old man to be there, wouldn't it be better for me to keep working on my writing in my deck chair, he said, laughing, and Daniel thought what a burden it seemed suddenly, the lightheartedness of these two elitist old men, Adrien and Uncle Isaac, the sky was so blue, Mai's flight wouldn't be delayed as was often the case on stormy days, Daniel thought, from above the clouds were thick as the plane circled the archipelago, Mai couldn't see the tiny island yet, a green dot in the ocean, she thought, it would be so nice to see her parents and her hometown again for a few weeks over the summer holidays, Mai was listening to Stars of Chaos, hallelujah, hallelujah, the lead singer, his name was Forever, his voice sounded so dark, almost restrained during that last concert before they found his lifeless body in his Los Angeles mansion close to where his wife and four children lived, they said his life was a fairy tale, Mai couldn't imagine, it seemed unacceptable, before he was found dead, he had hanged himself, no, those words had to be erased, surely it had been an accident, Forever was supposed to sing until the end of time, he was a god for Mai and so many other girls her age, he sang about hope and about the despair of youth, what happened, it was unacceptable, it was a mistake, no, it couldn't be true, Mai thought, she looked for Forever's face at eighteen, twenty, his blond hair plastered to his bony skull, he was so thin then, so handsome, Mai thought, singing *I can't love myself*, he had gotten a prize for artist of the year, and now this, what was happening, his face appeared on her tablet, tormented, singing about how he couldn't love himself, the same aching words so many teenagers shared, Mai thought, the years went by and with them the spiral of despair for Forever who sang in that video, *I can't break away from those addictions, I can't do it, the snake around my neck*, it did seem like he had a snake wrapped around him, some animal devouring him from inside, but everyone thought the detox would do him good, he would finally be able to put an end to the darkness gnawing at him, they said he's so successful, he's on top of the world, and in the meantime he was talking about the end, singing his own end, it was like he was thinking only of that, you'll find me some July morning, hallelujah, and his rough rock and roll voice became less delicate, less subtle, all you could hear was a scream, as if his voice was a broken instrument, crumbling, falling apart as he sang at the top of his lungs as if he were afraid we would stop hearing him, his face was changing and his body, he was less supple, his beautiful face became loose and awkward, *Give me a little more light*, he sang, over a year, I'm on the right track, he wrote, I'm not drinking anymore, I'm not doing drugs, but why is this such a struggle for me, every day feels like defeat, I can't forget every failure, perhaps life itself is just an uncomfortable condition, other musicians will do the same, you'll see, for so many people living is a struggle, it's not fair, I had a taste for opium too early, cocaine, amphetamines, and the snake faded inside the rings of smoke, I'll call it the snake of conscience, hallelujah, hallelujah, there's some tension in my blood, I can't break free, hallelujah, hallelujah, collapse on top of the world, collapse, you're just a cage of bones empty of flesh, hallelujah, you will hear a shock wave, wave, hallelujah, hallelujah, and Mai thought there must be some mistake, Forever had fallen, her idol, it couldn't be true, his kids would send up a message to the sky, they would fly a kite and say Daddy, you're free now, fly, we love you Daddy, from Texas to Los Angeles, your friends are thinking about you, fly toward the sweetness and warmth, dear Daddy, it was a broken voice, the voice of despair Mai heard in her headphones as the plane flew in over the archipelago, repeating to herself, no, it can't be true, I can still hear his voice, he's still alive, he can't stop singing for all of us, he can't, Mai thought, and suddenly she thought of Mère, her grandmother's death has been such a loss for her, she couldn't go kiss her anymore in her little house, she couldn't listen to music, hear her familiar words, you're getting home so late, little Mai, where were you, Mai felt like she had to lie so that Mère wouldn't have to worry, Esther, her name was Esther, it cut her heart, she thought, and now Forever, he would never sing again, Forever. As Daniel touched his sandalled feet to the water, he thought, Herta Oberheuser had predicted that it would be common practice in our time to carry out medical research on human subjects, she had sounded the alarm, she predicted that the same euphemisms would still be used to avoid the word torture, there would be talk of strategies, of procedures to heal vulnerable populations, the word healing meant a slow eradication, a degradation, the humiliation of the mentally ill, and so the doctor of all agonies would be reborn in another doctor of agony, this time in a mental health clinic in Ontario, in Canada, he experimented on psychopaths, and his experiments were a success, he would say, to further his own career, there was no doubt about it, he opened his own concentration camps in his clinics, other doctors helped him, they remembered his Capsule program, psychopaths were widely held to be insensitive to pain, it would be a boon to science to lock them up in small groups in enclosed spaces, in irons, hands and feet, and drown them in blinding fluorescent light day and night, they were to be placed naked in groups of seven in small rooms and a tray of food would be slid in through a slit in the door to see how these mental defectives would react to the torture of light and the lack of living space, the idea was to learn, to understand, the doctor also said, like the doctor who preceded him in other torture camps, there was also the strategy of solitary confinement, forced incarceration, segregation, he led all those trials with corrective authority and always he told himself that his human subjects never suffered enough, his authority had to become ever greater, more imposing, yes, solitary confinement was appropriate for that human trash, the doctor of agonies said, it was even ideal, according to his experiments, and like all the torturers who worked for him, his doctors and psychiatrists, he went home at night for supper, he kissed his children and his wife, washed his hands before the meal, with his utter and assured disgust for his patients, all those the maniacal torment of his hands had sullied during the day, their humiliation was an epiphany for him, for his vanity and pleasure, that was how he dominated those frail, wavering minds, perhaps that was how it was when the doctor of these new concentration camps went home at night, the camps of today and tomorrow, and the diabolical experiments went on and on, in step with the same scientists who had invented Agent Orange, that perfect killer, a herbicide and defoliant invented for warfare, used for ten years in Vietnam, 2,4,5-T and 2,4-D, the impact devastated the fields, the land, the forests of Vietnam, in Laos and Cambodia, not to mention the soldiers, winners and losers both, they developed cancers, leukemia, deformities, and their children too, but Agent Orange and the torturers who invented it had been forgotten, every day the chemical defoliant killed lake fish, it stripped bare the trees of Vietnam, it kept children from being born, almost four million people had been exposed to the chemical in Vietnam and another million suffered from chronic illness, animal species were reduced or eradicated in the forests and the ravaged fields, where were the torturers who had created Agent Orange, would there be a trial for them too, Daniel thought, Mai would be home soon, he said to himself, thinking of the planes soaring high in the sky above the clouds, she didn't know they were planning a party for her, Uncle Isaac had said, when you come out of the party room in the hotel, through the garden, you can head down to Caribbean Beach, that's what I called it, and Mai and her friends can dance all night, he always talked as if he were the sole owner, Daniel thought, my gardens, my beaches, though he probably couldn't do otherwise, since the first, humble hotel had been built as a residency for writers, Uncle Isaac hasn't stopped expanding, bigger and taller, his Grand Hotels had proliferated, they had prospered everywhere he had drawn and designed them, the enormously wealthy Uncle Isaac had planted his Grand Hotels in every legendary, beautiful spot he could, he said the Hawaii Grand was the most comfortable, although Daniel wasn't sure whether to believe him, Uncle Isaac lived inside his dreams of designing and building, even while he grew more isolated on the Island No One Owns with his animals, at least he used to have poets and artists with him, now all he wanted was his own solitude with the great eagles that soared over his tower, those eagles in the image of God flying just a bit too close, they weren't quite ready to grab him in their talons, as if he were just a sack of hair, a ready meal, Isaac said, yes, when they fly too close, I rush back into my room, didn't Uncle Isaac dream of taming those great eagles and eaglets gliding over the ocean, he was passionate about condor conservation, that majestic bird under constant threat from hunters, why are men such assassins, Uncle Isaac asked Daniel out of nowhere, his question landing flat in the hot afternoon silence while Adrien sipped his cocktail in a noisy clatter of ice cubes, and at Le Fantasque, in the bar, a couple of girls danced over to Petites Cendres, they had tattoos all over, words written on their bodies about love, *love is love* on a right arm, Léonie and Alexandra, in tank tops, tight jeans over their narrow hips, Petites Cendres also saw on Léonie's right arm, *who can live without love and sex*, we're here to celebrate our first wedding anniversary, said Alexandra, we renovated two cottages at the Acacia Gardens, we're going to take in two more families from Africa, Dr. Lorraine sent them, we're also taking care of the little ones, they're not infected, Dr. Lorraine said, it's just preventative, but the parents are very poor and very sick, and they could catch it, we're family now, said Alexandra, and no one will separate us at the Acacia Gardens, Petites Cendres hugged them and thought, Yinn doesn't say a word to anyone yet what a miracle worker, Yinn is miraculous, and I'm so hard on him, the Acacia Gardens are expanding far beyond the island, all the way to Africa, it's him, it's always him, Yinn, even though he never talks about it, oh, I thought I couldn't love him more, the kindness of his heart is our radiant gift, too bad he shares that boundless love with all of humanity and not just with me, or with his husband Jason, what can I do, it's always the same thing, I basically have to do what he does, love elsewhere and everywhere, droplets of gold spreading, just a little at a time, but they are precious drops of gold, thought Petites Cendres, the girls were dancing with Mick on the dance floor, Prince's face on the big screen undulating as if he were below the surface and on the second screen a silent film was playing, juxtaposed with heads, faces, and bodies moving as if they were underwater too, and black and white waves, voiceless, like the notes of a piano, it's all well and good, said Geisha, but you're a little early, girls, you too, Mick, we wanted to be here before it opened, said Mick, still dancing, his blue bangs flopping over his forehead, if we can do anything, said Mick, but Geisha was still thinking about the message they'd gotten that morning, it made the evening ahead seem strange, even though they got messages like that all the time, slurs against drag queens' freedom of expression, although a lot of people also wrote in admiration and friendship, life would be boring without you, they wrote, you're sexy and you're spiky, girls, we love you, thought Geisha, watching the dancers, may God keep them always so happy and trusting, they're so young, thought Geisha, and Robbie, Santa Fe, and I will get old, our legs won't be as spry and our minds won't be as open, that's for sure, with time everyone slows down, I've seen it happen, rancour pushes through like a rotten flower, we get jealous of others taking our place, I don't know that it can be any other way, thought Geisha, but in the meantime, dance, called Geisha to the hodgepodge group of dancers on the floor, in the meantime have fun, said Geisha, all dressed up in feathers, balloon in hand, it'll be a fantastic night for our Robbie, I promise, said Geisha, on Pelican Beach, Lucia, in her blue overalls, was tousling Brilliant's hair with her fingers, he was lying on the sand next to her, you've got to learn to comb your hair, you're a nurse now, you're looking more and more like Misha, Brilliant rolled in the sand next to Lucia, he laughed and called Misha over to them, he'll come back all wet and shake all over us, said Brilliant, the accident victims I roll onto a stretcher in my ambulance don't notice who I am, said Brilliant, we're rushing to the hospital, they don't even notice, nursing is a beautiful profession, said Brilliant, I often wake up in the night, Brilliant, said Lucia, worried, wondering if that young man I know, if you, but Lucia didn't finish her sentence, she started again, hesitating, yes, I wonder about the terrible day when someone asks me if I'm your mother or your older sister, you're all of that and more, said Brilliant, shushing her, his hand over her mouth, two people so different meeting like this is a real miracle, said Brilliant, he thought he heard his phone and got up, the wind messing up his hair, yes, I'm available, said Brilliant into his cell, where's the accident, I'll be there right away, on his day off Brilliant sadly left Lucia and Misha there, on Pelican Beach, he couldn't help but see Angel's little ghost running in the waves with Misha, he could almost hear Reverend Stone's voice proclaiming that Angel's true father had welcomed him into his celestial kingdom, I guess the reverend can only lie every time anyone is in mourning, Victoire had said, when Lena, Angel's mother, cried, a heartrending cry, don't take him away, don't take him away from me, through the flight of pelicans and white egrets on the platform by the sea, Eureka's ringing soprano led the Black Ancestral Choir, singing songs for Angel, oh, may he sleep at last at Jesus's feet, the cherub, may he find solace at last, sang Eureka, but Brilliant knew how much Angel loved Eureka's cuddles when she came to see him at home, she used to bathe him and rock him, wrapped in a blue towel on the balcony above the flowering jasmine, thought Brilliant, the smell of the orange and lemon trees, Angel would rather have spent longer being loved and cuddled by Eureka rather than heading off to join some unknown father people had told him was a loving god of children, he had never believed, even when Eureka seemed so convinced, she used to say, I preferred Jesus to God, he was more humble, he was a precocious twelve-year-old boy too, like you, my Angel, putting pretentious scholars in their place, telling them, you're false prophets, what are you doing in the temple, I alone am the truth and the life, that was how he talked to them, Jesus, and he wasn't wrong, said Eureka, luscious Eureka, Eureka the divine, and she said to him too, I'm not sure if you'll be with us then, my Angel, but one day the woman they call Donna Africa will fix it all up for us, every injustice, you'll see, and people will listen to her and worship her, and the world will come around to the first Black woman president, that's why I'm asking you to stay with us for a few more years, even if you don't feel well, your mama Lena would be so happy too, she talked to him like that before every spoonful of medicine Angel had to take each day, thought Brilliant, even if at the end Eureka and Lena spared him the drugs, Dr. Dieudonné said it was no use anymore, and Lena and Eureka listened to him, simply moistening Angel's lips with a bit of cool water, nothing more, and holding him tighter, thought Brilliant, that was what Angel wanted so badly, he wanted to come home, home to the Acacia Gardens, where he had been held and loved so well, he wanted Misha to come back to him like he used to, on his pillow, when the window was open to the blue sky, the intoxicating smells he wanted to smell again, the orange and the lemon trees, the jasmine flowers in summertime, it was almost time for his mother Lena to come home from work, in the blue bus with the words *Coral Coast: Protect Our Reefs* written on the side, there you are at last, Mama, he would say to his mother, opening the window wider. Stephen wrote to Daniel on his phone, not quite sure whether he would send the message, he wasn't sure of himself anymore, writing for him was suffocating, a mortification, it was terrifying, he liked living far more than he liked writing, my dear Daniel, Stephen wrote beneath the acacia arbour in Charles and Frédéric's house, the house they had bequeathed to young writers, in the luminous garden where Charles himself had written his books, reading snippets to Frédéric, dear friend, I look forward to your visit every Saturday, like before, your literary advice has been such a help as I write this biography of Charles and his poetry, I know how busy you are with all your children, and I know it will be your daughter Mai's birthday soon, thank you for your invitation to celebrate her eighteenth birthday at the Grand Hotel in town, I'm tethered to the book at the moment and I'm not sure yet if I'll be able to come, in spite of myself I've grown attached to the work, I'm not going out very much, it's not like me, I used to go out at night to all the clubs and the bars, I'm still doing a bit of coke, that's it, writing this book has been carrying me like a wave but I'm not sure yet where I'm headed, toward what confines, this wave, I think I can still hear Frédéric saying to Charles in the garden, careful, your writing is so beautiful I'm going to cry, hearing Charles telling Frédéric to stop smoking in his garden, and especially in his bedroom, chain-smoking, are you trying to burn the house down, and you should stop bringing Grégoire over, letting the old man dream about some sudden windfall, yes, you're taking him to the dog races, it's immoral, watching those greyhounds running in the summer heat, what are you thinking, Frédéric, and Frédéric replied by smoking one cigarette after another, compulsively, I'm thinking of making him rich, him and his family, that's what I'm thinking, Charles, this book you're writing is the most lyrical, the most beautiful, it's almost too cryptic, as if you're writing in code, what you're saying touches me, you're right, death doesn't exist, we are all alive but have known death and come back from it, not as ghosts but as real people enriched by our past experiences and even our mistakes, the dead are as alive as we are, perhaps the lesson of hope is too transcendental for your readers, I mean, dear Charles, my love, they might not understand, this time again, and so they spoke into the afternoon beneath the acacia arbour, jumping into the pool when the heat got to be too much, Charles wrote it all down in his journal, which I'm working with, and when the sun went down they played a Bach sonata together, I'm thinking of them, they were so united, dear Daniel, and I wonder, who did I spend my life with, just boors, and with Eli, that neurotic outcast who hung out at the prison selling drugs to the minors on the island, he wrote to me that my book, *Demons*, which was about him, it was at once so dark and gleaming, he found it amusing, he doesn't care about me, seeing you for an hour on Saturdays, dear Daniel, it inspires me to write, it gives me courage, just as you write your own books, that perseverance, even if your family and your friends do take up much of your time, and the environmental work you're doing to try to save the coral reef, I'm not as generous as you are, all I do is write and it's nothing but trouble, I'm such an ingrate, Charles was fifteen when he published his first book, the critics praised the eloquence of his poems, meanwhile I'm thirty and I've only written one book, the book I wrote to try to break free of Eli, I'm scared and silent here with Charles's biographical notes, the strength of his work, you travel a lot to lectures and conferences too while I stay chained to Charles's desk, or sometimes outside, here under the acacia arbour, frightened by the words I try to write, as if I knew how to write, I am and I will perhaps always be among the untold masses of mediocre writers, yet all I need is to hear your good advice and I come back to life, I'm ready to go on, you're a good influence on me and I love hearing you laugh, I do sometimes feel alone here, in this house, so full and sure of a couple's happiness, Charles was famous when his first books came out or at least he had been noticed as a literary prodigy, but I'm dragging my feet, I've never done anything much until now, if that's not reason enough to be discouraged, anyway, I can't compare myself to the man I'm describing as a poet, the poet of his generation, as I write about a life that the world shone on from day one, the privilege of birth, beauty, intelligence, and an aristocracy of thought already when he was young, I feel like as I write all that I'm fading, little by little, I feel like Charles is still in his house, he's watching me with that subtle irony of his, I think I can see his teeth gleaming, his kind smile, the fine hair on his wrinkled forehead, that wrinkle he always had, a mark of his insatiable intelligence, and his eyes lighting up, radiant, my dear little Stephen, they seem to say, dear little Stephen, just a little more courage, let's go, and especially try to snort a little bit less of that nasty cocaine, it's destroying your brain cells, you're deliberately killing them, believe me, I used to tell Frédéric the same thing, stop all that, those bad habits, what are they doing for you, life is so short, yes, you might well get a second or third shot but this life is guiding you toward all other lives so try not to have too much baggage, come on, relax and write, so I'm listening, I'm taking his advice even if it means starting the same sentence over and over again or wiping everything off my computer, that's how you write, probably, fighting for each word, and I'm thinking about that accident, the tragedy that caused such a rift in Charles and Frédéric's perfect relationship, when that actor appeared, Cyril, with his youthful ardour for Charles, Charles was monastic, that passion drawn out over them must have seemed unusually strong, discomfiting for a couple as secure as a safe is against a thief, the thief, fearless in the face of danger, running barefoot over the embers of an unbridled passion, it was Cyril, wasn't it, it must have been devastating, a comfortable twosome cannot accommodate a third, it's a perturbation in the planetary order, isn't it, and Brilliant drove the ambulance through town without turning on his siren, it was too bad there were accidents and disasters on a beautiful summer afternoon, he would've liked to sleep on the beach with Lucia and Misha, stretched out against them without a care in the world, nothing was as delicious as laziness for a lazy man, as love for a lover, was it the heat, the town slumbered in the long, muggy afternoon, the silence broken only by the raucous calls of birds, the parrots and parakeets perched on their keeper's shoulders, it was not yet time for him to head out to the pier with his birds, one of the colourful parrots burrowed its grey beak into its chest feathers without a sound, the bird seemed to be sleeping, the immobile city, that nervous, sleepy silence, there was nothing Brilliant liked less, he loved movement, singing and dancing in the street, everything seemed too quiet in the oppressively slumbering city, his heart tightened as he thought of his own flighty life, the oral epic he hadn't finished, though he still recited rough bits of it to his friends in the taverns, Lucia always came with him now too, hey there, Cajun man, tell us the story of your life, your fits and starts, the first time you ran away as a child when you hopped a train, the whole city was looking for you, especially your mother, the mayor, your nanny, your mother ordered her to beat you, to whip your backside raw, she was too much of a coward to punish you herself, tell us how it was, the first great devastation, the second devastation, when the helicopter came to save you from the water, you and Misha, when your brother, your half-brother, your Black nanny's son, you loved him so much, and he went out into the current alone, he didn't know how to swim, and you've always thought, it's my fault, I couldn't bring him back, what an image, all those pictures of your life, crushed and smashed into a thousand pieces, don't think about it anymore, it's too late, Misha had to stay at the vet's for so many months, yes, but you got him back, he'd already forgotten all his troubles, and the other ones who drowned with the nanny's son, my Black brother, I couldn't do anything about it, they dragged the ladder up into the helicopter, I had Misha on my shoulders, everyone else below like yellow creases in the stream, that's the rough story of the two devastations, once I was back on the island, I thought, in the end, your worldly parents have disowned you, they think you're a deviant, I'll finally have some peace here working quietly in the Café Español, when the third devastation came, another storm over my head, though I was already cracked in the head from all my adventures, I know, but Lucia forgives me, she says I am Brilliant, her Brilliant, and here we are happy together with Misha at the Acacia Gardens, Lucia says we should adopt Kitty, she's lonely without Angel, she'd be closer to her school, to her mother and her four brothers, they're still homeless, sleeping in their cars or in motels, they're drifters, they have debts so it's the cars or motels, Kitty wants to study math, yes, she could come live with us, it would be a little bit like seeing Angel again, seeing them play together, a little, yes, thought Brilliant, when I recite my epic to those guys at the tavern a few beers in it's a distraction for them to listen, hey, tell us more, you've got a gift, Brilliant, my name used to be Bryan and my life was miserable and I, no, that's not true, after the third great devastation, I met Kim and Fleur, the musician, I miss him, I miss Kim too, where are they, and Jérôme the African, destroyed by drugs, he used to sell water bottles, he was high all the time, he's in exile here, he said he was a child soldier in his country, the pain that man carried from having killed, they were all my friends, when they were hungry I brought them warm meals on the beach and blankets in the winter, but I don't see them anymore, and now I'm married, I've settled down, you fall one day and the next you get back up, should I turn the siren on, it's so nerve-racking, should I, it's such a beautiful summer afternoon, Mai headed toward her mother through the crowd at the airport, the bouquet of flowers Mélanie held out crushed against her face, she was so happy to see her mother, she couldn't wait to hug her, she loved her, she wanted the moment to last forever, it was like her grandmother was there too, and that reunion, Mère, Mélanie, Mai, life must never come between them, she had lost Mère and didn't want to lose Mélanie anytime soon, Mai could still hear the singer howling in despair, *I'm bursting*, listen to me, I am bursting like an underground sun, I'm sinking through the waves at the bottom of the sea, I'm bursting, bursting like a caged sun, let me out, and she thought, how come there was no one who held out their hand to him, how come Forever was so alone, even as he wailed with that voice, the despair, bursting, bursting, listen to me, why didn't anyone listen, why didn't anyone hear, Mai thought, someone would have said something, he might have given up on the idea, everything was dark and indistinct, we have a surprise for you, Mélanie said to Mai, I can't wait for you to see it, yes, but I don't want to say another word, you'll see, and Mélanie was thinking about Mère too, she wondered if she was there with them or whether she would come to them later, as if she were still alive, as if she were there to welcome Mai, as she had so often done privately in her little house, she had watched Mai grow up, her granddaughter, Mai thought her grandmother had always brought out the best in her, the more generous side of her, she also knew how to avoid the worst, yes, the tantrums, the anger when Mère let Marie-Sylvie de la Toussaint steal her jewellery, she didn't say anything, perhaps Mère was already too weak by then to speak out against Marie-Sylvie, she was bedridden, please don't tell your parents, she said to Mai, it's nothing, it's almost not even like anything was stolen, be tolerant, Mai, you can't understand that Marie-Sylvie is taking her poverty out on me, her brother's poverty too, the ocean crossing broke his spirit, we took them in, those poor refugees, in a spirit of tolerance and understanding of the past, they had lost everything, one day you'll understand, do I need my jewellery to get into heaven, tell me, granddaughter, and now Mai was so close to Mélanie, she could still almost hear Mère's words, they have lost everything, lost everything, even though she didn't feel sorry for Marie-Sylvie at all, she was a thief and had betrayed Mère's trust, but those words, *they lost everything*, caught in her throat like Forever's cries, his wounded melody, his lamentation at the end of a life that should have been crowned with success, the triumph of living, his death was no more triumphant than Mère's, no, Mai thought, it was a fall, but why, Mai wondered, why was that, she wanted the moment to go on forever, clasped against Mélanie's body, the offering of hibiscus in the noisy airport, she wanted the perfect moment of their reunion to be sealed, Mai remembered her grandmother asking, do you want to know what a successful life means, Mai, well, you see, every life has its share of success, more or less, that's what the living always ask themselves, how, with a breath of life, how to live with clarity, how to keep accomplishing what seems every day to just be some random project, misunderstood and incomprehensible, what's the good of living and why, perhaps the only answer is to love freely, even if some days it's a feeling we can't find, what do you think, Mai, and Mai replied to her grandmother that the only measurable success was happiness, avoiding unhappiness, that was all she wanted for herself, was that when Mère, in her room with the blue curtains, had pulled out of a drawer a photograph of Marie Curie with Einstein, she looked like she was talking to him, they had met by the lake in Geneva, Lac Léman, even if your life is a success you can still have doubts, Mère said, pointing to Marie Curie's face hollowed by cancer in the dark photograph, Mai only saw a grey scratch, her grandmother's lost memories, nothing seemed as alive to her as the haughty flutter of her own life, Einstein's back was almost completely turned to Curie, he was smoking his pipe, why isn't he listening to her, Mai asked Esther, she looks like a humiliated old woman, Mai added, she seems lonelier there with him than in her laboratory, he's stubbornly not listening to what she's trying to tell him, oh, Mère had said, he is knowledge and she is doubt, it's true, Marie Curie was a woman who always questioned everything, and she was always alone among men, there was never another woman as alone as she was, Mère told Mai, and Mai imagined her solitude, Marie Curie's numb hands tucked into her shawl as she walked through the radium factories between two men in that draining atmosphere or on the American president's arm at the White House, the president wouldn't even look at her, alone on the international commissions with contemptuous men, or perhaps her stiffness belied the attention she devoted wholly to her discoveries, a faraway, somewhat aloof expression on her face, they appreciated that she wasn't much of a woman, she didn't have an attractive femininity, unlike her male colleagues she wasn't trying to please anyone, all she wanted was to do her job, fiercely and with integrity, in a field dominated by the virility of the mind, and now who was she, was she supposed to feel grateful to be among those scientists, she was still young though her hair had gone white, she was a woman who didn't smile, how disagreeable, that austere mien, she seemed quite aggressive, there was never a woman so alone, Mère repeated to Mai, and as she thought of Marie Curie's dull eyes, ravaged by uranium, scorched by the blinding white beams, Mai vowed that her only goal would be happiness, there was nothing more serene, more gratifying, keep on shining, she wouldn't give in to despair like the singer she loved, Forever, no, Mai could still see her brother Augustino getting up at dawn to be like their writer father, from the attic of the house where he wrote the calm morning sea stretched out to the horizon, you could hear the lapping of the waves from there, the Atlantic on one side and the Gulf of Mexico on the other, Augustino was a pampered child, Daniel said, why did he need to write, writing troubled the soul, but Augustino, barely awake, got up and went to write, his writing was suspicious and mistrustful, Mai thought, his computer screen seemed to broil as his restless fingers typed away, do not believe in paradise, he wrote, our island will crumble in the fissures of the Coral Coast, beneath its phosphorescent waters there are strategic weapons hidden and controlled from afar by mad masters and you poor people know nothing about it, while we bask in the images of warm, soft sunsets, you in your blissful inertia will always pretend you had no idea when the choir of your destruction foretold rears its head in all its ugliness, controlled and wielded from afar by the governors and directors of your destiny in their evening clothes or beneath the military imposture of their costumes, during that time they dine in their mansions or gather for cocktails in their gorgeous gardens, you are nothing to them, always nothing, they smirk and laugh and take pleasure from your imminent destruction, as she kissed her mother Mai thought she could hear the words Augustino had written on his computer, where had Augustino's words led him, so far from his family, he had written to Vincent, I am inside the carcass of the world, we hear the true cries of the desolate, no one can soothe or heal them, it was so warm and sweet, the smell of jasmine floating up from shrubs by the sea, the airport was right by the water, and another smell, knapweed, such a sweet smell you could almost taste it, Mai thought, Mai took her mother's hand and said she would drive to the house, she knew how to drive now, she said proudly, but first she asked a million questions about her dogs, her cats, her birds, Mai had been raised with the utter certainty that the world she was born into was a paradise, she wasn't insatiable, simply glad of its bounty, content, a grateful contentment toward all those she loved, this isn't my child anymore, Mélanie thought, no, this tall young woman with piercings in her ears and in her tongue, this enigma I have to discover all over again, no, this isn't the child I knew, but I will learn her with all my heart, the smell of her hair is still the same and the sweat on her brow is the same, her smile is still a child's, candid yet watchful, she might be undone by the slightest thing and yet she's so strong, I will learn, Mélanie thought, Mai had always been small but she'd grown taller than her mother, she was less frail than Mélanie too, she looked more like Daniel now although she had Mère's delicate features, Mélanie would learn this new person, yes, she thought, Mai's face pressed against hers, her face seemed damp with tears and sweetly perfumed, and Uncle Isaac was saying to Adrien, who kept complaining about the heat, lifting his hat, if as Daniel says it's true that this is summer, how I aspire to autumn, to a winter without storms, how I would prefer to ignore summer entirely, I abhor this season for my animals, I could be alone at the top of my tower, my cook comes only once a week, people say I'm stingy because I don't eat much and perhaps it's true that I'm stingy, a man does need a few faults to get to such an advanced age, not to mention to get richer, at the top of my tower on the Island No One Owns suddenly my phone vibrated loudly, what did anyone want with me now in the torpor of the endless summer, alert, alert, there is a tornado warning in effect for your region, seek shelter, so, dear Adrien, I watched the petulant sky, I listened to the unpleasant bleating of my cell phone, a tornado has been sighted or indicated in your area, where was I supposed to hide in just a few minutes, I was outside, so close to the sky that I became its mercurial moods, I rushed down with my cane, my cook wouldn't make it, there was too much traffic in the sky and on the roads, I was alone, alone with a tornado, the cell phone screaming, danger, danger, shelter, quick, fine, if the cook couldn't come, I hoped he wasn't out on the freeway in the rain or on his boat on the way here, no cook this week, I'd save a bit more money, can you blame a man for being thrifty, no, am I stingy, it would be good to know, wouldn't it, and then, dear Adrien, as the wind crackled, strong enough to uproot my century-old trees, even the powerful gumbo-limbo tree, it would be reassuring to believe in a benevolent god, a merciful god, I swear, my friend, plowing beneath the winds, I am very light and slight indeed in the balance of the universe, prey to every madness, the wind tore my khaki shorts, should I buy another pair, what a useless expense, I've been wearing the same clothes for years, the wind could very well tear me to shreds, that would be unfortunate, I'd rather live, and if I were torn to pieces, where would my arms go, my feet, my head, especially, my head is good at trade and calculations, straight into the ocean to be with Jean-Mathieu, I hope, I could finally tell him, my poet brother, you, mysterious traveller refusing to tell us where you were going, I am with you now, you see, you were trying to hide for nothing, all poets are reserved, I don't hold it against you, and now look at our two heads full of ideas floating on the water, what do you think about that, let's travel together a while, though now as I walk into what is no longer my island but my jungle, a tangle of uprooted trees, I see a newborn iguana skittering as fast as it can on its little legs on a path it no longer recognizes, my rosebushes are black tangles uprooted by the wind, the orange trees and coconut trees are absolutely raining fruit, blackened by the furious winds, and my does and fawns fled in every direction, left and right, they didn't know where they were going, I could see the terror in the brown lakes of their eyes, how can we, the humble living, sink into such misery, oh sky, oh winds, when will you have mercy upon us, Uncle Isaac broke off suddenly, Adrien seemed to be dozing under his hat, his cheeks and his forehead were dark from the sunlight growing longer over the waves, swimmers played frantically in the water, my friend, Uncle Isaac said, although he knew Adrien hadn't been listening for a while already, my friend, I'm telling you, that's why I am an atheist, if there were a god, he would have mercy on the panicked does and fawns running off in every direction, their hearts beating out of their chests, during cyclones and tornadoes, and I'm not even talking about the hurricanes that grind up everything in their path, yes, just look at the damage that the tornadoes my phone tells me about can do, and in the eyes of that non-existent god, guilty as he is in his parasitic non-existence, those are merely minor catastrophes, microscopic events, aren't they, as for the fluffy little yellow birds, they have so few feathers they look like fireflies, the wind hurled them here from Cuba and they perched on the broken branches of the uprooted trees wondering how they would be able to fly away, and where, my little ones, come on, my friend, are you listening, Uncle Isaac asked suddenly with friendly impatience, and Adrien boomed indifferently, Isaac, you've known me for so many years, we crossed a whole century together, though often alas we saw too little of each other, can't you see it's time for my nap, my friend, well, since you're napping, I'll just shut up then, Uncle Isaac said, offended, he shrugged his shoulders, annoyed, and turned to Daniel, who was sitting in his own deck chair, saying nothing, Daniel seemed preoccupied, Uncle Isaac muttered into his ear, Daniel, this man, our friend, he doesn't have an ounce of congeniality, don't you think, nephew, I can see you're not listening to me either, look at that great blue heron soaring toward us, there's the wonder we were waiting for, Uncle Isaac said, it's diving for its catch of the day, it's so close, so close to us, Uncle Isaac said with a satisfied smile, seeing the great blue heron calmed his thoughts like a smile from the sky after the tornadoes, he thought, a rainbow of reconciliation, Uncle Isaac thought, even just briefly, some harmony reclaimed, a reward on this too-blue, torrid day. There are already almost two hundred people upstairs in the bar and on the ground floor everybody's dancing, said Geisha, but where's Robbie, he's not here yet, the party's just getting started and we can't even hear each other talk, said Yinn, he was wearing a flowing white party dress, tell the DJ to turn the music down a bit, electronica pouring out of the glass cage, Yinn was like a white butterfly or a giant Arctic bird, trying to keep the party from reaching quite that fever pitch, it could get way too loud too fast, he thought, through the purple light of the screens and the urgency in the singers' voices, the cascade of images across the two screens, they had to try to maintain some intimacy, familiarity, not too much noise, Yinn thought, to create space for embraces and kissing, people were dancing feral and free, whether by themselves or with a partner who appeared out of nowhere and who more often than not was a complete stranger, they had to create space for the miracle of an encounter, all of Robbie's Puerto Rican friends came, Geisha told Yinn, you look splendid, Yinn, Robbie will be so happy, it's basically a Puerto Rican party with all these friends of Robbie's, his faithful friends, hell-bent on pleasure, it'll be a hot, exciting night, our friends are already buzzing from the heat and that arousing closeness, Geisha said, although we keep getting messages on our phones, so much hurt and intolerance, we have Victoire, with her army background, she's our loyal defender, she's fearless and she has her dog Déesse with her, she'll be at the door, yes, everything's going to go as planned, the bar's become a ballroom, that's what we wanted, something majestic, yes, for our Robbie and his fans, balloons and decorations everywhere, through the northwest door a man came in, young, the man dressed in black they had seen earlier, his face was very pale, Victoire watched him, saying to herself, well, he came back, if he's a troublemaker, he'll be easy to swat out, that one, thought Victoire, maybe he was a customer, maybe he'd been there before, it was hard to know, there were so many people already inside, upstairs and downstairs, at Le Fantasque, Geisha had told Victoire, your dresses are a little too feminine for my taste but even under those sleeves everyone can see how strong you are, you must have been a sturdy soldier, impeccable, well built, they must've regretted throwing you out, you and all the others as courageous as you on those missions, they must have regretted that, and you were so decorated too, Geisha said, I'll be the old bag at the door, said Victoire, tell Santa Fe not to forget the fireworks, everything is going to go off at once when the music builds, Victoire told Geisha, she was melancholy now, it's no use thinking about the past, only the beauty of the present matters, but yes, it's true, Geisha, I was a good soldier, you were beyond honourable, said Geisha, who's that guy in black, he's covered up from head to toe and it's so hot in here, he hangs out sometimes I think, said Victoire, if he makes trouble I'll know what to do with him and you'll never see him again, said Victoire, Victoire watched the young man in black stride up to Yinn, she was surprised at how direct he seemed, the man wasn't very tall and he stood up on tiptoe to kiss Yinn on the cheek, so the little fake Judas is kissing Yinn, Victoire thought, really, I'm going to get him out of here, presumptuous brat, as if Yinn could belong to anyone, just going up to him like that, touching him, it's so possessive and it's downright indecent from a stranger, he's just a little squirt nobody wants, I've got my eye on him, I'm going to tell him to get out of here, but Victoire was distracted by Santa Fe, it's almost time, said Santa Fe, the sky will be all lit up with fireworks as soon as it's dark out, and just as he had come the young man dressed in black left through the northwest door, good, thought Victoire, I won't have to take him on, my hands are too strong, my fists are used to army fights, you should never abuse your strength or use it in vain, thought Victoire, I'm glad that's over but I'm still going to go watch the door in case he comes back, yes, thought Victoire, let's head back to the dance floor, said Geisha, have fun, where's Robbie, why is he so late, my firecrackers are ready, said Santa Fe, can we launch them already, and Brilliant thought as he drove his ambulance, I'm lucky, I'm a happy man, but I remember that during the second great devastation I thought, in a world of daily disasters there's often some corner that shows us some unexpected glimmer of hope, it was raining, pouring, and I remember a woman sheltering with her little kids, a refrigerator had washed up there by chance, right near the tiny space where her family was sheltering, the fridge was open and there were popsicles inside the top compartment, and as if destruction weren't hanging over her head the woman took the popsicles and gave them to her children and in spite of the torrent of tragedies they all seemed unaware and started eating the popsicles, smiling, savouring them, it was charming, an irresistible vision in the middle of the storm, sometimes it's like that, it often is, it's so natural for us to try to keep sadness at bay, I can still see them, the mother and her children, as if they were in a cave, safe from the rain and the wind blurring the landscape, I said to myself, they have been saved and Misha and I will be safe too, that was a sign of hope, we must never forget that there is often some sign of hope, how can we see it, it didn't seem so inaccessible, so far away, that feeling of tangible hope, it's often so close, at that moment my half-brother, my nanny's son, was drowning, he didn't know how to swim, thought Brilliant, suddenly sad, and in the bar, at Le Fantasque, Porsha crumpled against the wall, Porsha my love, my lovely flamingo, you can't fall asleep, the party's just getting started, get up, let's go dance, you had too much to drink, I told you to be careful, listen to this music, this driving beat, let's go dance, you and me, let me sleep a little, said Porsha, my wife, just a little, no, you can't fall asleep like that, my Porsha, no, you can't, I want to dance with you, where's Robbie, asked Porsha dreamily, where is he, my Portia, do you think our little piglets and lambs are okay without us on the farm, asked Porsha, we never leave them alone, it's only for a few hours, said Portia, my flamingo, darling, don't you want to dance with me, can you hear the fireworks, my Porsha, the sun has just barely set and already the stars are lighting up the sky with a bang, bang, I can't hear a thing, I'm so sleepy, said Porsha, oh, Porsha, my beautiful Porsha, get up, I don't want to dance alone, said Portia, from the second floor Portia heard a bang, I'm going to dance then, said Portia, you'll come join me, won't you, my Porsha, it's so noisy in here all of a sudden, it's true, Porsha, we can't hear a thing anymore, the DJ has got to change it up a bit, don't worry, sleep tight, my Porsha, I'll be right here, Alexandra said to Léonie, darling, I'm going to go see Bob in the DJ booth, up in his glass cage, maybe I'll make a few requests, he needs to turn it down a bit, did you hear a noise, asked Alexandra, it sounded like thunder, no, it's the fireworks, a bit too fiery, said Léonie, don't go, said Léonie, I've got a bad feeling, yes, something feels off, said Alex, I'll be right back, darling, Bob is all over the place and I know electronica, there's a truck pulling up across from the entrance, said Victoire, and a man in black clothes is getting out, he's coming in through the northwest door again, hey, you, what are you doing here, she yelled, I see you, I recognize you even with your black mask on, get out of here, but no one could hear Victoire's words and she wasn't armed, the intruder was already in the bar, there were gunshots and a muffled explosion, Victoire wondered if the short, sharp noise was really a bomb, maybe it was some homemade toy, dangerous though, now Geisha was shouting, the bar is on fire, the walls are on fire, everyone get out, everyone, get out, but no one seemed to be able to make it out to the street, in seconds the flames roared up, I'm dizzy, Portia, where are you, shouted Porsha, trying to get up and falling back against the wall, Portia, where are you, I'm going to text you, I'm worried I'll fall asleep again with all this smoke, Porsha took out his phone and texted Portia, she couldn't hear him, couldn't see him, Portia, my wife, I'm here, can you help me up, I'm afraid I'm going to pass out, I'm going to fall asleep for a long time, Portia, my love, husband, wife, can't you see me, I'm right here against the wall, I'm in the bathroom, I'm hiding, Portia wrote Porsha, my beautiful pink flamingo, I'm coming to you, there are lots of us locked in here, the door is locked from the outside, Portia texted Porsha, don't move, Victoire is going to break down the door and I'll be right there, my God, the smoke my God, wait there, I'll be right there, my Porsha, stay calm, wait there, there are so many of us locked in here, there are no windows, there's nothing, there's no air, we can't breathe, Victoire, Victoire, I can hear her trying to open the door, Portia could see a young girl panting and talking to her mother, goodbye, Mommy, goodbye, Daddy, I can't see anything, Porsha texted Portia, did they set off the firecrackers, I'm going back to sleep, Porsha sighed, maybe we shouldn't have left the house tonight, I don't like leaving them alone, there are lots of us locked in the bathroom, Victoire, where are you, Portia screamed, she could hear the girl gasping for breath as she talked to her mother on her phone, smoke rose up in front of them like a screen, Mommy, I don't know how I'm going to get out of here, I'm trapped, a bad man came, and, and, I can hardly breathe with all the smoke, Mommy, Daddy, goodbye, Portia could hear Victoire's voice on the other side of the door, don't worry, I'm going to get you out, she said, you have my word as a soldier, I'm going to get you out of there, try not to breathe, cover your face, don't breathe, it was Victoire's voice, thought Portia, and what sounded like a pickaxe or a hammer, Victoire was flinging herself against the bathroom door with all her strength, run, quick, girls, boys, when the door opens, run to the exits on the first floor, go, the gunman ran away, it was Victoire's voice, but we'll get him, the cops are already here, please, as soon as I get the door open run to the exits as fast as you can, don't worry, he's gone, Léonie, Alexandra typed from up in the DJ booth, I'm writing to you quickly, where are you, can you answer me, where are you, who could hate us so much they'd do something like this, darling, where are you, tell me, I can't see anything, it's so smoky, but Léonie didn't answer, the walls were burning, red flames curled up from the floor that just minutes before had been so lively, where should we go, a man's voice asked, can we take the stairs, go up to the roof, ordered Yinn, trying to brush sparks from the flowing white dress, I'm right here, I love you, you're not going to die, said Yinn, I can't believe they're murdering innocents in broad daylight now too, said Yinn, take the stairs, there's a door at the top, the gunman had fired a few rounds from his semi-automatic and from a handgun, climb the stairs, go up, shouted Yinn, propping up a Puerto Rican boy who had fainted, wake up, Pierro, said Yinn, wake up, we've got to save them all, using every ounce of her strength, Victoire finally managed to kick in the bathroom door but it was too late, there was nothing but a pile of bodies, boys and girls piled on top of each other, pale, lifeless, they weren't breathing, only Portia was still standing among them, kids massacred, happy kids burned alive, some of them still had sunglasses on, others were clutching their phones, let's go help the survivors, come quick, said Victoire, Porsha, where is Porsha, said Portia, her face was black with soot, they were my friends, they were my friends and they've been killed, they're dead, we were dreaming of a hot Latin night of dancing for Robbie, not a party at which all his Puerto Rican friends would die in a fire, it was a bad night, said Victoire, what a horrible night, those still standing were shaky on the dance floor, Yinn, Victoire, Porsha, as the club burned, the walls, the dance floor, Brilliant pulled up in his ambulance, he was the one they were waiting for, the sharp smell of the blaze, smoke billowing before him, he could hear the screams, the moaning, was it real or was it another bad dream, at night when he had bad dreams, when he had the feeling that some evil presence was pushing him away from Lucia and Misha, he loved them so much, he would turn on the light and see them there next to him in the bedroom, how had he ever doubted that they would be there, was love always intrinsically tied to a fear of loss, no, that wasn't how it should be, no, thought Brilliant, his sirens screamed seemingly beyond his control, this was real, he wasn't dreaming, Brilliant was used to having to witness murder scenes, but here he was too late, around him police officers and medics were already at work, maybe he was too late, there were already so many victims, burned bodies lined up on the sidewalk, he saw Portia bent over Porsha's body at the entrance of Le Fantasque shaking him, Brilliant ran toward the bar, my friends, these are my friends and they're going to die, wake up, Porsha, don't leave me alone, Porsha, I told you not to drink so much, wake up, my Porsha, are you hurt, talk to me, Porsha, I want to hear your voice, it was one of the flamingos, thought Brilliant, that blackened, motionless face, Portia was shaking him and begging but he wouldn't wake up, please, Porsha, my Porsha, wake up, Geisha ran up to Brilliant, quick, we have to get the stretchers out of here, quick, get them to the hospital, crying's not going to do any good, Brilliant, pull yourself together and help me, Yinn and Victoire saved a few Puerto Rican friends from the fire but they couldn't save them all, some people were hanging on to the windows and they were burned alive, my God, repeated Brilliant, this is horrible, what can I do, what, my God, come with me, said Geisha, stop crying, there will be time for that, it's a cruel god who runs this world, he doesn't deserve our tears, no, said Brilliant, this has nothing to do with God, the murderer is a man, he fled through the northwest door and hopped a truck out of town, we have to get the bodies, that's what you can do, said Geisha, as if giving an order, and Petites Cendres thought if Yinn had gotten a warning, why not tell us about it, why, yet again Yinn refused to believe in the human capacity for evil, he's always refused to believe that men are bad, there were over fifty dead, all those kids who just moments before had been on the dance floor, what did the message say, my religion casts you out, my religion, there was a second message after the murder, signed Lazaro, why, oh, why hadn't Yinn talked to the others about the first message, signed, I'm back, Lazaro, why hadn't he said anything, thought Petites Cendres as he helped Portia carry Porsha's heavy body toward the door, water, we need ice water for Porsha, said Portia, quick, cold water, firefighters were coming through the burned rubble, we can't breathe, said Petites Cendres, we can't breathe, you have to help them, some of them might survive, said Petites Cendres, help them all, through the smoke he could see Yinn and Victoire who had busted through the glass of the DJ booth and were pulling Alexandra's lifeless body out, she was still holding her phone in her hand after sending Léonie a final message, I'm coming to you, Léonie, I'm hurt but it's nothing, we'll get through it together, you and me, wait for me, Léonie, neither Geisha nor Yinn seemed dressed for a party anymore now, thought Petites Cendres, Yinn's white dress was in tatters, like a bird's wing hanging broken after a fall, you could see his body, he had always been lithe but now in the carnage he seemed downright fragile, yet the body still shone, beautiful, thought Petites Cendres, maybe Yinn in his calling as a lifesaving angel was nothing more now than a soul rising out of the flayed body touched by fire, a body wounded, he seemed to be bleeding black blood, while next to him Victoire stood like a soldier at vigil, watching over that soul, Victoire, victorious, she was there to raise the dead, there are so many dead, thought Petites Cendres, it would be in the news tomorrow, fifty Puerto Rican kids dead, Robbie had gotten the time wrong and showed up late to the opening of his own bar, when he got to Le Fantasque at midnight all he found was ashes. What a feat, what a great adventure I've managed, gathering all of them here together by the sea at the Grand Hotel, Isaac thought, loosening his tie, it was too much to have to dress up for the evening, the beige linen suit and the hat, any more and he would look like Adrien, they were looking more and more like each other, shuffling around with their canes, no, Isaac thought, I'm still spry, I'm younger than he is, Adrien is an old, hunched-over intellectual, he's never happy, probably he's chronically dissatisfied because he's very smart and very bitter, he's a man who knows everything, I don't have those delusions or that pride, Isaac thought, I'm happy with myself just as I am, a poor child glad of his riches, I'm reaping the rewards of my perseverance, I'm allowed to enjoy this, that's what I was telling my nephew, everyone was there, the lights turning on in the gardens, Isaac could hear the murmur of voices, the swimming pools' green water sparkled in the night, he would leave them to it on Caribbean Beach beneath the stars so that Mai could be with the other young people who were already dancing there by the sea to the rush of the waves, the music was too loud for Isaac, his right ear couldn't take it, after writing for so long up in the room Isaac had set aside for Jean-Mathieu at the top of his tower on the Island No One Owns now this was all coming true, the boat pulled up to the pier at Caribbean Beach and Jean-Mathieu climbed up to the platform where he would read his poems, Isaac had waited so long for this, but he wasn't alone, she was with him, Caroline, it was her, her quiet elegance, ready with her camera to capture the evening's aspirations, so much happiness, Isaac thought, they were together at last and he hoped they would be for long and for good, I always knew they would find each other here again after that unfortunate time in Italy when Jean-Mathieu caught such a bad cold, this is good, Isaac thought, everything is as it should be, there was something about the golden light over everyone's head, there was a gleam to the evening, the bodies were light, so light, everyone seemed to be waltzing, dancing, even Adrien who was so wary was different tonight somehow, Suzanne was back, she held her hand out to him, what was she saying, my friend, I told you I would go through the door, Dalet, do you remember, that's what it was called, and Adrien wept with joy as he walked toward his beloved wife, was he ecstatic or was he unhappy because nothing was ever perfect enough for him, over there, Adrien asked Suzanne, on the other side of the paper screen, that's where you were all this time, darling, wasn't it, are you finally writing the books that you wanted so badly to write, was that why you left me that terrible day in Switzerland, because I wouldn't let you write, was that it, is it, yes, but Suzanne had forgiven him long ago and she held her husband in her arms and said, don't you see I've always loved you, how are the children, not a day's gone by that I haven't thought about them, and Adrien fell silent, oh, yes, the children, he said, the children, they write me sometimes, they're busy with their careers, but you, tell me about you, how have we been apart for so long, *Dalet*, I've never liked that word, the name of that door, why did you leave me alone for so long, Suzanne, Isaac's thoughts came and went like melodious visions mingling with the song of the waves, he had done his best to bring them all together close to him that night for Mai's birthday, there was nothing he wouldn't have done, but he felt like a magician, not a rich man, just a magician handing around what was most precious to those around him, the fortune he held, expansive feelings of love freed at last, he couldn't even name it and no one seemed to see it in him, under his thin shell, how sad and awkward not to be able to express the breadth of it, even as effusive as he was, yes, Isaac thought, and as he walked over to his uncle beneath the palm trees swaying in the summer wind Daniel saw Isaac pensive, his knotty hands folded over the grip of his cane, the tip wedged in the grass on the lawn that had been mowed only that morning, it smelled fresh, Daniel wanted to thank Uncle Isaac for this incredible party, he thought, it was impressive, the sun was about to melt into the ocean like a red globe so slowly that no one noticed the night seeping in and yet as the blazing sun dropped languidly toward the sea Daniel was suddenly gripped by the sadness of a nightmare in which Mai was asking, Papa, what's going on, what's the smell of smoke, what is it, Papa, it was only a nightmare, a recurring dream Daniel knew all too well from his troubled nights, but the images came back to him, he remembered telling Mai, darling, today's your birthday, don't ask me these questions anymore, I'll explain later, I'll explain everything tomorrow, he did smell the smoke his daughter asked about, nobody else around him at the party seemed to be worried, it was a beautiful, fresh evening, in the glittering, rich feast, it was easy to feel only happiness at being alive, Mai was happy, and her mother, Mélanie, everyone, huddled together laughing and celebrating, as Daniel sank into his own thoughts, he was carrying his grandson Rudie in his arms, he was wondering if tomorrow he would be forced to carry a gun when he went in to the college, Rudolph was so sure of his own future, he told everyone he would grow up to be a pilot, he wanted to fly a big plane, that was his dream, the sky would be his, and Daniel watched Rudie's firm, calm face and said nothing, amazed at the child who looked a little bit like him, what was he worried about, Rudie took dance classes too, he was always with his parents, protected and loved, he would be a dancer too, a choreographer like his father, as creative as his mother was, Veronica, just like his parents he would be an artist in the constant throes of rebellion, he already was, wasn't he, he danced in his parents' work, he had played the child gagged and riding a bicycle through the suffocating yellow mist of the factories in Samuel's piece *China, Slow Movement*, so slow, pushing through the climate crisis windstorms, and who was that Daniel saw now through the night's procession, was that Stephen, the young novelist, Charles's future biographer, what a tour de force it was to write on Charles's work, his life, Stephen was becoming like Charles, he even had the same glowing, ironic smile, Charles and Frédéric felt very close in the white summer suits Daniel had often seen them wear, and Cyril, the actor Charles had fallen in love with in India, he was there too, laughing, he was so charming and Frédéric wasn't jealous at all, it was a peaceful night after all, all anyone could think about was dancing, as Daniel walked down toward Uncle Isaac's beach, Caribbean Beach, Daniel was glad that he didn't only have nightmares, he also had those crystal-clear dreams he jotted down in his journals, peaceful, limpid dreams, he could see Jacques cured and swimming in the green water of a huge swimming pool at the Grand Hotel, Jacques was saying to Daniel, we must set them all free from the Cemetery of Roses, their youth has been buried there for so long, and for what, I want them to join me here happily, I've discovered that the only paradise is this life on earth, the only harbour is our flesh, may we be easy in our skin, and Daniel thought he could hear Beethoven's oratorio "Christ on the Mount of Olives," Jacques had listened to it on his deathbed, at the end he could hear even though he couldn't see, so dies a man of the flesh, he said to Charles, I've had a good life, don't worry about me, were those his last words, Beethoven's oratorio floated up in the room to the dying body, the music unfolding beyond the gardens, beyond the Grand Hotel's pompous decor, among the bonfires on the beach, on the palm trees' gilded leaves, in the pine boughs arching in the wind, Daniel saw a bunch of the kids sitting in wooden chairs against the walls of the Grand Hotel, smoking and chatting like convalescents, like Jacques used to, they were wearing white bathrobes, there was a time when that was all Jacques could wear, the only thing he could tolerate on his shivering skin covered with sores, Luc and Paul would drape a robe over his shoulders, those two young men that Jacques called back out of the green water of the glistening pools under the night's twinkling lights to lives once so inexplicably interrupted, lives cut down by a divine sword, the image of God seemed shapeless to Daniel, abnormally cruel, it haunted him, like in his crystalline dreams, they would go meet Jacques, he was cured now, peaceful in the green water, the long fevers quelled at last, the birds sang all around and Tanjou would come too with his brushes to paint a portrait of the moment, he would say to Jacques, you remember me, Jacques, I was the Pakistani student you loved though you never told me, it was so hard for me, I was tormented, remember, Jacques, and Jacques would say, you're right, Tanjou, the greatest error of my life was not knowing how to love, I was too cold, yes, you're right, Tanjou, they would be calm next to each other by the pool, by Charles's river eternal, Tanjou would forget his fall that lovely late-summer day, the broken bones, swallowed up by fire as he leaped into the void that morning in New York, the blue sky was splintered by a thousand falling bodies, they had plunged through heaven's stained glass, Tanjou didn't remember anything but he remembered how cold Jacques had been before he got sick, with Luc and Paul, the friends who looked after him, he had never left Jacques's side, they listened to the oratorio together though there was no hope anymore, no, no hope, said Jacques, don't worry about me anymore, I was a happy man, but don't forget me either, and in an airport somewhere by the sea, Ari was telling Lou, you're heading so far away that I have to ask a flight attendant to look after you, how can I let my daughter travel to Mongolia all by herself like that to go see her godfather, it's crazy, I don't know why I'm letting you leave, good thing it's only for a month, but what's a girl going to do in a monastery full of novice monks, I want to go learn with him, with my godfather Asoka, Lou told Ari, Dad, I'm old enough, don't ask the flight attendant, I want to learn about a more spiritual world as my godfather Asoka says, it doesn't exist, said Ari, there is no more spiritual world, no better world, don't believe it, your godfather Asoka is a monk, and celibate to boot, what could he possibly know about life as we live it, but Daddy, weren't you one of his disciples when you were writing for that magazine *The Evolution of Consciousness*, weren't you, Dad, Lou asked Ari, that was a long time ago, Ari replied abruptly, a very long time ago, though Ari saw himself again just then in his sailboat crossing the Atlantic, bundles of hashish tucked under the deck planks, that was a long time ago too, was that after his friends were poisoned in Peru, he was almost poisoned too, that was when he converted to conscious evolution, the teachings of the mystic monk Asoka, he had made so many mistakes in his youth, it seemed like it might be time to change his life, but that call to transparency was false, thought Ari, he would never change, he was a man growing less mature, he had only one religion now and that was art, and, of course, as always, a sensual man's conquest of women, I told you not to dress like a boy, said Ari sternly, your godfather is going to see you dressed like your brother Julien and he won't understand anything about all the convolution in your head, he's a simple man, he's naive, don't tell him what you're telling me about how you want to be a boy, how you don't belong to your real sex, you know boys aren't as great as you think they are, boys grow up to be men like me, look at me, Lou, do you want to become a man like me or do you want to be what you should be, normal, a young woman like all the others, anyway, you don't have a boy's features, you look like your mother, what would you do in a boy's body, I will feel good, said Lou, but I won't talk about that with Asoka, I want him to teach me about the spiritual world, said Lou, I don't understand you, said Ari, here comes the flight attendant who'll look after you, you've got more than one flight and I want her to stay with you for each flight, I don't want you to be alone, Ari watched Lou leave with the flight attendant, he was distraught, yet again words had failed him, he hadn't been able to tell Lou he loved her, or him, whether tomorrow Lou was a girl or a boy or even one day a man like him, as ridiculous and awkward as that would be, he should have told Lou that even though he didn't like those dreams of metamorphosis, he wouldn't love Lou any less, but he thought maybe it was too late, it was better to trust Lou's godfather, the monk Asoka, it was better, yes, for Lou to seek out that spiritual world, though where was that world, wondered Ari, where was it, and they were all together by the sea in their white jeans and T-shirts, that was what Yinn had suggested everyone wear for the memorial by the sea on the pier where they would throw an armful of white roses into the night ocean, and orchids and birds of paradise, the offerings were getting repetitive, thought Yinn, as if the ceremony of offering flowers to the dead and disappeared only served as a reminder that Fatalité, Herman, Samantha, all of them were gone, their ashes dropping below the waves, the fight wasn't over, said Robbie, we're all going to go to the marches in Washington, in New York and Boston, after San Francisco, there were so many people there, don't cry, my friends, we'll keep on fighting for them, our Puerto Rican friends, the Fantasque martyrs, our resilience is contagious, universal, everyone was listening to Robbie deferentially, that night as they gathered to say goodbye to so many beautiful young girls and boys, so many of them barely teenagers, Reverend Stone said not a word, not a word about the kingdom and the father of all men, no, nothing, he was silent, he respected Robbie's words and dropped his head toward the water where the undertow dragged the flowers away, the young lives sacrificed, the very thought of that sacrifice imposed silence, he couldn't say anything, he was upset, though all at once, in a burst of hope, he called out to Robbie, I'm with you, I am with you, I weep with you, though he couldn't shed a tear and he knew Robbie couldn't hear a word he was saying in the din of the crashing waves, their names were spoken, Alexandra, Porsha, so many others, as the flowers floated out to sea, twirling above the waves, Brilliant, Lucia, and Misha had come, Brilliant wasn't sad, though he had grown up so much in a single day, he had become so watchful with those he loved, his new family, Lucia and Misha, they had adopted Kitty too, he would be strong, he thought, and that kind of tragedy would never happen again, oh no, no, he was so angry, he had to try to calm his beating heart, life was meant for joy, he thought, not for these atrocities and the sadness that followed, no, and Daniel noticed that Vincent would be late, he was always late, he worked too hard at the hospital, he kissed Mélanie and Mai, a quick, happy hug, Daniel thought, he would be there soon, with them, with Mélanie, she called him my big boy, Vincent, she remembered Augustino, she was sure she had seen him, his picture flashed by in a television documentary about Yemen, her son was there, he was pleading for medical and humanitarian help for cholera victims, it was him, she was sure of it, it was his face, for just an instant, she held him in her gaze and suddenly the image was gone as if it had been a blip, behind her back, when she turned to the television, seeing her son there pleading was like a slap in the face, but she was glad to have seen him, if that had been him at all, she would talk to Daniel about it that night, or maybe she shouldn't say anything, lock the gripping image deep within herself, Vincent had gotten to the party late and he kissed her as she thought of Augustino, and she caught herself, she was afraid suddenly that Vincent might tell her he had to leave too, that he was going to Jordan with his dermatologist friend, no, he couldn't, she would have wanted to keep them all here with her, especially her grandson Rudolph, he was away on tour so often with his parents, but Mère seemed to say, as if she had been there with her, she was everywhere, those we love are always with us, I am here too, she was saying, can't you see how radiant Mai is, how grateful, can't you see, she's not as dressed up as you would've liked, but the girls now, they're so young, dressed in barely a scrap of fabric, I'll have to get used to seeing her like that, with all her piercings, it's too bad, often we don't understand anything about our children, but see how radiant she is, and Daniel saw Tchouan too, Tchouan was pushing Olivier's wheelchair around a pool carved out of marble, another one of Uncle Isaac's eccentricities, all the marble, the torches by the sea, at least they were keeping the mosquitoes away, Daniel made a mental note to congratulate Olivier for his article in that morning's newspaper praising the presidential candidate, Senator Africa, she had said in a speech before an enormous crowd, the party of indifference would give rise to the party of terror, we have to pull together, to form a new conscience, a new humanity, lest we all be dominated, ready for nuclear extermination, one program among so many others headlined death, the death of the individual, the death of each person, the death of the universe, we had to face the terror that put us at such risk, Tchouan approved, it was too bad her son Jermaine wasn't there that night, he was in Hollywood for his film, Jermaine came to visit them all the time, she said, the situation with Olivier was a recent development, his paralysis, it was painful but their love got them through each day, the most important thing was that Olivier kept writing his articles every day, his editorials, wasn't it, yes, Tchouan said, and Daniel thought she was as beautiful as she had ever been, when she came to visit Mère at home or at those grand parties in the mansion overlooking the ocean, when Jermaine and Samuel were still small and their families so united, they spent all their time together, it was such a comfort that Jermaine was so close to his parents,

Daniel thought, he made films about his father's work, he was the worthy son of his father, and on the path up to the gardens, Daniel saw J'aime and his mother, J'aime was distant and contorted in his wheelchair while Olivier still sat upright, here are the poems I promised you and don't forget my exhibition, Daniel, the paintings will be up at the movie theatre where I've been working, his mother had the same blue eyes, she pushed him through the garden, it's true, he's been writing a lot and thinking of you, how encouraging you are to young poets, J'aime's mother told Daniel, and Daniel thought, so it's true, even while I'm writing, I'm not just thinking of myself, I'm thinking about J'aime too, and about Eddy over in Scotland, all of them, it's so wonderful to know that this world, my world, though it seems so closed, it's actually open to everyone, or at least to a few people, it was surprising to him, he would share that surprise with Mai, she always expected good news from her father, he was her guide toward the light, perhaps that was all he was, and Carlos couldn't believe it, as he came into the yard with Mama, his whole family was there, clapping, even Pastor Jeremy, his father, holding Rebecca and baby Trevor Junior on his lap, there was meat on the grill, everything was like it used to be, thought Carlos, the icebox in the grass, the roosters and chickens pecking pebbles in the yard, they would fly up and perch in the trees, everyone was shouting welcome home Carlos, welcome home, wasn't everything like it had been before, El Toque, his brother, whispering in his ear, how do you like the car, what do you think, brother, the vintage convertible, ask me where I got it, hey, ask me, I'll tell you everything, Carlos, and there, in the twins' arms, Deandra and Tiffany, there was Polly, Polly the third, not the first, you were gone so long, said the girls, they had grown so tall, and Polly pounced into Carlos's arms without a moment's hesitation, everything was exactly as it should be, as it has been before, thought Carlos, he had Polly back, yes, he had Polly, even Venus hadn't changed, she was as angry as ever and Carlos liked it that way, then there was that new thing, Venus has been going to night school after working all day at the hotel, she ruffled Carlos's hair lazily, saying, I've got my diploma, I'm going to be like Perdue Baltimore, she got your sentence commuted, she cleared your name, I'm going to work to defend all the delinquents like you, all the Black boys who mess up, he hadn't just messed up, protested Mama, it was serious, he was basically a criminal, yes, and Carlos repeated again that no, he didn't know that the Cuban's gun was loaded, he didn't know, that's all the past, Rebecca broke in, Uncle Carlos is back with us, he'll go find work tomorrow at the garage, said Mama, right, let's forget all about it, said Mama, let's thank God for the food on our table, Carlos was starving, he said, he was going to scarf down all the beans and the meat, he could smell it cooking on the grill, he thought everybody looked up to him because he was so manly, strong, so tall, his brother El Toque was just a scrawny gimp, though he had skills all the same, he could scrounge up old-school convertibles from who knows where, he had to admit it was a bit suspicious, Mama told El Toque he had to bring back the car to its rightful owner, tomorrow, that vintage convertible parked out in front of the house had to go, he would, wouldn't he, did he want to end up in that hole for juvenile delinquents too, was that what El Toque wanted, what a punk, said Mama, still complaining, and Venus said the Sunday coming up there would be a speech by the presidential candidate, Donna Africa, at the park by the water, everyone had to come hear, yes, said Venus, at the sports park, she's going to talk about reviving our souls, you've got to be there, Venus said to Pastor Jeremy and Mama, and her father replied, they say Donna Africa is too emotional, Venus looked mad as she listened to her father, nothing surprising there, thought Carlos, his older sister Venus was still the same, though most of all he was hungry and he loved them all so much, especially Polly, he would never leave her side again, this was the best day of his life, thought Carlos, because he had Polly back, yes, for sure, the best day of his life, and sitting in the sand against the husk of the boat that had belonged to her protector, Old Salt, with her daughter by her side, Kim swiped her phone open to read Fleur's unexpected message, it was him, he was there, in the video, he was explaining his new opera, his devout friend Claudio would conduct it in Brussels in the coming months, it starts off with a peaceful quartet, he said, all the students in the class focused on their studies, they don't have the slightest idea what's going to happen, and only when the cello comes in do they realize there's an intruder in the school, their usually quiet school in a little village in Germany, suddenly there's an intruder, yes, Fleur was telling Kim, he has spent so long composing his opera, he said, can you hear the cello, it's so precise, so crisp, Claudio was a generous man, he had urged Fleur to contact those he called Fleur's human family, Kim, Jérôme the African, Brilliant, all of them, Claudio was a musician who seemed to live only for music yet he had a family, a wife and three daughters in Rome, Andrew seemed too solitary, he should reach out to his family all alone over there in America, Kim, all of them, he should invite his mother Martha to his concerts, shouldn't he, and Fleur or Andrew had given in to Claudio's advice, though it was when he saw Pearl Saved from the Waters that he came to life, her round face, her budgie Orange, her rabbits, it was Pearl Saved from the Waters who brought him back to his true family, Fleur's face seemed to quiver on the screen, he was wearing a hoodie like he used to, Kim listened to the song of the cello, Fleur's voice cracking against the thundering waves wove its way into her heart, they would never be apart again, thought Kim, no, never, and as he walked to Caribbean Beach where Mai and Mélanie were waiting for him, and all of Uncle Isaac's guests, Daniel saw he had a message from Eddy in Scotland, he was invited to the twenty-first international festival of writers for peace, come to our mountains, dear friend, we'll be waiting, Eddy wrote, as we do each year, dear Daniel, we'll be waiting for you, that was the message Daniel wanted to show Mai, he, her father, Daniel, was invited to that conference at the top of a mountain in Scotland, all those people coming together for peace, Eddy's invitation soothed him just then, it was soothing for all of them even though for the time being it was only one of his crystalline dreams among so many, another one of his limpid hopes.

Appendix

MAIN CHARACTERS IN THE SOIFS CYCLE

Adam (11 years old): A young admirer of Jessica the pilot.

Adrien (93 at the end of the cycle): A famous poet in Daniel and his family's circle. Adrien is also a friend of Charles and Frédéric, Caroline and Jean-Mathieu, and Uncle Isaac. At first he is happy with his wife, Suzanne, and later he grows old alone on the island.

Alan (30): An exiled AIDS victim.

Alfonso (55): A priest who denounces the hypocrisy of the Catholic church, and a friend of Martha, Fleur's mother.

Amos: A child with AIDS who Nora cares for.

Andrés: A victim of police violence during the refugee crisis.

Andrés (60): A doorman at the cabaret.

Andrew Adam: Goes by the name Fleur. After years of homelessness, the musical prodigy takes back his birth name and embarks on a new life as a virtuoso in Europe.

Angel (12): A young AIDS victim who was expelled from school due to pressure from parents afraid of contagion. He and his mother are taken in at the Acacia Gardens.

Angelina (23): A young pregnant woman who Tigli and Daniel meet in Guatemala.

Angelina, Angie, and Annette (7, 10, and 16): Three Black sisters who sing on the street; Brilliant notices them several times on his way to Pelican Beach.

Anna (48): A pastor and one of the victims of the Young Man's carnage at the New Hope Methodist Church.

Antoine (50): A reverend, and Pastor Anna's husband. They are a close couple.

Ari (about 30 at the beginning of the cycle): A sculptor committed to his art who once lived a bohemian, adventurous life as an artist. Lou's father.

Arnie Graal: A Black choreographer and dancer who died very young of AIDS at the height of a remarkable career in New York. He was Samuel's dance teacher. Critics dubbed him the Snow Queen.

Aryan Brotherhood: A white supremacist gang Carlos encounters in juvenile detention.

Asoka: A Buddhist monk who collaborated with his friend Ari on the magazine *The Evolution of Consciousness*; a pilgrim who is active all around the world. Asoka is Lou's godfather, enfolding him from afar in his spiritual protection.

Augustin: A small refugee child who survived a stormy crossing.

Augustino (3 or 4 at the beginning of the cycle): Daniel and Mélanie's son. After publishing his first book, *Letter to Young People Without a Future*, he travels to India to work and live with those plagued by poverty.

Bertha: A young woman who sells cocaine in Guatemala.

Brilliant (Bryan; 37 at the end of the cycle): Lucia's friend; he feels protective of her, and they eventually marry. He works at the Café Español. He often hangs out with unhoused teens on the beach at night, bringing them food and comforting them.

Bryan: See Brilliant.

Caridad: Lazaro's mother and Mama's friend. She left her husband to settle in the United States and rejected his religious oppression as well as her son's political and moral orientation. She sells handicrafts on Bahama Street.

Carla Eva: A criminal sentenced to death.

Carlos (13 at the start of the cycle): Pastor Jeremy and Mama's son. He fights injustice in a juvenile detention centre before being released thanks to his lawyer Perdue Baltimore.

Carmello and Grazie: The owners of a farm in Spain near a monastery where Daniel retires to write.

Carmen: See Mark and Carmen.

Caroline: A talented photographer renowned for astonishing portraits of destitute Black families in the South during the 1950s; she also published books on modern poets with her partner Jean-Mathieu. She dies shortly after him, at the age of sixty-seven.

Casey: A child of refugees, rescued from the water during a storm.

Charles: Frédéric's partner and a great poet who had a big impact on Daniel. He dies at sixty-seven.

Charlotte: A piglet rescued during the refugee crossing.

Charly (Charlotte; around 30 or 35): A Black woman who works for Caroline as her chauffeur and as her photography model in Jamaica; she takes advantage of her; Charly subsequently works as Adrien's chauffeur. Little is known about her past, though it is suggested that her father is a white soldier who seduced her mother.

Cheng (22): A Chinese queen apprenticing with Yinn.

Chris (24): A young Russian musical prodigy. Claudio's friend.

Christiensen: An economist working in Africa. Nora's husband; the two make a handsome couple, and Mère notices their beauty.

Christina, Sister: A nun who tries to save criminals from the death penalty.

Christophe (Désiré Lacroix; 30): A Black actor who ends up in prison after killing five people in a bank. Frédéric, who tries to protect him from the harshness of the legal system, calls him the Black Christ of Bahama Street.

Clara: A child musical prodigy who becomes a friend of Fleur after they meet at a concert in New York.

Claude: A young New York judge and Renata's husband. He is in favour of the death penalty, a position that shifts over time, not least because his wife is firmly against it.

Claudio (25): A conductor who introduces Roman audiences to Fleur's music and becomes his friend.

Cobra (27): A young trans friend of Yinn.

Cornelius: A musician who lives in a trailer by the sea. He fought in the Korean War and is Venus's uncle.

Cristal (17): Kitty's friend. Cristal and her family, who are Black, live in their car. The father is in prison.

Cupid (17): A young queen who works at Yinn's cabaret.

Cyril (35): A comedian who falls in love with Charles in India.

Daisy: See Marguerite.

Damien: Kim's beloved mongrel dog.

Daniel (30 at the beginning of the cycle): Daniel arrives on the island with his family to start a new life as a writer, having given up the hard drugs of his pampered youth. He begins a long autobiographical novel entitled *Strange Years*, which he never stops reworking and editing; several of his early books published under that title are quite successful, though he remains discreet.

Daphne (20): Peter's fiancée, whom Daniel meets during the international writers' conference in Scotland. She is a somewhat distracted reader of Daniel's books, though he is touched by her joie de vivre.

Deandra: See Tiffany and Deandra.

Désirée (also called Harriett): Caroline's Black governess when she was a child.

Dieudonné (around 45): A Haitian doctor and medical clinic director. He is very much a humanitarian. Petites Cendres is his patient and friend.

Donna Africa (50): A Black American presidential candidate inspired by Martin Luther King who calls for freedom and rebellion. She is a rising political star admired by people from all walks of life, including Mélanie, Venus, and even young Rebecca and her grandfather, Pastor Jeremy.

Dorothea: An old Black woman, born in the Bahamas, who was hired as Adrien's attendant, but who feels close to him and became as much a companion as a caregiver. Adrien holds her in high esteem and has taught her to read, though he repents somewhat when he finds out that Dorothea's reading material is entirely religious.

Eddy: A young bartender at the hotel in Scotland where an annual writers' peace conference is held. Eddy is a keen traveller, curious about people and different cultures; he is especially interested in the writers he has been serving for several years at the hotel bar. He is a free-spirited, sensual man, a sensitive foodie open to the arts and with an ear for poetry.

Eduardo (40): A Mexican who fled a difficult past as a drug addict. He works as a gardener for Frédéric and Charles and becomes Frédéric's confidant and protector.

Eli (25): A hooligan who sells drugs to minors. Eli's transgressions inspire Stephen to write a book about evil.

Emilio: A Cuban boy who Mai plays with on the beach.

Emma and Juliette: Two young friends of Lou.

Escobez brothers: Hoodlums who end up in prison.

Esther: See Mère.

Eureka: A pastor and caregiver who often visits Angel and tries to console him with her songs. She is a member of the Black Ancestral Choir and one of the ensemble's most radiant, inspiring, hopeful voices.

Ézéchielle: The pastor of the Community Church. A generous and tolerant Black woman who takes the unfortunate, the poor, and the sick, as well as prostitutes like Petites Cendres and Timo, into her church.

Fatalité: A queen who had AIDS and died of an overdose. She is never forgotten and is featured in videos shown every evening at the Porte du Baiser Saloon.

Flavian (25): A young AIDS victim, a friend of Robbie's.

Fleur: See Andrew Adam.

Franz: A composer, concert pianist, and conductor. The arc of his career unfolds from the beginning of the cycle, from his past as a child prodigy in Europe through his professional and personal life.

Frédéric (Fred): A writer, musician, and painter whose artistic skill, generosity, gentleness, and humanity left a deep impression on the young Daniel. He dies at sixty-nine, shortly after his partner, Charles.

Geisha (30): A prominent queen who works at Yinn's cabaret.

Gracyn and Kaylin (15 and 16): Two of the victims of the Young Man's racist rampage at the Methodist church.

Grégoire (85): An old Black man who wants to help Frédéric.

Greta (30): Nora and Christiensen's oldest daughter.

Harriett: See Désirée.

He Who Never Sleeps (40): A Haitian refugee who suffers from dementia and is taken in by Daniel's family. He is Marie-Sylvie de la Toussaint's brother.

Heidi: The dog that belongs to the owner of the artists' residency.

Henri (35): A writer Daniel meets at the international writers' peace conference in Scotland.

Herman: A committed artist and LGBTQ activist whose socially satirical work shows intelligence and sensitivity. He dies of cancer at the age of thirty and is fondly remembered.

Ingrid (40): Lou's mother and Ari's ex-wife.

Isaac (almost 100 at the end of the cycle): Daniel's uncle. An architect who has always played a creative role in the town and who, like Isaac, remains active in his old age. He is a wealthy man and is trying to save wildlife on the Island No One Owns, a wild island that he owns.

J'aime (James; 20): A young poet with cerebral palsy whom Daniel takes under his wing.

Jacques: A writer and literature professor who dies of AIDS at the age of fifty. A central figure in the group of writers and a sociable, sensual man.

Jamie (50): A friend of Yinn who works at the cabaret, supporting the dancers and singers.

Jason: Yinn's husband. He runs lights and sound at the cabaret where Yinn dances.

Jean-Mathieu: A widely admired poet. Charles and Frédéric's friend, and Caroline's partner. Jean-Mathieu is an avid traveller who dies accidentally at sixty while visiting Venice. He was born into a poor family in Halifax, and remained something of an outsider in the privileged world of his writer and intellectual friends.

Jenny: A refugee taken in by Daniel's family, who becomes the children's governess. At the beginning of the cycle, Jenny studies medicine and later works for Doctors Without Borders.

Jeremy: A Black pastor and family man, and Venus, Carlos, El Toque, Deandra, and Tiffany's father. He is a religious, domineering man, and devoted to his children's education, as is his wife, Mama.

Jermaine: Olivier and Tchouan's son. He is a filmmaker whose work is inspired by his father's fight against racism.

Jérôme the African: A young unhoused African immigrant. Fleur and Kim's friend.

Jerry: Mabel's surviving parrot after her other pet parrot, Merlin, is killed by a vicious child.

Jessica: A young pilot who dies at the age of twelve during an air show. A heroic figure whom Augustino admires.

Jill: An unhoused woman who lives with her little boy, Jonathan, after leaving her abusive husband, Rodriguez.

Joë (20): A sailboat owner.

Johann: Mayor Martin's partner, who dies of AIDS at the age of twenty-five.

John Kevin (11): A young pilot.

Jonathan (4): Jill's son.

Joseph (60): Daniel's father, president of a marine biology laboratory. Daniel's grandfather's name was also Joseph.

Julien (14): Ingrid's son from her first marriage. He grows up with his mother and his half-brother, Lou, after Ingrid leaves her first husband, Ari.

Julio (about 25 or 30): A Cuban refugee taken in by Mère, Daniel, and Mélanie. His children, Oreste, Nina, and Ramon, and their mother, Edna, drowned during the crossing. He later works for refugees in New York.

Justin (55): Born in China, the son of a pastor, he is a writer and a pacifist, and a friend of Charles, Frédéric, Jean-Mathieu and Caroline.

Karin: Adrien and Suzanne's daughter.

Kevin: A prisoner who spends years on death row.

Kim (17): Fleur's friend, she is unhoused for much of the cycle. The mother of Pearl Saved from the Waters.

Kitty (13): Angel's unhoused friend; they become closer as Angel gets sicker.

Lamberto: A progressive poet and a friend of Martin and Johann.

Laura: A woman who killed her son Sugar Candy; Renata is her attorney.

Laure (50): A smoker Daniel meets in an airport while waiting for his flight to the international writers' conference.

Lazaro (12 or 13 at the beginning of the cycle): A Muslim immigrant who lives on Bahama Street. He is a playmate of Carlos, but the friendship becomes conflictual.

Lena (35): Angel's mother. The two are warmly welcomed at the Acacia Gardens after being shunned elsewhere.

Léonie and Alexandra (Léo and Alex): A young couple Petites Cendres meets on Atlantic Boulevard and befriends. They go on to work as carpenters at the Acacia Gardens.

Lilia (50): A pianist and Franz's sister.

Lily and Line (12 and 14): Jason's daughters from his first marriage. They are like family to Yinn and his mother.

Linda and Toki: Dogs that followed their owners out to sea and were rescued.

Lizzie: A musician and a friend of Fleur.

Lola: A little dog found in a sleeping bag in Las Vegas by an unhoused man who decides to rescue her.

Lorraine (55): A doctor at Dr. Dieudonné's clinic who used to treat AIDS patients and their families in Africa. She contracted HIV while performing surgery.

Lou (Marie-Louise): One of Ari and Ingrid's two children. Lou slowly comes of age throughout the cycle. He eventually identifies as a boy and chooses the name Benjamin.

Louisa (25): A young prostitute and drug addict, a friend of Robbie and Petites Cendres.

Louisiana Diva (around 65 or 70): A talented drag queen who dances and sings at the cabaret at Yinn's invitation.

Luc: Jacques's friend and caregiver during his brief illness.

Lucia (68): A woman who is taken in at the Acacia Gardens. She was kicked out of her home by her sisters, who thought she couldn't be trusted with her own life.

Mabel (65): Owns the house where Petites Cendres lives while waiting to be admitted to the Acacia Gardens. Mabel is a Black woman who has suffered considerably from racial segregation. She has a large family who live in another town. Mabel is often accompanied by her birds, which she shows off to tourists in the evening on the pier, where she also sells flowers and lemonade.

Mac: Jacques's red cat, who distracts him from his suffering.

Mai (18 at the end of the cycle): Daniel and Mélanie's youngest child. She is still in school at the end of the cycle, studying art and photography. Acutely aware of the world she lives in, she yearns for radical change and already shares her parents' humanitarian concerns.

Mama: Pastor Jeremy's wife and the mother of Venus, Carlos, El Toque, Deandra, and Tiffany.

Mama Yinn: See Somo.

Manuel (20): A young man who takes drugs and with whom Mai falls in love.

Marcus (27): Louisa and Virgil's brother, whose life was derailed by hard drugs.

Marguerite (22): A young transgender AIDS victim.

Maria (12): A girl who sails with Luc, Jacques's caregiver and friend.

Marie-Louise: See Lou.

Marie-Sylvie de la Toussaint (55 at the end of the cycle): A Haitian refugee who Mère took in. She becomes the nanny of Daniel and Mélanie's children.

Marius (25): A friend of Fleur who still smokes crack.

Mark and Carmen (20 and 22): New York artists who befriend Daniel during his time at an artists' residency in Spain..

Martha (45): Fleur's mother. She works in a pub by the sea.

Martin: The long-time local mayor, a progressive politician who dies of AIDS in his fifties.

Matupali: One of Asoka's two younger sisters, who dies at the age of thirty during a war in her country.

Max: Fleur's dog, a German shepherd that becomes Kim's.

Mélanie (like Daniel, 30 at the beginning of the cycle): Daniel's wife, an activist leader who is concerned about the oppression of women.

Mère (Esther): Mélanie's mother, who has had a profound and positive effect on her children and grandchildren, even after her death. Daniel, who remembers her vividly, sees her in his dreams and continues an almost constant spiritual exchange with her.

Michael (40): A prisoner on death row.

Mick (18): An androgynous teenager. He and his sister Tammy were both disowned by their parents, well-known and well-to-do writers who feel nothing but disdain for their children.

Miracle: Samson's dog, who guides his master through the city.

Misha: Brilliant's dog, saved by his master from a hurricane.

My Captain (Thomas; 35): A handsome friend of Yinn who ferries tourists around on his boat.

Nadine: The daughter of a woman killed by the Young Man in the church.

Nanny (60): Brilliant's Black governess during his youth in New Orleans. Brilliant adores her and is heartbroken when her son Victor, who doesn't know how to swim, drowns following a hurricane.

Next One: See Cheng.

Night Out: Lucia's beloved parakeet.

Noémie (30): Ari's lover, an art critic for a newspaper, for which she writes about his work.

Nora: Christiensen's wife and a painter who goes to Africa to work with children with AIDS. She constantly questions her destiny as a woman artist.

Old Daddy: One of Robbie's lovers, a much older man who supports him for a few years and eventually leaves him for a younger man.

Old Ogre: See Wrath.

Old Salt: A captain who offers Kim and Fleur his boat as a haven. At the age of eighty-five, he is murdered by two thugs, who are never caught.

Olivier (65): A Black journalist and a friend of Daniel. He witnessed the riots against Black people during the 1960s. Even after he gets sick, he remains active.

Orange: The name of a budgie that belongs to Pearl Saved from the Waters.

Oreilles Coupées: An abandoned and abused dog rescued by Carlos's twin sisters, Deandra and Tiffany.

Our Lady of the Bags (13): An unhoused girl on the streets of New York. Samuel is moved by the sight of her. She is something of an oracle, foretelling the destruction of the Twin Towers.

Paul: Jacques's friend and caregiver. Works at the local library with Luc. Luc and Paul remain devoted friends throughout Jacques's illness.

Paul: A trumpeter who plays with his jazz band on the beach where Fleur and his friends sleep while they are unhoused.

Pearl Saved from the Waters (also Pearl Redeemed from the Sea): Kim and Rafael's daughter. She loves all animals, especially birds.

Pedro Zamora: A young activist who dies of AIDS at the age of twenty-two.

Perdue Baltimore: The lawyer who defends Carlos against charges of manslaughter.

Peter: Daphnée's fiancé, who is in Scotland.

Petites Cendres (between 30 and 40): A young prostitute who hangs out with the queens at the Porte du Baiser Saloon.

Polly: A puppy Carlos steals and which becomes his companion.

Portia and Porsha: Portia is the woman and Porsha the man, although Porsha also loves dressing as a woman. Known as the flamingos for their typical pink outfits.

Rachel (30): Franz's young wife and Yehudi's mother.

Rafael (40): A craftsman who seduces Kim after Fleur leaves for Europe, and the father of Kim's daughter, Pearl Saved from the Waters.

Raoul: Luc and Tanjou's tennis partner.

Rebecca: Venus's daughter. The cycle traces her childhood and adolescence, particularly her relationship with her mother. Unlike Venus, Rebecca believes in a promising future.

Rémi (50): A journalist and a friend of Daniel.

Renata: Mère's younger sister, she becomes a lawyer and a judge. She has a long affair with Franz before marrying Claude. She campaigns against the death penalty and represents victims of rape and infanticide.

Richard (Rick; 30): Captain Williams's caretaker during his marriage to Venus.

Rising Sun: See Su.

Robbie (35): One of the transvestites at the Porte du Baiser Saloon. He is also known as the Puerto Rican.

Robert: A young Black model who hangs out with the cabaret artists.

Rodrigo (60): A Brazilian poet Daniel meets at an artists' residency in Spain, and again at the international writers' conference in Scotland.

Rodriguez: Jill's husband, who beats her and their son Jonathan.

Rosalie: A young female soldier who dies in combat in Iraq.

Rosie (5): A childhood friend of Lou.

Rudolph (Rudie): Samuel and Veronica's son. Although his passion is aviation, he becomes a dancer and choreographer like them.

Samantha (30): A drag queen who is a friend of Yinn and the dancers at the Porte du Baiser Saloon. On her way to visit her parents in Georgia, Samantha meets a man who kills her.

Samson (25): A soldier who develops amnesia and mental illness after a tour in the Middle East.

Samuel: Daniel's great-uncle, who was shot by Nazi officers in Poland during the Second World War.

Samuel (12 at the start of the cycle): Mélanie and Daniel's oldest son. He grows up to be a dancer and choreographer in New York. His works are inspired by current events: for instance, he creates a disturbing piece on pollution in China.

Santa Fe (30): One of the queens who works at the Porte du Baiser Saloon.

Seamus: A musician and a friend of Fleur.

Simon (29): A waiter at the Grand Hotel who is curious about Adrien and the writing life.

Sluttie (20): A prostitute and a friend of Petites Cendres.

Somo (Somiko; 65): Yinn's mother. His friends call her Mama Yinn (sometimes Mama One).

Sophia (11): A classmate of Lou.

Stephen (30): A New Yorker and a great admirer of Charles's poetry. He is writer-in-residence at Charles and Frédéric's house, which they bequeathed to young writers.

Stone, Reverend: An open-minded religious man who strives to help all communities, including AIDS victims. He works for social justice, is present at memorials, and supports gay marriage. His thinking is superficially conservative, based on his belief in a benevolent paternal God, though his rather simplistic theory of divine compassion develops more widely over time.

Su: A young musician who dominates Wrath with a pernicious yet loving influence. A Japanese exile who Fleur wants to save from drug addiction. Wrath sometimes refers to him as Rising Sun.

Sugar Candy: A child murdered by his mother, Laura.

Suicide bomber (12): A young Afghan girl sent on a suicide mission wearing an explosive belt.

Sunbeam: A dog that gets lost during a festival in the city.

Suzannah (13): A young girl who dies as a result of her father's violence.

Suzanne: A writer and poet, and Adrien's wife. Suzanne published several books with her husband in her youth, then gradually stopped being published, though she continued to write in secret. Daniel loved her a great deal and will always remember their beautiful friendship. She dies quite young.

Tai (24): Wrath's much-younger lover. Wrath claims to have purchased Tai in Asia during one of his religious missions.

Tammy (between 15 and 18): Mick's sister and Mai's friend, a child tormented by her parents' lack of love. She dies of an eating disorder.

Tania: Suzanne and Adrien's daughter.

Tanjou: A painter and Jacques's Pakistani student. Jacques resist the painter's love.

Tchouan (55): Olivier's wife and designer who creates pleasant, artistic surroundings for her friends. Her parents died in Hiroshima, about which she talks very little, but Daniel is aware of her private sorrow.

Thomas: See My Captain.

Tiffany and Deandra: Pastor Jeremy and Mama's school-aged twin daughters.

Tigli (30): A wild young man Ari meets and befriends in Guatemala.

Timo (30): A friend of Petites Cendres, he is a thief and a drug addict who makes his living as a prostitute. He disappears one day in Mexico, and Petites Cendres never sees him again.

El Toque: Carlos's brother, Pastor Jeremy and Mama's son. He walks with a limp; when he was small, his father had to carry him to the school bus, a memory that has stayed with Carlos.

Trevor (35): Venus's second husband, a Jamaican musician. He is affable and sensual and, after losing her first husband, Captain Williams, Venus learns to love him.

Trevor Junior: Trevor and Venus's infant son.

Valdés: A doctor and a friend of Dr. Dieudonné.

Vanquished Heart (later called Triumphant Heart; 30): A transgender friend of Yinn.

Venus (15 at the beginning of the cycle): Carlos's older sister, Pastor Jeremy and Mama's daughter. As a teenager, she sings at the Coral City Temple, her father's church. She also sings at her Uncle Cornelius's mixed club. Her life changes when she begins studying law at night in order to defend Carlos.

Veronica Lane: A dancer and choreographer, like her husband Samuel; the two met when they were young.

Victoire (27): A transgender artist, formerly an engineer and a soldier. As she awaits gender affirmation surgery, she is welcomed at Yinn's cabaret among his singer and dancer friends.

Victor: Nanny's son. Brilliant loved him like a brother.

Vincent (a baby at the beginning of the cycle): Daniel and Mélanie's son. Vincent suffered a great deal as a child from shortness of breath and acute asthma. His desire to cure children with the same condition leads him to become a doctor.

Virgil (20): A thief. Marcus and Louisa's younger brother.

Vladimir and Pete: Unscrupulous young men who work with Brilliant at the Café Español.

Williams, Captain (around 55 or 60): Venus's adoring, generous, much-older husband. He appears to be involved in drug trafficking, conducting shady deals at sea. He comes to a tragic end.

Wrath (Old Ogre): An extraordinarily intelligent disgraced priest. He meets Fleur under a bridge in Paris when Fleur is preparing for a concert and tries to bewitch him. He shows Fleur and Su the social hell in which he lives, with thousands of men, women, and children as miserable as he is.

Yehudi (5): The son of musician and composer Franz. He also becomes a musician.

Yinn (around 35 or 40): The artistic director of the Porte du Baiser Saloon, which features nightly song and dance drag shows. His father is American and his mother is Korean.

Young captain (30): He has been sailing since he was seventeen. He is a friend of Luc and Paul, who are the same age.

Young Man (17): He dreams of being the youngest white supremacist leader. He murders parishioners in a Black church and is sentenced to death.

Photo by Jill Glessing

MARIE-CLAIRE BLAIS (1939–2021) was the internationally revered author of more than twenty-five books, many of which have been published around the world. In addition to the Governor General's Literary Award for Fiction, which she won four times, Blais was awarded the Gilles-Corbeil Prize, the Médicis Prize, the Molson Prize, and Guggenheim Fellowships. She divided her time between Key West, Florida, and Quebec.

KATIA GRUBISIC is a Canadian writer, editor, and translator living in Montreal. Her collection of poems *What if red ran out* won the Gerald Lampert Memorial Award for best first book of poetry. She has been a finalist for the A. M. Klein Prize for Poetry and twice for the Governor General's Literary Award for *Brothers*, by David Clerson, and *A Cemetery for Bees*, by Alina Dumitrescu. She won the Cole Foundation Prize for Translation for Clerson's *To See Out the Night*, and the Governor General's Literary Award for Marie-Claire Blais's *Nights Too Short to Dance*.

Also available from House of Anansi Press

The Soifs Cycle

These Festive Nights
Book 1

Thunder and Light
Book 2

Augustino and the Choir of Destruction
Book 3

Rebecca, Born in the Maelstrom
Book 4

Mai at the Predators' Ball
Book 5

Nothing for You Here, Young Man
Book 6

The Acadia Gardens
Book 7

A Twilight Celebration
Book 8

Songs for Angel
Book 9

Together by the Sea
Book 10